FATAL RESONANCE

CHRIS BERKNESS

CHAPTER 1

July 2nd, 2016 - Rindville, Wisconsin

"Welcome to Rindville: Population 1,563," thirteen-year-old Maddie Schwarz reads aloud from the archway at the edge of town. She lets out a sarcastic snort and tosses her chocolate-brown ponytail over her shoulder before turning back to her cell phone. "More like, welcome to the middle of nowhere."

"You used to love visiting," her mom, Debbie, says from the driver's seat.

"Used to," Maddie mutters.

"I can't believe it's been five years since we saw your parents," Debbie says to her husband, David, who's staring out the passenger-side window. "Five years since we were last here."

"Looks the same." David squints into the glare of the setting sun, taking in his small hometown as their Chevy Suburban creeps down Main Street. Downtown Rindville is a lame tourist trap. Western-style wooden sidewalks and planters in front of tiny boutiques and restaurants with tavern doors. They pass a restaurant called Pig in a Fur Coat. "See? That place is never going to close."

"How much longer?" Maddie whines, propping her army boots up on the back of the driver's seat.

Debbie frowns and glances in the rear-view. Grace, her youngest, is asleep with her thin neck bent sideways, head on her shoulder. Soon, she'll be too old to find that comfortable, but a sleepy six-year-old has little qualms about where she naps, and the concept of sore muscles is still foreign. Grace's light brown hair is stuck to one cheek with drool. Maddie's eyes are glued to her phone, so Debbie has to swat Maddie's fatigues to get the teen to clue in and drop her feet back to the floormat.

"We're almost there, sweetie," says Debbie with as much cheer as she can muster. She's learned that she must pick her battles with Maddie. Feet on the seat isn't worth starting a screaming match over.

"At least Barry's is still here," David says, twisting in his seat as they drive past his favorite burger joint.

"Maybe we can take your parents out tomorrow night," Debbie says. Barry's butter burgers *are* delicious. Plus, David and his father, Stan, are less likely to get into one of their arguments in public.

"If we're still here tomorrow night," David grumbles.

"We will be," Debbie assures him. "Did you call Kevin yet?"

The downtown street ends abruptly, spitting them out into a residential area that's basically open fields with houses dotted every ten miles or so. Rindville is a Northern Wisconsin dairy town. There are more cows than people.

They drive for a solid minute before David finally says, "No."

"Why not? He's your best friend," Debbie says disapprovingly.

"Used to be."

"It's been two years since we saw the Schumers in person, and with everything that family is going through, the least you can do is—"

"I'll call him tomorrow morning, okay?" David rubs his neck, grimacing with irritation. As he shifts in his seat, his muscles strain against his cotton button-up. Debbie is always having to fix popped stitches and buttons. The man works out too much for his own good, in Debbie's opinion. But it does give her some peace of mind knowing her detective husband can take care of himself. Detroit is an unforgiving place for a cop. She can't complain about his daily martial arts training with Maddie either. A girl should know how to defend herself. In a year or two, he'll start lessons with Grace.

"You two have known each other since first grade," Debbie says.

"Yeah, and I couldn't get out of this shit town fast enough after high school," David says. "I haven't lived in Rindville in..." He pauses to do the math. "Twenty-two years."

"But you and Kevin always kept in touch. Is this about...?"

"It's complicated." David avoids his wife's gaze.

Debbie rubs David's forearm. "I know. Joey's not getting any better, is he?"

"No. The last time I talked to Kevin, he said that none of the treatments are working. Chemo, radiation, stem cell... nothing."

"What about his blast count?" asks Debbie.

"It keeps getting worse." David's knuckles go white on the dashboard.

Debbie shakes her head. "I'm so sorry to hear that. He's so young."

"Yeah." David pauses and rubs at his stubble. "Joey is Maddie's age."

Debbie nods. "We should stop by tomorrow."

"Mom would like that. I bet she'll make a pie or two."

Thinking of her mother-in-law makes Debbie smile. "I can't wait to see your mom. She's one of the sweetest women I know. She's always been so kind and welcoming to me."

"Are you saying my dad isn't?" David chuckles, but the sound is dull, devoid of any real mirth.

"Do you think he is?" says Debbie, an eyebrow jumping.

"I know what my dad is. It's why I moved away after high school." *And why we haven't been back here in five years,* he finishes inside his head.

Debbie nods. "I am so glad you did move away or we would never have met."

David thinks back to the fraternity party at the Univeristy of Michigan where they first met. Things were so much simpler then.

David has a complicated relationship with this place. He loves his mom and hates his dad, and so he looks at Rindville with a mix of warm nostalgia and cold disdain. The closer they get to the farm, the more he vibrates with tension.

"Your mom wanted us here," she says quietly. "She thought you could talk to him—"

"I know exactly what my dad wants to tell me," David says in a voice that's deceptively steady. "I know exactly what I'm going to tell him."

A glance in the backseat tells Debbie that Maddie is

secretly listening. The teen's brown eyes flick back down to her cellphone the second they catch her mom's. Debbie changes the subject.

"Your mom's making a roast, right?"

David responds with the closest thing to a genuine smile that she's likely to get out of him for the next week. "Yup."

Debbie leans back in her seat, imagining the perfectly spiced beef is already melting on her tongue. Her stomach rumbles for her to cut it out. "Can't wait, I'm starving."

"Me too. And I hope she makes her cinnamon rolls for breakfast tomorrow morning."

Debbie lets out a soft "oooh." She looks in the mirror again. Homemade cinnamon rolls are Maddie's favorite. But Maddie either hasn't heard or is doing her best to act like she doesn't care.

For a few minutes, there is no sound but the purr of the engine and the occasional bump of the tires falling into notches in the unkempt road. Then, David sees the turnoff to his family's five hundred–acre dairy farm up ahead. The wooden sign by the mailbox is splintered and partially bleached, proudly displaying its age. The sign and the family have been here for four generations.

They won't be here for much longer.

After seven hours in the car, David's legs are restless. He bounces them in anxious relief as Debbie pulls onto the long driveway leading to the farmhouse. What kind of welcome will he receive when he steps onto that porch? What kind of welcome does he want? What does he deserve?

Grace stirs as the tires bump over a divot in the dirt driveway. "Are we here?" she asks, smearing a hand over one drool-stained cheek as she looks out her window.

"Yes," says David, turning to give both girls a tight smile.

Maddie has her cell phone raised over her head and pressed to the window, brow furrowed. "I don't have any reception!" She glares at David like he's the source of the shoddy connection.

"Not surprising. Like you said before, we're in the middle of nowhere. Guess you'll just have to spend time talking to your family." Maddie crosses her arms with a huff. Satisfied that he has given his sullen teen a sufficiently bad time, David wiggles his brows at his wife, who shakes her head.

"Can I feed the cows?" Grace asks.

"You'll have to ask your grandfather," says Debbie.

Grace presses her forehead to the window, searching for the herd as the rust-red barn appears on a hill in the right field. "Daddy... all the cows are sleeping!"

David snorts. "That's impossible, Gracie. They wouldn't all be sleeping at the same time... *goofball.*"

When he turns to look at her, she taps the window. "Yes, they are... *look.*"

David glances out the passenger window. Instantly, his blood runs cold. "Stop the car!"

Debbie slams the brakes. "What's wrong?" she asks as the dust cloud settles outside the Chevy Suburban.

David gets out of the vehicle, heart hammering in his throat. As he jogs to the woven wire fence, Debbie and the girls open their doors. David shields his eyes from the setting sun for a better look into the pasture. "What the hell?" he whispers, eyes drifting over spotted lumps clustered in the grass under a large oak at the field's center.

Debbie's hand on his back startles him, but he turns to squeeze her fingers as she asks, "What is it?"

"Dad's herd... they're..." He can't finish the thought. The implications are too great. "We need to get to the house...

now!" David ushers the girls back toward the car as they crane their necks to try and see around him. He hops in the driver's seat and revs the engine the moment Debbie shuts her door.

The white two-story farmhouse with an elegant wrap-around porch materializes over the next hill. As he whips around the circle drive at the front of the house, David counts the pickups parked off to the side. Three: his dad's truck, his mom's, and the newer one that was supposed to be his, if he'd chosen to move back here five years ago. A peace offering he'd refused to accept. They'd kept it, just in case. His mom's idea, no doubt.

David twists to fix the girls with what he hopes is a calm but serious look. "Wait here. Let me check on Grandma and Grandpa."

Grace's face immediately crumples with worry verging on tears, and Maddie's mask of teenage nonchalance is slipping. David feels frantic, adrenaline coursing through every limb. With a shaky sigh, he tries to offer a smile and then pushes open the door as casually as he can manage. The moment his feet hit the driveway, though, he starts jogging. Across the gravel. Up the wooden steps to the front door. His hand trembles on the knob. Unlocked, as usual.

With the girls' eyes off him, David sprints through the open living room and dining room combo to peer through the peek-a-boo wall into the kitchen. "Mom... Dad?!"

The smell of burnt beef hits him as he enters the kitchen. A thick plume of smoke is spewing through the oven vent. David flips it off and coughs as he opens the door to release a gray wall of smog.

Margaret Schwarz has never burnt a roast in her life.

David can hardly breathe, all his training and years on the job forgotten. He races up the steps two at a time, vague memories of sprinting up them to escape unseen monsters in the dark tickling his brain.

"Mom! Dad!"

The house is much too silent. The floors creak their protests as he opens all the doors along the hall, but no one answers his calls. David slows as he approaches the master bedroom. Fear constricts his chest, but he grits his teeth and swings the door open. He takes a single step inside and then sways left, bracing himself on the doorframe.

His mother is lying on the hardwood at the foot of the bed, eyes closed. Her body is too rigid for sleep, her skin too pale. One shoe dangles off her toe, while the other is still in its rightful place. She's still wearing her red apron.

Behind her, propped against the side of the bed, is David's father. His dirty overalls are unbuckled on one side, as if he'd just started to change clothes after a hard day's work.

David staggers forward, some small part of him whispering instructions in the matter-of-fact voice of a seasoned homicide detective. He presses his fingers to his mother's neck and wrist first. No pulse. The tears blind him, and he has to crawl on hands and knees until his fingertips brush his father's leg. He, too, is growing cold, the blood stilled in his veins.

Dead. His parents are dead. The word feels wrong, as though he's forgotten how to pronounce it.

The detective inside him starts logging details. *No blood. No signs of forced entry. Natural causes, then? But how could this be natural? Both of them at the same time? And what about the herd?*

The questions become a buzzing in the back of his brain. The answers don't matter. Nothing can change that awful word.

Dead.

David clutches his aching chest. Everything inside him is begging to cry out, to release his grief into the open air.

But when David finally lets himself scream, the pain doesn't flee. It only digs deeper.

CHAPTER 2

David stares at his callused fingers, head bent because he cannot find the strength to lift it. He does not want to look up and meet the fearful eyes of his wife and daughters, though he can feel them staring at him from the safety of the Suburban. What they would find in his face would only make things worse.

Three patrol cars flank the Chevy. David can hear the officers' heavy boots stomping around in the house at his back. One set approaches David, but still he does not look up. Not even when Kevin sits beside him on the top porch step.

"I'm so sorry, David," says Kevin.

David stares at his old friend's brown pants, standard issue for sheriff's deputies. "Thanks."

There's a moment of awkward silence before Kevin asks, "When did you get into town?"

"Just before..." David clears his throat. "It was last-minute. I was planning to call you tomorrow." David hears the lie in his own voice and figures Kevin does, too, but he's too weary to care.

"You can't stay here," Kevin says after a beat. "The investigation..."

"We'll get a room in town."

Another long pause. "You guys can stay with us. We have plenty of room."

David stiffens. The desire to be alone, to feel no pitying, questioning eyes on him, has rooted deep in his gut. "I'm sure the last thing you need is the four of us invading your home. I don't want to be a burden."

Kevin sighs. "I already told El. She's making up the beds for the girls. In fact..." Kevin gestures to the Suburban, making David's head lift for the first time. "You should probably head over now. No sense in staying here. We'll update you as we get new information."

"I'm not going anywhere," David snaps immediately. He takes a breath, trying to get his flare of temper under control. "But you're right. I can send Debbie on ahead. Thanks."

Standing is like lifting two hundred pounds of dead weight onto his shoulders, but David manages to find his feet and follow Kevin to the car. Debbie slides out and takes a hesitant step toward David with arms rising slightly, a question in her eyes. David drags one foot closer, fighting the burn of tears, and she rushes into his arms. She says nothing, only buries her face against his neck—a welcome warmth.

"Why don't you take the girls to Kevin's," says David, voice gruff and raw from screaming his grief into every corner of his parents' home. "It's getting late. I'm going to stick around here for a little longer."

Debbie kisses his cheek and withdraws a little, her movements slow and careful, as though he is a wild woodland creature she fears startling. "Are you sure?"

He nods.

She chews on her cheek. “Don’t stay too long,” she whispers as she climbs back in the Suburban.

David leans in through the back window. The girls are wide eyed and pale, and their silence is louder than any tantrum or cry for help. He longs to hold them, but he knows he’ll break down, and he still has work to do.

“Try to get some sleep, okay, girls? I’ll be there when you wake up tomorrow. I promise.”

“But, Daddy—”

Grace’s protest is cut off by Maddie’s touch. She wraps an arm around her little sister, giving her a tight squeeze that Grace leans into with a look of utter surprise. Maddie meets David’s eye, and for the first time, in place of his little girl, he sees the woman she’ll grow up to be. Her understanding nod fills David with enough strength to stand upright.

“See you in the morning, Dad,” she says softly. “Love you.”

“Love you,” he says, turning to hide his tears.

Debbie waves as she drives down the long dirt driveway, and he waves back to try and ease her worry. Then, he turns to face the farmhouse.

“Chief deputy,” he says to Kevin, nodding his approval without taking his eyes off the home where he grew up. “Suits you.”

“Funny.”

“I’m not kidding. Congrats on the promotion.”

Kevin gives David a side-eye. “You still think we’re just a bunch of Mayberry hick cops, while you’re Mr. Big-Shot Detective with the Detroit PD. Plus, you’re stalling.”

David doesn’t dignify that accusation with a response. But the goading does get his frozen feet to move. The two men climb the porch steps as a deputy begins to cordon off the house with crime scene tape.

"You sure you're up to this?" Kevin asks at the front door.

David draws himself up to his full height. "Why wouldn't I be?"

"Come on, man. Your parents just died. You're allowed to—"

"Let's just get on with it."

Kevin shrugs as David pushes open the front door. "Okay, then. What do you think happened here?"

David stops to put on blue latex gloves from a box placed on the table in the foyer where his mom keeps—no, *kept* a bowl of potpourri. As he snaps the gloves into place, he scans the scene. He does his best to disconnect from the familiar sight of his mother's faded red crockpot, the baby pictures over the mantle that he can spy through the peek-a-boo wall opening, and his father's truck keys dangling from the open cupboard door by the stove. He tells himself this is just another crime scene... but is it a crime?

"Did you call CSRU?" he asks.

Kevin shakes his head. "The sheriff wanted to be here before the Crime Scene Response Unit showed up. He's on his way now."

"You're chief deputy," David says derisively, "and you still have to run your calls by your dad?"

Kevin scowls at him.

As if on cue, a short, black-haired deputy enters the kitchen. "The area has been cordoned off. What do you want us to do next, sir?"

"Nothing right now."

The man nods and heads back outside.

"Sir? That's what they're calling you now?"

Kevin grits his teeth. "Busting my balls at a time like this.

Seriously, what is wrong with you? You're acting like you did when Lizzy—"

"*Don't.*" David bites out the word.

Kevin rubs the back of his neck. "Sorry. I'm just worried about you, is all."

David hardly hears Kevin's apology. Now his head is filled with hospital rooms, the smell of sanitizer, the beep of machines, and his sister's skeleton-like form beneath thin sheets. The anger rises fast and furious, but he chokes it down. Screaming at Kevin isn't going to do anything but get him kicked out of the house.

Before the two men can snipe at each other any more, a burly man tromps through the door, spurs jangling as he adjusts the gallon hat atop his head, a sheriff's emblem affixed just above the brim.

"David!" The wrinkles in the sheriff's face stretch upward as he strides into the kitchen. David holds out a hand to shake, but Jack Schumer grabs him in a crushing hug instead. He takes his hat off as he steps back and places it over his heart in a show of respect. His face sobers as he says, "It's great to see you, boy. I just wish it were under better circumstances."

David nods, unable to speak past the sudden lump in his throat.

The sheriff shakes his head. "I'm so sorry, David. Your parents were two of this town's finest. They'll be sorely missed."

"Thank you, sir."

"You're not six any more... you don't have to call me sir." He swats David's shoulder with his hat. "You're a big-city detective, for God's sake. Call me Jack."

David manages a grin. "Okay, Jack."

"That's better." The sheriff turns to point a finger at

Kevin. "Except you. You still have to call me sir," he says with a wink. "What do you have for me, *chief deputy?*"

Kevin returns a stony look and points upstairs. "We found the bodies—" He flinches and looks to David. "Sorry. We found Mr. and Mrs. Schwarz upstairs on the floor in the master bedroom. There is no sign of blunt trauma. No forced entry." He broadens his stance and sets his jaw with more severity as the deputies he's overseeing come in through the front door. "There's something else. I've had my team walking the property. It seems like the entire herd is dead."

"What the hell?" Jack curls his lip in an open-mouthed grimace. "How many?" he asks David.

"Three hundred and twenty-five."

"I'll be damned." The sheriff shakes his head. "Any theories, Kevin?"

"Could be the well water?"

Jack scratches the stubble on his skin and neck, making a sound that grates on David's frayed nerves. "No, that doesn't explain the entire herd dropping dead on the same day. Better call CSRU."

Kevin does an admirable job of pretending the idea of bringing in the forensic team hadn't crossed his mind until his father suggested it. "Yes, sir."

Jack pulls latex gloves from his pockets and struggles to get them over his large hands as he heads upstairs, Kevin and David right behind him. "Did you call the coroner?"

"Not yet," says Kevin, and this time, David can detect the tiniest hint of impatience in his voice. "I know you like me to talk to you first."

Every stomp of Jack's boots on the stairs is loud and strong. The man hasn't lost any of his vigor while entering his sixties. At the top of the stairs he turns to Kevin. "We can't use the Lincoln County coroner. They don't have a forensic pathologist. You better call Marathon County."

Kevin nods, and they follow Jack into the master bedroom. He sucks in a shaky breath, taking his hat off once more. "What the hell happened here?" He doesn't wait for an answer. Instead, he crouches between the two bodies for a better look. He glances up at David. "This has gotta be difficult for you, son. Why don't you wait downstairs?"

David raises his chin. "I'm fine, sir. *I mean, Jack.*"

Jack stands up, places his hat back on, and walks around the whole room in less than ten strides. "Is there anything out of place?" he asks David, standing by the bed with thumbs in his pockets.

David shakes his head as he looks around the room. "Not that I can see."

Jack sucks his teeth. "Anything odd happen recently?"

David nods, his mother's frightened voice echoing in his head.

I don't care to think what your father will do. I haven't seen him mad like this since Lizzy's doctor told us... well... you know.

"There was something," he tells Jack. "It's actually the reason we decided to visit."

Both Schumers look at him with wide, interested eyes.

"My mom called a few days ago. She was worried about Dad. She said that Gordon Muller has been pressuring him to sell the farm."

Jack narrows his eyes. "Pressuring... *how?*"

"He keeps calling, and apparently he stopped by last week with a contract." David lets out a puff of air. "He's offering above market."

Jack scrunches one eye. "What the hell for? Wisconsin dairy farms are struggling. There must be a reason for the offer. I've known Gordon to be a pretty savvy businessman."

David shrugs. "Yeah, I have no idea. All I know is, Mom was genuinely worried about Dad. He was pretty worked up about it. That's why we're here."

"You would think he would be excited about the offer," says Kevin, giving David a curious look. "Knowing that the farm has a future...?"

David scowls, unable to stop himself. "This farm has been in the Schwarz family for generations. Dad would never sell it. He was probably planning to ambush me while I was here. I bet Mom was in on it." His throat tightens and his head swims, thinking about the tough conversation—argument, more likely—that will never happen now. David never intended to follow in his father's footsteps. He was never going to take over the family business. That was always Lizzy's—

His throat tightens up on him. He takes a step backward, and then another. "I'll be in the hall," he chokes out, trying to save face. He won't break down in front of his childhood friend and his surrogate father-figure. He *won't.*

In the hallway, he leans against the wall, steadying his breath. David isn't a man who likes to show his emotions. Hell, he barely likes to *feel* his emotions. That's why he used to drink.

He stays by himself long enough for his drowning grief to turn into blazing anger. With the anger comes a sense of purpose. David is a police detective. If someone did this to his parents, he won't stand by and let other people—even people he's known for decades—solve the crime. This is his responsibility now.

When Jack steps into the hall, he turns to David. "We'll figure this out, son. I promise."

"Thanks," David says grimly. To himself, he vows, *I'll make sure we do.*

* * *

David waits in Kevin's patrol car while the deputies finish giving their reports from their canvass of the property. Leaving them to wait on the coroner and forensics team, Kevin waves goodbye over his shoulder and gets in the driver's side. He rolls down the windows as they pull down the dirt driveway. "A/C's broken," he says, nodding toward the console.

David doesn't respond. In the light of the full moon, he watches the retreating house in the side mirror until the next rise blocks it from view. He will never again come up this road to find his mother waving from the doorway. He'll never again eat her cooking. Never listen to her singing while she tends to the garden out back.

God, that fucking garden.

If he lets his thoughts wander any further down that road, he'll start to sob. To ward off the unwanted blubbering, David turns to Kevin. "Is your dad planning to retire anytime soon?" he says, surprising himself with how casual he sounds. "What is he, like, sixty-seven?"

"Sixty-five. He's planning to serve out this term, and then step down." Kevin lets a beat of meaningful silence pass before adding, "He wants me to run."

David sits forward to catch Kevin's eye. "Are you going to?"

Kevin purses his lips. "I'm giving it some thought."

"You should. You would make a great sheriff."

"Maybe," Kevin says. "Maybe not."

"What's the problem? This is what you've been groomed for, man."

Kevin gives him a look. "How'd following in your dad's footsteps work out for you?"

That shuts David up... until Kevin hits the stereo's media button, and a classical number, "Orchestral Suite No. 3 in D Major," blares through the speakers, the violin notes long and high.

David flinches and sticks a finger in his ear. "Jesus, Kevin... seriously?"

Kevin chuckles. "What?" he says, clearly knowing damn well what.

"Whatever happened to Queen or Aerosmith? When we were kids, you listened to classic rock."

"We're not kids anymore."

"You got that right."

Both men are quiet for a few minutes. Kevin takes the turn that will lead to his lakeside property. It's like muscle memory, driving between his place and David's parents' farmhouse, even though he hasn't made the trip in five years. You do something enough times, and it becomes a habit.

Eventually, David reaches over and turns down the music. "Gordon Muller was pressuring my dad to sell the farm," he says slowly. "Mom called me, scared. She said she was afraid of what Dad would do, how he would react if the Mullers kept pushing. But what if..."

Kevin raises an eyebrow but doesn't interrupt.

"What if she was afraid of something else?"

Kevin still says nothing.

"What if she was afraid of Gordon Muller?" This time, when Kevin doesn't respond, David blurts, "Say something, Goddamnit."

"Of course we'll include the Mullers in our investigation. They're your parents' closest neighbors."

"By proximity, not friendship," David grumbles. "Anyway, you should get a subpoena. Search their home. Search their attorney's office. There's something there. I can feel it."

"I'll stop by their place tomorrow and ask some questions," Kevin says.

"That's not good enough," David barks.

"I *said,* I'll question Gordon Muller tomorrow."

"And his boys. Ben and... what was his brother's name?"

"Bradley."

"Right. Bradley. That little prick." David rolls his shoulders, picturing the two Muller boys in his mind's eye. His anger is simmering again, and it wants a target. "I'll go with you tomorrow," he says.

"No, you won't."

"They were my parents," David insists. "I'm a detective."

"This is not your jurisdiction." Kevin's jaw is clenched. "You have to trust me to do my job."

David holds up both hands. "Fine." But his surrender is only outward. Inside, he's already plotting his next move.

The road winds closer to the lake, and Kevin's driveway appears up ahead, the reflective strip on the mailbox warning them not to miss the turn. The three-story lake house soon comes into view. It's old but well kept. Jack and Lily, Kevin's mom, lived here before Kevin and Ellie got married. Then they transferred the deed and moved to an apartment downtown, near the Sheriff's Office. Jack lives there alone now, since his wife passed a decade ago.

David has so many childhood memories at this house. They're honestly among his better memories of Rindville. Kevin was one of the few things he didn't want to leave behind.

They park in the driveway behind the Suburban. Kevin turns off the car but doesn't get out. "You realize you haven't once asked me how Joey is doing?"

David closes his eyes and takes a deep breath through his nose. "You're right. I'm sorry. I was thinking about him on the way over. It's difficult... his situation..."

"You mean his leukemia. Call it what it is, David."

"Yeah." David clears his throat too loud.

"I'm just saying, you could've asked about him."

"It brings back memories of Lizzy." David stares out the windshield, contemplating a quick sprint to the front door.

"I know... for me too."

David snaps his head toward Kevin. "Yeah, well... she wasn't your sister."

"Doesn't mean I didn't care for her."

David remembers Kevin standing in the corner of Lizzy's hospital room, a hand over his mouth to hold in a scream of rage and despair—a stance David had recognized because he'd adopted it many times himself.

"She was my little sister, and she suffered so much."

"My son is suffering right now. My *friend*—" Kevin puts a lot of emphasis on that word. "—should be there for me. The way I was there for you."

David's eyes are wet. He just wants to make it inside and shut the guest room door before he loses it. When he catches Kevin's eye, he sees a haggard, hurting man looking back at him. He imagines Kevin in another hospital room, at the foot of a much smaller bed. "Sorry," he says gruffly. "It's one thing watching your sister suffer... I can't imagine watching your kid go through it. I didn't say anything because... well, I don't know what to say."

"I of all people know this brings up a lot of bad memories for you. And I know it's a terrible time." Kevin sighs. "Just don't shut me out."

"I won't," David says, knowing he will. That's what he does. It's the only way he knows how to cope.

Kevin finally pops open his door. "Let's get you settled in."

The front porch offers them welcoming seats—rockers and a big wicker swing—but the men pass them by. Kevin lets them in, and suddenly Debbie's arms are wrapped around David. "How are you doing?"

He kisses her as he squeezes back, thankful for the warmth of her in his arms. "I'm fine."

Ellie, Kevin's wife, appears from the living room and gives David a hesitant one-armed hug. "I'm so sorry for your loss." She is so thin, David feels like he's hugging a willow. She tugs at a strand of her long, black hair, and fixes him with shy, sympathetic eyes.

"Thanks, El," David says. He looks up the stairs. "Are the girls in bed?"

Debbie nods. "They went down about an hour ago."

Ellie gestures down the hall to her right. "I made up the downstairs bedroom for you two."

Debbie squeezes Ellie's forearm. "You're so sweet, thanks."

Ellie brightens, some of the awkward tension falling away from her shoulders. "Of course. You need anything at all, just let me know."

A ding makes Kevin look at his cell phone. "The CSRU team just arrived at your parents' house."

"Which department?" David asks sharply. "Milwaukee?"

"No, Wausau."

"Do you have to head back?" asks David, already preparing to return to the car.

"No, my dad is there. He's got it covered." Kevin yawns. "I think I'll turn in. Long day tomorrow."

"Goodnight," Debbie says.

David wavers, feeling the tug of an investigation-in-progress, until Kevin pats him on the shoulder. “Goodnight, bud.”

With that dismissal, David’s pent-up energy begins to leak out, like the helium from a balloon. All of a sudden, he’s so, so tired. “Goodnight,” he says quietly as Kevin and Ellie head upstairs and Debbie pulls him down the hall.

CHAPTER 3

July 3rd, 2016

David awakes to blinding sunlight burning one retina through a crack in the curtains. He rolls slowly, blinking in surprise at the clock on the nightstand. It's already 9:30, and he rarely sleeps past six.

That's when he remembers: his parents are gone.

His first instinct is to roll over, to pull the blankets over his head, to cocoon himself from this world without his mom and dad. But then he thinks of the promise he made them… and himself. He will figure out what happened to them.

If necessary, he will avenge them.

He sits up. He slides out one limb at a time, like a child emerging reluctantly from the warmth of the womb. He sighs heavily, and then he stands. Today, he must start a new life, one in which his parents no longer exist, and his first steps into this strange new world are wobbly.

He goes to the window. He opens the curtain all the way to see that Kevin's Jeep is already gone. He presses his head to the cool glass, shoulders falling. Kevin probably thought he was doing David a favor, letting him sleep in. But he should have known that David wouldn't want to be left behind. Not on this. David looks over at his family's Suburban. Driving it seems like a monumental task, but he'll have to do it. Just... not right this second.

He has to steel himself before he talks to anyone. He has to get his thoughts in order. He has to be able to think like a police detective, not like a grieving son.

David goes over to the bag he didn't unpack last night, other than to pull out his pajama bottoms and his toothbrush. He digs around until he locates the journal Debbie bought him for Christmas, the one he's supposed to use to record his innermost thoughts. It's still pristine. He hasn't been able to bring himself to crack the spine. He'd rather work out his feelings in the weight room than in writing. But today, he's glad his wife packed the thing.

He sits on the bed and begins to jot down every detail he remembers about yesterday's events, in sequence, from the "sleeping" cattle to the 911 call, and beyond. He makes notes on what he wants to investigate, too. Everything from his parents' medicine cabinet to the Mullers' interest in his family's farm. He'll even test the damn well water, like Kevin suggested last night, if that's what it takes.

He loses himself in the minutiae of the case, and he feels less adrift. There's a wrong in the world. He is going to make it right.

* * *

In the kitchen, Debbie watches Ellie whisk eggs in a cup and then flip the hash browns and bacon already sizzling on the stove's central griddle insert. She expected David to be up hours ago. Surely the smell of breakfast will draw him. Debbie looks toward the hall, but she hears no sound of footsteps. Turning back, she catches Ellie watching her son, Joey, out the bay window by the sink. He's sitting on the dock, feet dangling over the edge.

"It's sweet of you to make us all breakfast," says Debbie.

Ellie looks over her shoulder. "It's the least I can do." She bends her head over her work, tipping the cup of scrambled eggs into the waiting skillet.

"And letting us stay with you..." Debbie looks around the homey kitchen. The cabinets have been repainted since the last time they were here, five years ago. "We really appreciate it. David won't say it, but it means a lot to have you and Kevin take us in at a time like this. Especially after the two of them... lost touch." It's a euphemism—both women know that David is the one responsible for the radio silence—but Ellie is kind enough not to push the issue.

At least, not yet. Not today.

"I feel for him," Ellie says. "Losing his parents that way. And being the one that found them—that's gotta be difficult."

"Yeah, I would be a mess," Debbie says. "But David... he internalizes everything."

"Kevin is the same way. He finds any excuse to be at the office instead of being here with us."

Debbie is surprised by the vulnerability of the sentiment. She and Ellie were always friendly because their husbands had grown up together, rather than because they'd bonded in their own right. They never used to share confidences. But maybe, now that both families have been touched by tragedy, all that's about to change. Debbie slides off her stool and moves to put a hand on Ellie's back. "I'm so sorry. I should have said so sooner, but last night was so..." She shudders, getting back on track. "How are you holding up?"

Ellie's lower lip trembles, and she turns her head away. "When I look into his eyes... I still see that beautiful little baby that I held in my arms, seconds after he was born. When he was perfect in every way." She gestures out the bay window. "I still see that little boy running down the dock with his friends. He always had so many friends here at the house." She swallows loud enough for Debbie to hear. "Now he sits on that dock alone each day. *He is so lonely*. It just hurts my heart to watch him sitting there all alone." She covers her mouth to hold in a sob.

Debbie's eyes are watering. "Couldn't he still have friends over? Or is it too risky for him to be around them?"

Ellie's mouth shifts into a scowl. "It's not that. His friends all dumped him last year."

Debbie gapes at her. "What? Why?"

"I honestly don't know. If I didn't know any better, I would swear they are... *afraid* to be around him. Like he's contagious." Ellie stirs the eggs a little more vigorously than necessary. "But that's not even the worst part of all of this. Thinking about the future..." Ellie sets down the spatula and braces herself on the kitchen counter, nails scratching at the granite.

Debbie rubs Ellie's back. "Maybe there's still—" She sucks her words back in as Joey walks through the front door. He shuffles into the kitchen, looking drained. His skin is nearly white. He doesn't move with the vigor of other thirteen-year-old boys; the chemo has stolen that from him, along with his once dark, shaggy hair. Debbie finds herself staring at the frailty of his chest, so thin and flat.

Ellie regains her composure and smiles at her son as he hoists himself into a chair by the dining table, rather than tackling one of the high stools lining the island. "Do you want something to eat? I'm making breakfast for everyone."

Joey grimaces. "No, my stomach doesn't feel well."

Ellie tries to hide her worry with a little smile, but Debbie sees the way she sucks in her cheeks and the sorrow in her eyes. "Why don't you drink some juice, sweetie." Ellie pours a glass of orange juice and brings it to him without waiting for a reply.

"Hi, Joey," says Debbie.

"Hi, Mrs. Schwarz. I'm..." The awkward pause makes Joey seem more like a normal teen than anything about his appearance. "I'm, uh, sorry about what happened to Mr. Schwarz's parents."

"Thank you, sweetie."

"Is Maddie okay?" he asks.

"Why don't you ask her yourself?" Ellie suggests. "It might make her feel better to be with someone her own age right now." She glances at Debbie, and Debbie gives a slow nod. Maddie has been extra prickly since she got up this morning, but Debbie suspects that's just how she's handling the news about her grandparents. Maybe Ellie is right. Maybe Maddie would rather talk to another teen.

"Okay," Joey says, picking up his orange juice glass. Ellie's shoulders relax slightly when he takes the juice with him in his search for Maddie.

Joey takes small sips as he moves slowly around the house, looking for her. As he walks, his stomach fills with butterflies. He's known Maddie his entire life. The Schwarzes used to visit every year, sometimes twice a year. He and Maddie told ghost stories by the light of a single flashlight out on the dock. They had ice cream eating contests in town, betting on who could make their cone last the longest without it melting away. They chased each other through the fields at the Schwarz farm and curled up together to watch the fireworks Joey's dad has always loved to set off over the lake.

But five years ago, the Schwarzes stopped coming to Rindville. Joey's family visited them in Detroit twice after that, but the last time was two years ago.

Joey wonders what Maddie looks like now. What kind of stuff she's into these days. They haven't seen each other since... *before the diagnosis*.

He wonders if she'll stare at him the same way everyone at school does: like he has the plague, like touching him will give them leukemia. His former friends never invite him to do anything anymore, knowing he won't be able to shoot hoops or skateboard without having to sit down for a breather while they all fidget in the awkward silence. Each time they laugh at a shared joke, their eyes flick to him, as though it might be offensive to be happy in front of a dying kid. By the end of the school year, Joey had stopped joining them at lunch just to spare himself the stomach-churning awkwardness.

Maddie won't be like that. He and Maddie had a different kind of bond.

He finds Maddie on the living room couch, engrossed in something on her phone. She's dressed in a white t-shirt and fatigues, with her long legs stretched out over the length of the couch. She looks older. Stronger. Also… harder.

"Hey," he says. "I was looking for you."

She doesn't move her eyes from her phone.

There's a sliver of cushion open by her feet. Joey sits there, accidentally nudging her toes with his hip. That makes her look up. Her gaze skims the smooth top of his head, and her legs immediately curl inward. She sits straighter to scooch further away.

Joey shrinks, even though he now has more couch space. Maybe Maddie isn't any different from his local friends, after all. But he's not ready to give up yet. "What are you looking at?"

Maddie holds up her phone. "What does it look like?"

Joey huffs. "I know it's a cell phone."

"Then why did you ask?"

Joey crosses his arms and then uncrosses them, not wanting to let her see how much she's hurting him. "I'm sorry about your grandparents."

Her head snaps up so fast, Joey is surprised her neck doesn't pop. "Like you care."

"Of course I care. We used to spend a lot of time over there, when you visited."

Maddie snorts.

"Plus," Joey insists, "my family actually lives here. So, like, we saw them in town. Your grandma sent a bunch of casseroles over when I was in the hospital the first time—"

"Don't you have something else to do?" Maddie spits.

Joey shakes his head, glaring back.

Maddie harrumphs and stands up. Ponytail swishing hard enough to swat a fly, she stalks out of the room, nearly barreling into Grace, who's standing in the doorway. Maddie jukes around her sister and shouts, "What are you staring at?!" with her arms splayed wide.

Grace glares at Maddie, hands on hips. "You're mean. I'm telling Mom."

"Be my guest." Maddie points in the direction of the kitchen then stalks off down the hall.

"Hi, Joey," Grace says, before turning around to stomp off to find Debbie.

"Hi, Grace," Joey says to the six-year-old's back. He sinks into the cushion, mumbling to himself, "Well, that went *great*."

In the kitchen, Debbie cuts off midsentence as Grace enters and bellows, "Mom, Maddie was mean to me!"

Debbie massages between her brows with a sigh. "What did she do?"

"She yelled at me."

"What did she say?"

"She asked me what I was staring at. But she said it really, really *mean*."

Debbie holds in an inappropriate snort of laughter. Even at a time like this, her daughters find a way to be at each other's throats. She holds out her hand for Grace's. "Your sister feels bad about Grandma and Grandpa. Just give her some space."

"I feel bad too, but I'm not mean like her." Grace stomps her foot but takes Debbie's offered hand anyway.

Debbie kisses her on the forehead. "Not everyone grieves the same way."

"What does that mean?"

"Just stay away from your sister."

Grace wrinkles her nose and storms back out of the kitchen.

Ellie watches her go and then raises a brow at Debbie. "So, how are the girls doing?"

Debbie makes an exaggerated exhale and puts her face in her hands. "It's rough. Grace hadn't seen Stan and Margaret in person since she was a baby, so she only knew them on the phone—and it wasn't like we called that often, after David and his dad had their falling-out. But she was really excited for this trip. I told her a lot of good things about her grandma, especially."

Ellie nods. "And Maddie?"

"Who knows, with that girl. She's just like her father. She's angry, and she's hurting, but she doesn't want to show anyone her soft underbelly..." Debbie sighs. "I don't know how much David told her about his relationship with his dad, either. They talk sometimes, during their training."

"Training?"

"David's got Maddie learning martial arts."

Ellie's eyebrows go up, but she just says, "Ah."

"Anyway. I'm the last person Maddie would tell her feelings to these days."

"Teenagers," Ellie says softly, shaking her head. She starts dishing out eggs, potatoes, and bacon, popping one plate into the oven on low heat to stay warm for David. "Did David get a chance to make up with his dad? Is that why you're here?"

"No. We're here because his mom asked us to come. I don't know if Stan even knew to expect us until yesterday." Debbie takes the plate Ellie hands her. "Thanks. Did we ever tell you and Kevin exactly what happened?"

"Only that Stan and David had a fight." Her work finished, Ellie gives Debbie her full attention, a fist propped on one hip.

"It all started going downhill when David lost his partner at work. They were close. He had a difficult time dealing with the loss."

Ellie puts her hand over her mouth. "Oh, my God, did he get shot?"

"No... he actually had a heart attack."

Ellie's eyes widen. "How old was he?"

"He was only forty-five."

"That's so young."

Debbie nods. "David took it pretty hard, and of course he internalized everything. He started drinking and... *gambling.*" Debbie takes a deep breath, looking around for the kids before continuing, in a low voice, "He lost our entire savings. All of our credit cards were maxed out."

Ellie bites on her lip. "I'm so sorry. We had no idea."

"David had to ask his dad for a loan in order to pay our mortgage. His dad told him that he would buy us a house here in Rindville if he would agree to take over the farm one day."

"What did David say?"

"You can guess, given that we haven't been back here in five years."

The two women eat their breakfasts quietly for several minutes. Then Ellie says, "When we visited you guys two years ago, you never mentioned any of this."

"The last time you visited, David was still drinking quite

a bit. He hasn't had any alcohol in over a year, though. I guess it's easier to talk about now that he's doing better."

Ellie takes Debbie's hand atop the island. "I'm so sorry."

"Sorry for what?" says David as he trudges into the kitchen, making the women break apart with a start.

"The loss of your parents," Debbie says, before Ellie can reveal their actual topic of conversation. Her husband is sensitive about the past few years. He doesn't like her airing his dirty laundry.

David nods grimly. "Speaking of which… I'm going over to the farm this morning."

"Are you sure?" asks Debbie.

"Yes. I'll take the Suburban."

"Have some breakfast first. Ellie made eggs and hash browns."

David looks like he wants to march right out the door, but after a second, he takes a seat. "Any coffee?"

* * *

David pulls off his parents' driveway into the grass to avoid blocking the crowd of government vehicles lined in a row in front of the house. He spies Kevin's Jeep parked between a white van labeled "Wisconsin Crime Laboratory Bureau" and a brown van that is the property of the Marathon County Coroner.

No one is outside, so David makes his way to the open front door. Strangers bustle back and forth through the living room and call to each other from the stairs. A woman in a green windbreaker swishes in front of David as he steps inside, and he reads the words "Marathon County" on her back. A man in latex gloves totes a camera up the stairs, chatting with a similarly clad man with a sketch book.

David hasn't seen this many people in his parents' house since his sister's memorial.

He finds Kevin and his deputies in the kitchen, listening intently to the low tones of a broad woman with long, dyed-blonde hair. She cuts off at the sight of David's approach, making Kevin look around. His face flickers with emotion, like he'd hoped David wouldn't show up but had resigned himself to the fact that he absolutely would. Then his expression is all business once more.

"David," he says, waving him closer, "let me introduce you to the coroner. This is Janet Aguilar. Marathon County. Janet, David Schwarz—son of the..." He clears his throat. "The deceased."

David shakes Janet's hand. "Nice to meet you."

"Nice to meet you too. Sorry for your loss," says Janet.

"Thanks. What's the status this morning?" David asks briskly. "Where are we with determining cause of death?"

Janet looks a little surprised at the barked questions. "Sorry, do you work for the sheriff's office as well? I was led to believe that Kevin here would be my point person on scene."

"I'm a detective with the Detroit PD," David says.

"Ah." Janet gives David a polite nod and turns to address Kevin again. "We'll be in touch as soon as we have a report for you." She brushes past David with a quick, "Nice meeting you."

David watches her leave through the front door. "What's her deal?"

"What did you expect? You walk in here like you own the place and try to pull rank..." Kevin shrugs. "She doesn't report to you."

David grunts. This is going to be tougher than he thought. His badge means nothing here; in fact, it might be more of a hindrance than a help. Small-town officials hold their jurisdictional rights very close to their chests and don't appreciate outside police snooping around—even if those outside police have a personal connection to the case. David walks away to survey the living room with a scowl and notices the crime scene investigators walking down the stairs. "They're already finished with the photos and sketches?" he asks as Kevin appears at his side.

"Yes. Although they're still gathering evidence."

"Have they found any?"

Kevin nods. "Some prints, some hairs. But most likely, they're your parents'... or yours, from when you were here yesterday."

David grunts again. He knows this is how it usually goes —the painstaking evidence-gathering, the slow ruling out of suspect after suspect. But he'd still hoped to show up this morning to learn that Kevin's team had already found the smoking gun. "Have they examined the herd?" he asks.

"The vet will be by today. He'll be performing the necropsy later this week."

"Good. And the well water?"

"Marathon's sending someone to run those tests."

"Seems like you thought of everything," David begrudgingly says.

Kevin snorts. "Believe it or not, I know how to do my job."

"I didn't mean—"

"I know what you meant." Kevin watches the investigators examining the windowsills in the dining room. "A few of the cows' bodies were attacked by a mountain lion last night," he tells David.

"Mountain lion?"

"Yeah... we've had a few attacks recently, mostly along

the river. Gordon Muller actually reported one of his animals being mauled last month."

"Gordon Muller." David scowls. "We need to search his house."

"I'll be interviewing him later today."

"Can I tag along?"

Kevin shakes his head. "I don't think so."

"Why not?"

"Because I know you too well. You've already made up your mind."

The barb hits home, but David shakes it off. "Don't worry about me. I can be objective."

Kevin cocks his head, arms crossed. "Can you?"

David nods, mouth tight.

"Well, like I said before, you don't work for the sheriff's department. The answer is no."

David's fists clench. He suddenly wants to punch something. He wants to put a hole in the wall, right between his parents' framed wedding photo and the antique mirror his mom had found at a thrift shop when he was a kid and had lovingly restored. "I'm gonna take a look around upstairs," he manages to say through clenched jaw and gritted teeth. "See if I can spot anything your team might've missed."

"Sure. Suit up, man." Kevin gestures toward the table of PPE: disposable gloves and booties, as well as face masks and protective goggles. "I'll be out front if you need me."

Still grumbling, David slides on a pair of latex gloves and slips plastic shoe covers over his sneakers. He heads upstairs as two forensic techs are on their way down. He passes one more deputy on his way to the master bedroom, and then he's alone.

He stands in the doorway to his parents' room. Their bodies have been removed, but he feels like he can still see them lying in their final resting places. It's like a double-exposure on an old film camera, their ghostly images captured for all eternity. He shudders, squares his shoulders, and gets to work.

He starts in the en suite bathroom, with the medicine cabinet. He pulls his journal out of his back jeans pocket and takes note of every prescription bottle: what it's for, when it was issued, how many doses remain. Then he jots down the over-the-counters. Finally, he opens up every shampoo and soap he can find, studying and sniffing for anything that seems amiss.

When he glances at himself in the mirror over the sink, he looks away quickly. He doesn't like this version of himself, unshaven with dark circles under his bloodshot eyes. It reminds him of a time in his life he would prefer to forget.

He moves back out into the bedroom. His parents haven't redecorated since he was a teen, which is actually helpful. Even though David hasn't been here in five years, the furnishings are familiar. He feels like he'll know if anything is out of place. He riffles through drawers and moves knick-knacks from their spots on the shelf, checking for hidden papers or tucked-away treasures. He goes through both nightstands and crouches to look under the bed. He even lifts the mattress.

Finally, he picks up the book his mom was reading, which sits atop a bedside table. It's a mystery, a popular one. One of Debbie's friends was reading it recently, he thinks. There's a bookmark sticking out of the top, about a third of the way in. David gets an unexpected lump in his throat at the thought that his mom will never know how the story ends.

He picks up the book and flips to the page where she left

off. She's made a note in the margins, her handwriting clear and distinctive despite her age: *Not everything is as it seems.*

Damn right it's not, David thinks, beginning to skim the page.

Soon, his detective sense starts tingling. "Poison," he murmurs. "Of course." At the end of the chapter, he slams the book shut. He has to talk to Kevin.

CHAPTER 4

"The book my mom was reading... it reminded me of a story she would tell Lizzy and I as kids," David says to Kevin. They're sitting side by side on the porch, eating sandwiches Kevin had one of his deputies pick up for lunch. "It got me thinking about this case."

Kevin nods. "Really? Well tell me the story. I always loved your mom's stories."

David smirks. "It's about this woman who was married to this man for twenty-eight years. He was the only man she had ever loved. They were high-school sweethearts. They met when they were sixteen and married when they graduated high school, but they never had kids."

"Sad," says Kevin, wondering if this is a true story or some sort of fable, but not wanting to interrupt to find out.

David snorts. "If you say so... Anyways... the husband was a rather frugal man and wasn't very romantic. She had tried for years to talk him into buying her jewelry or taking her out for a nice evening. Maybe dinner and dancing. But after twenty-eight years of marriage she had given up. Then one day when she was shopping in their small town, she saw her husband in a jewelry store. She was excited at the thought of him buying her a necklace or ear-rings. Afterall, in three weeks she was turning fifty. It was an important birthday and maybe he was finally going to get out of his comfort zone and buy her something romantic. The next day, she decided to make him a special dinner. She made a roast with mashed potatoes, his favorite. She had it ready by 5:30 p.m. because in the last ten years, the man had always come home from work at the same time. He was obsessive compulsive about schedules. She had the table set with her fine china and had lit candles to make it romantic, but he didn't walk through the door until 8:00 p.m."

Kevin smirks, shifting back in his seat. "I can see where this is going."

"I'm sure you can. So, when he walked through the door, she asked him where he was and he told her that he had to work late. Well... he was late the next two Thursdays, but she didn't complain because she was excited about her birthday gift. The next day, she finally got her gift, but it wasn't jewelry. It was a blue scarf. She didn't know what to think. Maybe, he was planning to give her the jewelry on their anniversary; which was next Wednesday. Next Wednesday came, but she was once again disappointed when she opened the gift and saw that it wasn't jewelry. She was extremely hurt and disappointed. Who did he buy the jewelry for, she wondered?"

"The next day, when he didn't walk through the door at 5:30 p.m., she had decided enough was enough so she drove down to his work to check on him."

Kevin narrows her eyes. "Let me guess, he wasn't there."

"Would you let me finish?"

Kevin throws his hands up in surrender.

"Alright...," says David, sporting a big, boyish grin, "so

she talked to her husband's boss and he told her that he wasn't working late and didn't know where he was. She went straight home and cried for hours. When he walked through the door at 8:00 p.m., she asked him where he had been the last few hours, and he said working late."

"She spent the whole night obsessing over his lies, and she decided there was only one thing she could do to the man who had betrayed her trust, who had broken her heart. When she looked out the window the next morning, she knew it was a sign. A complete white-out. Something the small town hadn't seen for over a hundred years." David's fingers dance above the railing in a mimicry of falling snowflakes. His voice was hushed as he said, "She poured some poison into his bourbon. She knew that he was a creature of habit, and that at 5:30 p.m., he would make his special drink."

Kevin's scoff breaks any sort of tension David was trying to create.

"That's ridiculous... there's *no way* she would poison her husband of *twenty-eight years* without first talking to him."

David chuckles. "You mean there's no way *you* would poison someone. I've spent ten years in homicide. Trust me, people kill for a lot less than that. The truth is, we are all so different. We react differently to different situations. What makes a person irrational is their life experiences and their DNA. Just because you wouldn't poison him doesn't mean she wouldn't."

"Whatever," says Kevin with an eye roll.

David's smile makes his low, suspenseful tone moot as he continues, "The husband wasn't able to go to work due to the storm and had been depressed all day. At 5:30 p.m. he walks out of their bedroom in his nice suit and tells his wife to get dressed. She asks him why they are getting dressed up if they can't go anywhere because of the blizzard. He tells her he has a big evening planned tonight and wants to celebrate. She goes into the bedroom and comes out a few minutes later in her nice dress. She walks into the kitchen and sees the man making dinner, something he has never done in their twenty-eight years of marriage. She asks him what he is doing and he tells her about the special evening he had planned. He had made dinner reservations at the finest restaurant in town and afterwards they were going dancing. He had spent the last five weeks learning how to dance. Each Thursday evening, he had a two-hour dance lesson. He then shows her the small gift-wrapped box with a bow on top. She covers her mouth and starts to cry. She opens the gift and sees that it's is a heart shaped pendent with an inscription that reads, 'Happy 30th anniversary'. She asks him why it says thirty years when they've only been married for 28 years and... not to mention that their anniversary was a few days ago not today. He tells her that today is a special anniversary. It's the first day he laid eyes on the love of his life. The first day they met. He tells her that he can't wait to spend the next thirty years with her."

David glances sideways at Kevin, who is leaning toward him in curiosity despite himself. He puts on his best ominous voice, with all the theatrics of a kid telling a ghost story around a campfire.

"He hands her a drink and proposes a toast. When he brings the glass to his mouth, she panics and knocks it out of his hand. He asks her if she has gone mad. She doesn't want to tell him why she knocked the drink out of his hand."

"He stares at his wife in disbelief as she empties his bourbon in the sink, but before he can ask her why; he doubles down in pain. He had a drink of bourbon earlier in the day; at 5:30pm while she was getting dressed. When she finds out what he did, she immediately dials 911, but the lines are down due to the blizzard. She can't drive him to the hospital. A few minutes later, his eyes close, and she starts to sob uncontrollably."

"What a sad story," says Kevin through a frown. "That doesn't sound like one of your mom's stories to me."

"It's not over yet. So, after a few hours, she decides she cannot live without him. She can't live knowing she killed the love of her life. So, she swallows the entire bottle of poison. Within an hour, she dies. But a few hours later, her husband wakes. He had only had a very small glass of his special drink. Not enough to kill him. He wakes to find the love of his life, dead."

Kevin blanches, nose wrinkled in distaste. "Good, Lord, that is not how I thought it would end. What exactly is the point of that story?"

David smirks. "According to mom, it was to teach us a lesson, that sometimes things aren't always as they seem."

Kevin cocks one brow. "Really? You would think there would be a better way to teach that lesson."

David chuckles. "Maybe. But it got me thinking about this case."

"I'm not understanding how that story has anything to do with your parent's death."

"It got me thinking about Bradley Muller."

"What?"

"What do you remember about Bradley Muller?"

"Not a ton, other than that he was awful."

Gordon Muller's older son, Ben, was Kevin and David's age. David and Ben were... not friends, exactly. But something like buddies. When you live in a small town, and your family farms border each other, it's hard not to hang out.

Bradley Muller was another story.

"He was a psycho," David says.

"He was... troubled," Kevin agrees.

"Remember when we were, what... ten?" David presses. "Bradley poisoned their German shepherd with wolfsbane."

Kevin's grunt of acknowledgement is more like a growl. "Yeah, his dad thought we did it."

"What a crazy fuck." David pauses, taking a breath before getting to the heart of the matter. "I always thought it was Bradley that killed those Guernseys when we were kids."

"Maybe. I wouldn't put it past him," says Kevin. "But it could have just been a mountain lion, like the good old boys said."

David slowly shakes his head. "It definitely wasn't a mountain lion."

"How can you be so sure?" asks Kevin.

"I saw those Guernseys not long after it happened." David will never forget those red-and-white spotted corpses laid out in the valley, their legs sprawled over one another and their tongues bulging through their lips. "There were no bite marks. They weren't attacked."

"Why didn't you report what you saw?" asks Kevin.

David shrugs. "I told my dad, but he didn't believe me. Anyway, first the Mullers' German shepherd, and then a half-dozen cattle."

"That was years ago."

"Where's Bradley living these days?"

Kevin side-eyes David for the too-casual way he asked the question. "Not sure. He's been gone almost as long as you have."

"Maybe he's home. Maybe he's helping his dad out with some... *business*."

"David..." Kevin begins, his tone a warning.

David looks in the direction of the Muller farm. "He was capable of killing animals as a kid. What if he's capable of more than that now, as an adult?"

"It's one thing to kill a mouthy dog. You're accusing a man of killing not only an entire herd—someone's livelihood—but also two people. That's a big leap."

David forges on with his argument, feeling more and more sure of himself as he talks it through. "Why take out my parents? Well, maybe Gordon assumed I'd be more likely to sell. Maybe I'd even give him a good price, just to get the property off my hands fast."

"If the herd is dead, the value of the property drops," Kevin points out.

"So maybe there's something else he wants the land for." David stands, surveying the miles and miles of pasture visible from the farmhouse porch. "I'm coming with you to speak to the Mullers."

"No, you're not."

"Bradley Muller poisoned my parents," David says bluntly.

Kevin shushes him, eyes darting around to make sure none of the deputies overheard David's accusation. "We don't know that."

"Yet."

Kevin sighs. He massages his temple with his thumb and forefinger. "I'll call you after I complete the interview. That's the best I can do for you."

It's not what David wants, but he knows it's all he's likely to get—and if he pushes his luck, he'll end up with even less. "Thanks."

* * *

Gordon Muller has the leathery skin and wiry muscles that come from decades of hard work outside. When he answers the door for Kevin, he's in his undershirt and suspenders. "Let's get this over with," he says, by way of greeting. "I can spare you half an hour."

"How's it going today, sir?" Kevin asks, walking into the kitchen to take the chair Gordon is pointing at.

"Three of my best cows went lame, and a handful have mastitis," the old man spits out. "Been a hell of a day."

"It could be much worse."

Gordon sits across from him at the wooden table, squinting in his direction. After a beat, he gives a sharp nod. "Shame what happened to the Schwarz herd. A crying shame. You figure out what killed those cows yet?"

Kevin notes that he doesn't mention the human loss. "Not yet. We're working on it."

"So, you're here to see if I got anything wrong with any of mine. Well, like I said, some mastitis, some lameness, but nothing like what you've got over there at Stan's..." Gordon pauses and begrudgingly adds, "May he rest in peace."

"Did you, your family, or your employees notice anything unusual around the Schwarz farm lately?"

Gordon grunts. "No."

"When was the last time you saw Stan and Margaret?"

That question earns Kevin a keen look. "I know you know I was over there last week, deputy."

Kevin shrugs. "I may have heard that, yes. Can you tell me why?"

"I want to expand," Gordon says.

"Why now?"

"It's a good time to buy land."

"And why the Schwarz property?"

"Besides the fact that it's next-door to mine?" Gordon

raises his tufty eyebrows. "Stan and Margaret aren't—I mean, *weren't* getting any younger. Their kid's been away for years. Seemed like a safe bet."

"But Stan wouldn't sell?"

"He is one stubborn sonofabitch," Gordon says. "I mean, he was." He shakes his head. "Do you think the same thing that killed the herd got Stan and Margaret?"

"We're trying to investigate every lead," Kevin says blandly. He looks around the kitchen and sees that there are multiple coffee cups in the dish rack by the sink. "Is Bradley back in town?"

Is he imagining it, or do Gordon's eyes go shifty at the question? David must be rubbing off on him.

"For a couple months now," Gordon says.

"Is he staying here with you and Ben?"

"Yeah, but he usually sleeps in the bunkhouse out by the barn."

"Did either of your sons come with you when you visited the Schwarzes last week?"

Gordon's eyes narrow. "Why do you ask, deputy?"

"We're taking forensic evidence from the property. We need to rule out everyone who was there who might've left some kind of trail behind. It helps us determine if foul play was involved in the deaths."

"Right, right. Foul play." Gordon raps his knuckles against the kitchen table. "Ben and Bradley went with me to talk to Stan."

Kevin nods. "We'll need all three of you to drop by the sheriff's office so we can take some samples."

"Samples of what?" the old man asks warily.

"Hair, saliva..."

There's a pause, and then Gordon says, "Fine, fine. Is after the holiday all right?"

"Holiday… oh." Kevin had almost forgotten tomorrow is the Fourth of July. He thinks of the stockpile of fireworks in his shed by the dock and wonders if it would be insensitive to ask David and Debbie if they can still set them off tomorrow night. "Come by first thing on the fifth."

"Will do." Gordon looks at the clock and stands up. "I gotta get back out there. Vet'll be here soon to take a look at my sick cows."

Kevin stands and holds out his hand. "Thanks for your time."

Gordon shakes his hand, adopting a solemn expression. "Of course. Stan and I might not have seen eye to eye on much, but we were neighbors. Talking to you, helping you figure out what happened… it's the neighborly thing to do."

Kevin nods, thinking of David's insistence that these so-called good neighbors poisoned Stan and Margaret Schwarz, along with three hundred and twenty-five cows.

As he gets back into his Jeep and starts down the long driveway to the main road, Kevin replays the conversation. He's been in law enforcement long enough to suspect that Gordon Muller didn't tell him everything. But that doesn't mean the old dairy farmer is part of a murder plot. And then there was the expression on the man's face when Kevin asked about Bradley…

David's instincts may be right. There's something there. But what?

CHAPTER 5

July 4th, 2016 - Atlanta, Georgia

Thomas Murphy makes it to his cell phone just before the call goes to voicemail. "Hello?" he says, putting it on speaker so he can juggle the tongs, the spatula, and the tray of meats he's been marinating for the barbecue later.

"Thomas. It's William."

"Oh. Hello, sir. Happy Fourth." Thomas sets down everything in his hands and grabs the phone, turning the speaker mode off again. When William Frieden, director of the United States Centers for Disease Control—and Thomas's boss—calls, nothing else takes precedence. "What can I do for you?"

"We're monitoring a developing situation in Wisconsin," the CDC director says. "Might turn out to be nothing. I *hope* it turns out to be nothing. But I wanted to make you aware."

"Of course, sir. Go on."

"We have a possible pathogen on a dairy farm. Three hundred and twenty-five dead cattle... and two dead humans. The farmer and his wife."

"Did local law enforcement contact us?" Thomas asks.

"The coroner called the Wisconsin Department of Health Services. She's having trouble establishing a clear cause of death and wanted to flag the case for follow-up. WDHS called us."

"I see. And you want me on site?"

"Possibly. Go ahead and pack your bag and alert your team, just in case."

"Yes, sir." As the CDC's lead epidemiologist, Thomas spends most of his days sequestered in the lab, but every once in a while, he'll be sent out into the field. Despite the dire circumstances, he always feels a little thrill at the idea of being on site at an investigation. This is what he trained for. "Can you send me the brief?"

"It's already in your inbox," William says, never one to waste time. "You'll get updates as soon as we have them."

"Thanks." After William hangs up, Thomas logs into his email. Sure enough, there's a new secure message waiting for him. He has the presence of mind to put the tray of marinating meat into the fridge and then jogs to his office, where he starts opening files on his laptop. It may be a national holiday, but the barbecue can wait.

* * *

Rindville, Wisconsin

The iced tea glass bites at David's palm with a chill that spreads up his arm and cools his whole body in the July heat. The setting sun grows orange blossoms on the lake as David takes a sip and strolls along the back deck toward Kevin and the grill. Kevin salutes him with his own glass full of frozen margarita and then flips the line of burgers with a theatrical flourish.

"Tell me again what Gordon Muller said to you," David says without preamble.

Kevin groans. "We went over this last night."

"Tell me again," David insists.

"He wants to expand his operation and needs the acreage. He feels like now is a good time to buy land."

David scowls. "Bullshit... there's got to be another reason he wants my parents' property."

"Well, that may be true, but—"

"We need to get a subpoena and search the Mullers' house... and their attorney's office."

Kevin rolls his shoulders back, trying to match David's bulk and height. "We don't have just cause."

David huffs through his nose like an angry bull.

"When the toxicology report comes in, maybe..." Kevin allows. "If there's something in your parents' systems that shouldn't be there."

"There will be," David says darkly, taking a drink of his iced tea. He grimaces, wishing it were something stronger.

Before coming outside to talk to Kevin, he'd stood in the kitchen, staring at the two pitchers—margaritas and tea—side by side. His eyes had drifted to the icy lumps in the left one. He'd salivated, already able to taste the lime juice. He used to love a frozen margarita on a hot day.

But he knows good and well that, for him, one leads to far too many. He also knows that the numbness a margarita would provide would only last through the second round, and then all the emotions he's been trying to avoid would slam into him at once. He would no longer be able to shove his parents' deaths into that locked-away chamber deep in his head. The door would burst open.

"At least the Mullers agreed to give samples for DNA testing," he grumbles to Kevin.

"They're supposed to drop by the sheriff's department tomorrow morning." Kevin starts transferring burgers to a nearby plate.

David wonders what Kevin would do if he got up early and beat him to work… if David was there waiting when Gordon, Ben, and Bradley Muller showed up. It's a tempting idea. He could catch the Muller men off guard. Ask them some questions before they had a chance to square their stories.

Of course, that could throw a wrench into the whole investigation. Nothing David learned would be admissible, since he doesn't have jurisdiction here. He'd never forgive himself if it was his fault his parents never got their justice.

The sun isn't close enough to the horizon for the nearby oak to shade the entire deck, so David plops in one of the lounge chairs beneath two large blue and white umbrellas. He grimaces when he leans back and feels his shoulder blades stick to his shirt thanks to the dense humidity. When the breeze comes off the lake, he leans forward and closes his eyes to savor the refreshing sensation.

A bang startles his eyes back open.

"Oops," says Ellie with a tipsy giggle.

She and Debbie readjust their grips on the card tables and successfully navigate them through the door this time. They drop them with loud thuds in the very center of the deck and bend to begin unfolding the legs.

"Not there. You'll block the stairs," says David. "The kids will come charging through here and knock everything over." He motions with his glass. "Move it toward the railing there a little, and back some."

Debbie straightens with hands on her hips. "You want to help us?"

David waves his hand. "No… I'm good."

She gives him a look that says, *Watch yourself.*

She won't say it out loud, but she's worried about him. Just like she's worried about the girls. David's wife is a worrier, and David hates to be worried over. He's strong. He can handle himself. He scowls at the glass in his hand and looks up just in time to see Debbie's eyes dart from the glass to his face.

She walks over, far too casually, and takes the sweaty glass. "Need a refill?" she asks. Before he can answer, she slurps down the last of his iced tea herself. He watches as she swishes the liquid around in her mouth.

He knows what she's doing. He grinds his teeth to keep from snapping at her.

She still doesn't completely trust him.

Then again, he doesn't completely trust himself.

"I'll bring you another glass of tea," she says out loud. Her face says, *I'm not sorry I did it. I'd do it again.* But her shoulders are relaxed as she heads inside, flip-flops smacking the deck.

"What was that all about?" asks Kevin, who spent the whole awkward interaction laying out sausages on the grill.

"She was checking up on me."

Kevin's eyebrows go up.

"A few years back, I went through some... *stuff.* I started drinking. About a year ago, I stopped. I promised Deb that I wouldn't drink again."

"El mentioned that you guys went through a rough patch," Kevin says, looking back down at his sizzling bratwursts.

David scoffs. "That's Deb. She's always sharing too much. So... you must know we lost our home."

"No... she didn't mention that." Kevin flicks sympathetic eyes up from the grill. "Sorry."

"Yeah... I started gambling and... well, you know." David's gaze wanders to the lake. Joey is swimming. Maddie is lying alone on a towel on the deck, phone in hand. "I asked my dad for help but... he refused. Well... I should say, he offered to help if I moved back here to Rindville, to take over the farm."

"And obviously you told him—"

"To go fuck himself," David finishes with a joyless laugh.

"You never told me any of this when we visited you guys in Detroit two years ago."

"I was too embarrassed at the time to talk about it."

High, happy shrieks turn both men's heads toward their younger children. Grace is on the oak's tire swing, leaning back with legs extended, hands clasped on the rope, and her long hair trailing the ground as Bethany pushes her in wide circles. "Let's swim!" Grace suddenly shouts, bouncing off the swing and racing toward the dock. Bethany follows, squealing with glee.

The two girls are a marked contrast to the teenagers. Maddie and Joey are silent and solitary. They haven't spoken to each other since their failed conversation yesterday morning.

But as David watches, Joey paddles over to the slippery plastic stairs bolted to the wooden dock. He climbs out of the water and approaches Maddie.

"Huh," David says, shading his eyes with his hand. "Look."

Kevin turns and smiles. "Hey, maybe there's hope for those two again after all."

* * *

"I'll race you to the buoy." Joey points to the white, bobbing structure about fifty yards into the water.

Maddie doesn't even bother to look up from her cell phone. "No."

"Come on... it'll be fun. If you beat me, I'll do dishes when it's your turn."

Maddie props herself on an elbow. The aggression in her glare makes him take a half-step back. "Leave me alone."

Joey steels himself and reaches down for her hand, dripping all over her towel. "Are you afraid you'll lose? Come on."

Maddie yanks her hand away before he can touch it and jumps up with surprising speed. "Leave me alone... *freak!*" She storms away, nearly pushing her little sister into the water as she goes.

Joey watches his former friend run as fast as she can away from him, a knot forming in his throat. Part of him wishes he'd knocked her phone out of her hands and onto her face, instead of trying to be nice. The rest of him is just lonely.

Grace tugs on his finger, holding a donut float around her waist with one hand. "Bethany and I are gonna swim now. I'll race you to the buoy."

Joey shakes his head with as much of a smile as he can manage. "No, thanks."

Grace shrugs, plugs her nose, and leaps into the water with Bethany, both of them nearly coming out of the floats when they smack the surface of the lake. They come back up through the holes laughing.

Joey looks on in envy. Then he turns and trudges across the lawn, into the house, and up to his room.

* * *

After dinner, Debbie pushes away her paper plate, smeared with the remnants of potato salad and ketchup spilled from her burger, and grabs the last cube of watermelon. The porch light and a handful of tiki torches illuminate the dark yard where David and Kevin are setting up the fireworks.

"Should we make Joey a plate?" she asks Ellie.

Ellie presses her lips together as she sighs. "He said he wasn't feeling well. I'll save him something, but I doubt he'll eat it. The chemo really does a number on him."

"Is he coming down to watch the fireworks?"

"No, he wanted to stay in his room, in case he got sick."

Debbie's heart constricts. "Poor kid." Despite the delicious meal and the margaritas and the beautiful weather and the promise of fireworks to come, this is the most melancholy Fourth of July she's ever experienced. Everyone's good moods are only surface-deep. They're all walking on eggshells.

Except for Bethany and Grace, of course. Watching her younger daughter bond with Bethany has given Debbie her only genuine moments of joy since driving up to Stan and Margaret's house forty-eight hours ago. "It's going to be hard to separate them," she observes to Ellie.

"Well. Good thing you aren't leaving anytime soon," Ellie says in a bittersweet voice.

"Right. The investigation, the memorial..." Debbie feels the weight of it all press down on her again. She tries to shake it off. The fireworks are almost ready.

Down in the grass, David steadies a pipe mortar and looks sideways to make sure he's lined it up properly with Kevin's.

Kevin rubs his hands together. "I think we're ready. Do you want to do the honors?"

David grabs the lighter, feeling a flicker of excitement in

his chest. He can't wait to see Grace's face. She's never seen one of Kevin's shows. "Is everyone ready?" he calls up to the deck.

Debbie, Ellie, Grace, and Bethany cheer. Maddie gives a sarcastic thumbs-up without looking away from that damn cell phone of hers.

The wick hisses at David as he lights the first firework. He and Kevin jog backward as it shoots off into the heavens and explodes with a bang that heats David's blood. Red, green, and blue fire outward in a perfect circle and then rain down, winking at them all.

"That's a beautiful sight," Kevin says appreciatively, and David has to agree.

Fireworks bring back nothing but good memories, and his weary heart drinks them in like a tonic: shouts of delight, his arm around Debbie and his eyes on her red shorts, good food, happy kids, summer nights sparkling with blues and silvers to rival the stars.

From the highest back window, Joey looks on at the fireworks from the edge of his bed, smiling as one last tear rolls free from his cheek.

CHAPTER 6

July 5th, 2016

David wakes early, jolted to consciousness by the realization that the Muller men are supposed to report into the sheriff's office this morning to have their fingerprints taken and their DNA sampled. He wants, desperately, to be there. But his rational detective side reminds him that his presence won't help. It might even hurt the case.

Still, now that he's awake, he can't do nothing.

"I'm going over to the farm," he says to Debbie, who's yawning and stretching in bed beside him.

"I'll come with you," she says, sitting up.

"You don't have to. Stay here with the kids." David begins changing from his pajamas into a gray shirt and jeans.

"Ellie can watch the kids." Debbie goes to her suitcase and begins pawing through the clothes she brought for the week.

"Doesn't she have work or something?" David grumbles,

for no reason other than that he's not in the mood for company.

His wife shoots him a look. "She quit her job at the bank when Joey got sick, to take care of him."

"Oh," David says, flustered by the mention of the situation he's been trying not to dwell on, despite his conversation with Kevin in the Jeep on their first night here. "Right. Well. I need to do some looking around at the house and on the property. You won't want to tag along after me."

"I won't bother you. And I won't disturb anything the deputies are doing," Debbie adds quickly, knowing that's her husband's next argument. "But I do need to go over there."

David snorts. "Why?"

"Your mom has a recipe that I need for tonight. I want to make her lasagna for dinner. I already promised Ellie. She's been doing all the cooking."

David knows he's losing this battle, but he can't help trying one more tactic: "You can't remove anything from the house."

"I won't. I just need to take a picture of the index card. Your mom kept all her recipes on those index cards, remember?"

David looks up at the ceiling and shakes his head. "Can't you do it some other time?"

Debbie kisses his cheek. "You won't even know I'm there."

* * *

The yellow tape stretched across the porch steps is now the only thing David can see as he pulls up the driveway. The once familiar silhouette of his childhood home feels twisted by it, like an invading kudzu constricting the foundation. As he tears his gaze from the bold canary hue, David is surprised to see only one deputy car parked out front.

He parks behind the truck that would have been his and gets out of the Suburban. Debbie hurries out of the car and walks close to his side. Despite their bickering this morning, he takes her hand as they walk up the steps and he lifts the tape for her to duck under.

The dark-haired deputy walks out just as they are about to enter, and an awkward, sidestepping dance ensues as they trade places. The deputy tips his hat to them as an apology.

"Where is everyone?" asks David.

"CSRU finished gathering evidence."

"And your people?"

"Sheriff Schumer has us on a rotation here now," the deputy says. "My partner and I are about to swap out with our replacements."

"Oh." David takes a deep breath, knowing that it's Jack's call on how many personnel to keep on site. "Thanks for checking up on the place."

"Sure. I'll let them know you're inside." The man goes down the porch steps, meeting his partner as he comes around the side of the house. They get into their patrol car and drive off, presumably to meet the next shift at the end of the driveway.

David puts on blue latex gloves and plastic shoe covers and motions for Debbie to do the same. He nudges the front door open. "After you."

Debbie spins in a circle in the dimly lit living room. "Wow... this place seems so..." She shakes her head with her fingers resting against her lips, not wanting to say the first word that popped into her mind: *lifeless*. "I'm used to it always smelling like your mom's cooking."

David clears his throat and strides into the kitchen. On the counter sits a green recipe box painted with faded pink flowers. David's fingers tremble as they run along the top and his throat closes up. This box holds so many memories. His mother was really a tremendous cook. She showed her love through food.

Composing himself with a small but rough shake of the head, he opens it and flips through the cards. "Here it is. 'Baked Lasagna.'"

Debbie smiles as she rushes over, phone already in camera mode.

"I'm going to look around a bit," says David as she snaps photos.

"Okay. I'm going to get a few more recipes while I'm here. Then I'll find you."

"Okay."

David leaves his wife in the kitchen and heads upstairs. He does a sweep of the master bedroom, looking for any clues he may have missed two days ago. Nothing jumps out at him. He scans the other upstairs rooms, including the one that was his bedroom as a kid. It's now a guest room that bears no resemblance to the space he remembers. He definitely didn't have floral wallpaper and matching throw pillows. Shaking his head, he returns downstairs. He treads carefully through the living room, imagining the meeting between his parents and the Mullers happening on these very sofas. His mother would have set out tea or lemonade, with coasters to protect the table. She would have offered cookies or scones. There was always something fresh-baked, in case of company.

Thinking of the Mullers in this house, acting innocent, makes David's blood simmer with resentment.

He pulls out his phone and texts Kevin: "Any news?"

When several minutes pass without a response, he puts the phone away and stalks out the back door.

He finds Debbie sitting on the hand-carved wooden bench in his mother's garden. Her body blocks out the words he knows are carved into the backrest: "Lizzy Schwarz, Our Angel in Heaven." He almost turns around immediately and goes back inside—he's not ready for this—but before he can sneak away, Debbie looks up and spots him. Her eyes are glistening with tears.

David's chest clenches with emotion. "No," he tells himself through gritted teeth. His eyes don't obey the command. Instead, they begin to prickle with unshed tears. This garden was his mother's pride and joy. But the flowers will wilt now. The strawberries will dry up and shrivel. And that bench...

The headstone...

"This is where your mom took me to talk, when she realized we were serious about each other," Debbie says in a shaky voice. "I think she wanted... I think she wanted your sister to be a part of the conversation."

David shakes his head, trying in vain to hold back the tsunami of emotion rising up inside him.

"'Thank God he found you,' she said. 'I couldn't hardly get him to take a shower, much less get such a snazzy haircut.'" Debbie pauses, her smile watery. "Like anyone could ever make you do anything you didn't want to do."

David snorts.

"Come over here," Debbie says softly. She holds out a hand, and then pats the seat beside her. "Talk to me."

His feet walk him to her against the wishes of his brain. He sits, even though he doesn't want to. Or maybe, deep down, he does. His heart is overriding his mind. "This place was sacred to Mom and Dad," he says after a long moment.

"The whole garden, but especially this spot." At the center of a field of white edelweiss flowers sits Elizabeth Mary Schwarz's final resting place.

"Losing a child so young..." Debbie says, staring at the dates etched into the headstone: 4/21/76 to 6/22/90. "I can't imagine pain like that."

David makes a noise of agreement. Neither of them mentions Joey, but they both think of him—and Kevin and Ellie.

Debbie's neck is sweating, but the breeze blows gently on her nape, keeping her comfortable. It blows the fluffy clouds overhead, offering moments of shade sliced by razors of sunbeams. She looks up to see a sky full of light gray puffballs promising rain later in the day. "I asked your mom a few years back why she plants this garden each year. She said it had something to do with her grandparents."

"Yeah."

"What's the story behind it?" she asks, scooting closer to loop her arm through his.

He sighs. "You've seen *The Sound of Music*, right?"

"Yes."

"It's basically the same story. Her grandfather was a munitions specialist living in Austria near the border of Switzerland. The Third Reich were going to force him to join their army. So... he took his family... his wife and three kids... and left Austria. They crossed the border to Switzerland."

Debbie nods. "Just like the Von Trapp family."

Though his shoulders remain stiff, David interlocks his fingers with hers as he continues. "Her father was twelve when they crossed the border. He met my grandmother six years later. Apparently, it's customary for Swiss men to climb steep rocks to gather edelweiss flowers to demonstrate their love. Although he wasn't Swiss, he still gave my grandmother a bouquet of edelweiss when he proposed. She saved the flowers. When they moved to the U.S., my grandmother planted a garden to remind her of the Alps... and the day my grandfather proposed. She saw it as a symbol of his love for her."

"How sweet. And your mom kept the tradition alive."

David nods.

"Did the flowers always bloom?" Debbie asks.

David abruptly crumples, putting his head in his hands.

Debbie puts her arm around his shoulders in concern. "David, what is it?"

"There was one year..."

Debbie hears him swallow hard and rubs his back. "Take your time."

"June 28th, 1990." He looks over at Debbie, unable to stop the tears now.

"Your birthday?"

"Yeah, my sixteenth. Mom promised me..." He can barely get the words out. "She promised to take me to the DMV to get my driver's license. I had been looking forward to that day for months."

Debbie glances to the second date on the headstone. "But your sister had just died."

"Yup, June 22nd." He takes in a shuddering breath. "I was so fucking selfish."

"David—"

"She wouldn't take me to the DMV. Or couldn't. She was grieving. I know that. But I was tired of my mom ignoring me and spending all of her time in this fucking garden. So... I went to the shed and started up the riding mower."

Debbie stiffens with her hands on his shoulders. "Oh, my God."

David covers his eyes and starts to sob in earnest, each inhale violent, each cry a wail. Debbie clings to him as he chokes out, "I miss Lizzy... *so much*. And now Mom's gone too... I can't..."

He turns his head into her shoulder, and Debbie runs a hand over the back of his head and neck, as she does with their girls in times of sorrow or distress.

"I'm so sorry for what I did that day," he says, voice muffled by her shirt.

"You were sixteen. Your sister had just passed away. That was a confusing, emotional time."

He looks up at her. "Yeah... well..." He sits up and wipes away his tears with two swipes of his large hand. "Anyway, that was the year the edelweiss didn't bloom. But there's something I left out."

Debbie braces herself. "What?"

David grimaces as if she's twisted a knife in his gut. His

chest shudders with new sobs. Drawing in an enormous breath, he says, "My sister was cremated, and..." He sweeps a hand over the garden.

Debbie puts a hand over her mouth. "Oh no... they spread her ashes in the garden?"

"Yeah. The day before my birthday. The day before I destroyed the garden with the mower."

"What did your mom do?"

"She didn't say a word to me... she couldn't even look at me for days."

"And your dad?"

David's smile is bitter, his eyes so hollow he looks wooden, and Debbie's stomach flips with unease. "He completely lost his mind. He beat the shit out of me. I couldn't go out in public for weeks. I thought I was going to lose the vision in my right eye." He brushes away the hair from the right side of his forehead. "You see this?" Debbie knows the two-inch scar's shape well, but never knew its origin. "That was my dad's work."

Debbie swallows hard, choosing her words carefully. "You said your mom didn't talk to you for days, but... your dad had just beaten you."

"Oh... she yelled at him for it... but she still ignored me."

"What about your dad?"

"He felt guilty for what he did. He apologized over and over, but I never let him off the hook."

Debbie squeezes her knees, taking it all in. "Wow... why didn't you tell me this before?"

David shrugs. "I was just... *too embarrassed.*" He pauses for a moment and says, "That brick fence around the garden. My dad built it a week later."

Debbie feels a cold droplet on her face and raises a palm

to the sky. The beginnings of a sprinkle wet her skin. "Looks like it's going to rain."

David looks up at the gray skies. "I still want to walk the property a little. Do you want to wait in the car?" It sounds more like an order than a request.

"Okay," Debbie says reluctantly, not sure she wants to leave her husband alone when he's in such a vulnerable state. "But don't take too long."

"Half an hour," David says, pushing on his knees to stand up. He kisses his wife's cheek and strides off toward the barn.

* * *

It's properly raining by the time Debbie shuts the Suburban door. She dries herself off with some paper napkins she finds in the center console and settles in to wait with her phone. That's when she sees that she has a text message from Ellie: "Call me when you have a chance. Thanks."

She calls right away, but no answer.

She glances at the sky, noting that the rain has slackened a bit. She opens her door and heads for the barn to get her husband.

David walks past the old red barn, the one that looks like something out of a storybook. Over the rise beyond is the farm's real base of operations, a larger free-stall structure that's open at the sides but covered on top. This is where the cows stayed when they weren't out to pasture. Many of them died here three days ago, but those bodies have already been removed.

The place still smells, though. As he steps inside, the pungent stench of manure and rotting hay makes David's eyes water. He lifts his t-shirt up over his nose and walks carefully down the center of the barn, keeping his eyes peeled not to step on any existing footprints. He's sure CSRU has already taken photos and plaster casts of the clearest prints to compare with his dad's old work-boots and the shoes worn by the farm's other employees, but it can't hurt to be careful.

He can hear flies buzzing around in some of the stalls. It's an unsettling sound, given that there's no other noise. There's nothing alive in this place that was built solely to care for living creatures.

Huh. David stops as something occurs to him. *There's nothing alive here,* he thinks again.

But there *should* be. Birds, for a start. And rodents. One of his jobs as a teen was pest control. David moved around the fake predators that scared off the birds and fixed the netting that blocked off common nesting sites. He set the mouse traps and made sure the barrels of feed were properly sealed. When pests did get in—and they always did—David was in charge of calling the exterminator.

But today, the barn is too silent, too still.

David makes his way over to the nearest milking stall. He scans the space and then zeroes in on a pile of loose hay in the corner. He squints, wanting to get closer but not wanting to disturb the scene any more than he already has. Are those...?

"David!"

He turns to see his wife approaching from the fields, hands on her hips. "Stay there!" he shouts back. Then he's unnerved all over again: the sound of his shouting voice should have sent sparrows and starlings bursting from the rafters.

"We need to get back to Kevin and Ellie's!" Debbie

shouts, putting her hands around her mouth to carry the sound.

David waves her off, snapping on a spare glove he tucked in his jean's pocket earlier and reaching for a rake that's hanging from a nearby beam. He maneuvers the rake over the stall fence and pokes at the pile of hay. He jostles it again. And again.

His phone buzzes in his pocket. With his free hand, he grabs it, expecting it to be Debbie calling him so she doesn't have to shout. Instead, he sees Kevin's contact on the screen. He answers. "Hello?"

"Hi, David," the chief deputy says. "The Mullers were in first thing this morning, and we've already heard back from Wausau Crime Labs."

"And?" David prompts, still gently raking the hay in the stall.

"The patent fingerprints we lifted from your parents' coffee table were a match for both Gordon and Ben Muller."

David's heart leaps. "What about Bradley?"

"No match yet, but Gordon already told us his sons were both with him that day."

"Is it enough for a subpoena?" David asks.

"If we find any of their prints anywhere other than the main living room or entryway, maybe," Kevin says. "But I'd still rather wait for the toxicology report."

"Jesus, Kevin, what's the holdup—" David breaks off, jaw dropping open.

"David? Did I lose you?"

"Kevin, I'm at my parents' farm. You should get back down here. And call CSRU again too."

"Why?"

David moves to the adjacent milking stall and uses his

rake to move around some of the piled-up hay there. He does the same for the next stall, and the next.

"David, what's going on?"

"Just get here," David says, shaking his head. He can't believe what he's looking at.

Dead birds. Dead mice. Dozens and dozens of them, scattered across the floor, covered in loose hay. If he hadn't looked closely, his eyes would've slid right over them. Brown mice and brown birds on a brown floor. There's no blood. No mess. Just a horde of tiny bodies.

Well, David thinks to himself, gesturing for his wife to stay back, *that explains all the flies.*

* * *

The moment Debbie walks into their hosts' living room, she knows something is wrong. Mumbled conversation cuts off, and Kevin and Ellie stare somberly at David and Debbie from the couch. Kevin's hand lays atop Ellie's, and she looks like she's been crying.

"Everything okay?" asks Debbie, doing her best to sound cheery.

Ellie stands up, nostrils flaring as she takes in a deep breath. Debbie expects her to yell, but instead, her voice is weary and defeated as she says, "We found out why Joey didn't come outside to watch the fireworks yesterday." She clears her throat, eyes fixed on the floor. "And why he spent the entire day in his room."

Debbie walks over to Ellie and takes her hand, hoping to lift some of the weight from whatever burden she's shouldering. "What is it?"

Ellie slides her hand free and says, "Apparently, Maddie called Joey a *freak* yesterday, while they were on the dock."

Motherly rage flashes behind her eyes as she lifts them to Debbie's face in a defiant stare, daring Debbie to contest the statement. "Joey is used to that kind of talk from the kids at school, but he felt safe around Maddie. He's known her his entire life. So... it really hurt his feelings."

Debbie makes a guttural sound, punched in the gut by embarrassment, shame, and righteous anger. "I am so sorry. Where is Maddie?" she says, voice clipped as she tries not to scream for her daughter from the living room.

Ellie points. "She's in the family room watching TV."

Debbie nods and walks with heavy footfalls across the foyer. She glances over her shoulder to find David heading for the kitchen, and her blood boils. She'll deal with him later. In the family room, Maddie has taken up the entire couch, her head propped on one side and her feet the other. Grace and Bethany sit on the plush rug, heads tilted back to see their cartoons.

Debbie smiles at Grace and Bethany, then puts a hand on Maddie's shoulder. Maddie looks up from her phone with her typical annoyed, eternally bored expression, but when she sees Debbie's face, she sits up in a hurry. "Follow me, young lady."

Maddie rolls her eyes, but her voice is childish and frightened when she says, "What?"

"Now!" Debbie can feel her face burning as she squints her eyes to angry slits.

Grace jumps at Debbie's outburst, but when she sees Debbie's attention trained on Maddie, she smiles wide.

"Relax," says Maddie with a huff as she gets off the couch.

Debbie leads her out the back onto the deck. Maddie leans against the rail furthest from the house and puts her phone back in front of her face.

"Hand it over," Debbie snarls, gesturing to the phone.

"What? Why?!" She tucks the device to her chest like a baby.

"Now!"

Maddie takes her earbuds out and slams her phone in Debbie's hand. "What did I do?"

Debbie crosses her arms and breathes deep, trying to regain her composure. "Why did Joey spend the day in his room?"

Maddie throws up her arms . "How should I know?"

Debbie shakes her head. "You realize he stayed in his room last night and missed fireworks because of you."

Maddie's mouth pops open in a disbelieving scoff. "Me? What did I do?"

"You don't even realize what you did?" Debbie raises one brow as high as it will go. "I don't know what makes me more upset. The fact that you hurt that boy's feelings... or the fact that you don't even care."

Maddie begins the teenage shrug dance, bobbing her shoulders up and down with a goofy look of feigned outrage on her face "How did I hurt his feelings?"

"You don't remember calling him a freak?" asks Debbie.

Maddie closes her eyes. "I did but..."

"But what?!"

"Let me finish." Maddie puts her hands up.

Debbie taps a finger on her elbow. "I'm waiting."

"He wouldn't leave me alone... and he kept asking me if I was afraid to race him."

Debbie narrows her eyes. "That's it? That's your excuse?!"

"After last year..." Maddie shakes her head. "... forget it, you wouldn't understand."

"You're right... I don't. There is no excuse for what you did." Debbie's glare is cut short by the sliding door opening.

As David walks toward them, Debbie shoots him an "about time" look that he doesn't seem to register.

With a huff, Debbie looks back to Maddie. "You need to apologize to Joey."

"What? No!" Maddie stomps her foot.

David steps in between them. "Are you sure that's a good idea?" he asks Debbie.

Debbie grinds her teeth, doing her best to burn a hole through his forehead with her eyes.

David takes a step back. "No, you're right. She should apologize."

"That's not fair!" Maddie whines.

"This isn't up for debate. Follow me," says Debbie.

Maddie doesn't budge. "Can I have my phone back?"

Debbie looks back and says, "What do you think?" in her deadliest voice.

She heads back into the house, not needing to look back to know David and Maddie are both close behind.

She leads Maddie to Kevin and Ellie, still on the couch, and nudges her in front as she says, "Maddie has something she would like to say to Joey."

Ellie nods and says, "He's in his room."

David watches Debbie and Maddie walk up the stairs, loitering in the hopes Debbie won't notice him missing.

"I have some news" says Kevin, making David sigh in relief.

"What is it?" Surely any news is better than all the drama going on upstairs.

The two men walk outside. "We did find Bradley's fingerprints," says Kevin after the two men take a seat on the porch.

"Where?"

"Upstairs bathroom."

David stands up. "I knew it!"

"Whoa, whoa." Kevin holds up a hand. "You can't still seriously think Bradley Muller did this. All those dead birds and mice... it makes me think we're dealing with something else."

"They were collateral damage," David says. "He was going for the cows, but he ended up taking out everything in the barn. Maybe we're looking for something airborne or waterborne—like he sprayed it over the whole area."

"Or maybe I was on the right track testing the well water. This just doesn't seem like a murder case, David." Kevin leans forward to rest his elbows on his knees. "Think like a detective. Does this scream 'murder' to you?"

"I *am* thinking like a detective," David says stubbornly. "And yes, it does."

Kevin shakes his head. "I heard that the coroner looped in the Wisconsin Department of Health Services. This might be a public health thing, man."

"It's not."

"Honestly," Kevin says, staring out at the trees in front, "I hope you're right. And I hope we figure it out soon. Before anyone or anything else gets hurt."

CHAPTER 7

July 6th, 2016

It's 1:30 in the morning, and David can't sleep. Not even the sound of Debbie's breathing, slow and smooth, can lull him into dreamland himself. When he can't stand it a moment longer, he flicks back the covers and slides out of bed. Debbie's muttering makes him freeze, but she simply rolls over. Grabbing a pair of jeans and his discarded shirt from the floor, he dresses quietly and then walks on the balls of his feet to the front door, where he puts on his shoes. Kevin doesn't lock his doors, so David's only obstacle is the creaking hinge. He opens the door just wide enough to squeeze through and makes it to his Suburban without a hitch.

I hope we figure it out soon. Before anyone or anything else gets hurt, Kevin had said. Well, if the sheriff's office won't take the threat of the Mullers seriously, David will take matters into his own hands.

Using his GPS, he makes his way to the office of Hemming & White, Attorneys at Law. He parks down the street and then jogs to the parking lot, slipping around the building as he extracts a lock-picking kit from his back pocket. He slows as he approaches, looking for cameras. Nothing on the outside. He puts on latex gloves and inserts his tools into the lock. He enters the two-story joint office building and braces himself for an alarm, but none sounds. A quick scan shows no cameras here either. Thank God for small-town trust.

The building smells of must and old man cologne. The stairs are carpeted and full of dander gathered over decades. David suppresses a sneeze as he reaches the top. Down the long hallway, he finds the door for "Hemming & White." He stares at the gold plaque, steeling himself. Perhaps this goes against many of the oaths he took as a police officer, but not the most important one: to serve and protect.

There is something dirty here, he can feel it. There's no way he's going to let Kevin keep poking around the edges of this mess instead of getting a subpoena. He's bound to spook all those involved, without ever making a real move, and there will be nothing to keep them from destroying evidence. With a cautionary glance down the hall, he makes quick work of the lock and enters the office. The row of filing cabinets lures him, and he pulls open the drawer labeled with an M. Flipping through the folders inside, he hunts for the name Muller. The cabinets give him hope that these good ol' boys keep hard copies rather than going the fully digital route.

With a soft exclamation, he snatches the Muller folder out and sets it on top of the cabinet. His fingers are feather light, flying over the pages to peel them up just long enough to scan the contents. The words "Geological Survey" jump out at him, and he pulls the document free. David uses his phone for better light and sees that the entire first page is a map marked with longitude and latitude. One spot is circled, and David's gut somersaults. It's a patch of land that straddles the border between his parents' property and the Mullers'.

The next page of the report has photos paperclipped to it. The Muller lot and his parents' lot are both depicted in the images. David recognizes a spot in the back acreage near the rock cliff he used to try to scale as a kid, much to his mother's distress.

"What the hell?" he mutters.

He skims the report. According to the landscape inspector the Mullers hired, the location has an estimated fifty-thousand tonnes of IOCG. There are extensive breccia-vein sheets within the host stratigraphy. Iron enrichment of siliciclastic rocks by metasomatism.

David has no idea what any of it means.

The next page is a little more helpful. It states that the IOCG deposit has a grade of five percent copper and three grams per tonne of gold. David's eyebrows jump. *Gold and copper deposits? On his parents' property?!*

It's a motive. A good one.

David's dad wouldn't sell off the secretly valuable land, and so Gordon Muller schemed to take the elder Schwarzes off the board.

David snaps pictures of every page in the report with his cell phone and puts the folder back. The filing cabinet slams harder than he expected, and he pauses at the office door, trying to listen for any sounds of movement over the pounding of his own heart. Stepping into the hall, he risks a smile as he nears the stairs. Home free. But the creak of a door behind him seizes his muscles. He turns his head over his shoulder to see the janitor tugging his cart out of a door at the other end of the hall. He's whistling to music from his headphones, and David knows it's now or never. He sprints down the stairs two at a time, but the old steps scream a warning to the janitor above.

"Hey!" shouts the janitor, and David can hear him thundering down the hall. He never looks back, determined not to show his face, and flies through the door. He uses the remote on his keychain to unlock his car doors and jumps into the driver's seat before the janitor even makes it to the bottom of the stairs. Breathing hard, David slams the car door shut and drives away.

* * *

After a few hours of fitful sleep, David rolls out of bed to go wake his older daughter. He and Maddie haven't trained together since they got here, and he doesn't want her to lose her edge.

Plus, he saw how she looked last night when Debbie took away her phone. There's nothing like a vigorous Krav Maga session to work out some anger and aggression. David should know.

He drags his reluctant teenager out onto the lawn between the Schumers' house and the lake. They stretch and jog in place to warm up, and then they get to it.

Time flies as they kick, spin, and flip. They both sweat buckets, even though the July heat hasn't set in this early in the morning. They're so engrossed in their training that it takes David a while to register that he has an audience.

"Kevin," he grunts, extending a hand to help his daughter up from the grass.

"Wow, that was like watching an action movie," Kevin says, only half joking. "Remind me, how long have you been working on that?"

"Since she was six," David says, wiping his brow with the hem of his shirt. "I'll start with Grace soon. Two hours a day, six days a week."

Kevin blanches. "Jesus, David. That's a little overkill, don't you think?"

"No daughter of mine is going to be a victim," David says crisply.

David gestures to the house as Maddie runs inside to shower. "You should teach Bethany."

"Maybe." Kevin clears his throat. "I came out here to talk to you about something."

"About the case?"

"You could say that. There was a report of a break-in at the Hemming & White office early this morning. The night janitor saw someone leaving the office."

"Really. Any idea who it was?" David says, voice even. Maybe too even.

"As it turns out… the man fits your description." Kevin stares at David until the other man blinks.

David rolls his eyes. "All right, you clearly you know it was me." He pulls out his cell phone and opens the camera app. "I have something I want to show you." He hands the phone to Kevin, open on the picture of the survey. "Take a look at this."

Kevin widens the picture with his thumb and index finger. "Geological Survey?"

David nods. "It's motive."

Kevin scrolls down. "What is IOCG?"

"I had to look it up. It stands for Iron Oxide Copper Gold. There are fifty-thousand tonnes of this stuff under the surface of the Mullers' lot and my parents' property. The deposit borders our lots."

"Damn!" says Kevin. "How much is it worth?"

David shrugs. "I have no idea. I'm sure it's valuable or else Muller wouldn't be so desperate to buy my parents' lot. It's the motive we need to get a subpoena."

Kevin scratches his head. "That's not motive. It's not like he inherits your dad's lot if they die."

David sighs. "He knew my dad wasn't going to sell, but I would."

"Maybe. I'll tell you what. Let me talk with my dad and see what he says. But we have to figure out a *legal* way to acquire this information." Kevin gives David a stern look. "You know I can't use cell phone photos from your late-night break-in."

"Obviously." David puffs out a breath, like, *I did my job, now you do yours.*

"In the meantime, you should talk to a geologist. Find out how much of the deposit is on your parents' land and how much it's actually worth."

"I'll call someone later."

Kevin nods toward the house. "Have you told Deb?"

"Not yet."

"Why the hell not?"

"Well, for a start, she won't like what I did to get this information. But she's also busy this morning with the..." David fades off as the adrenaline of having made a break in the case leaches out. In its place, reality seeps back in. "She's handling most of the plans for the memorial."

Kevin's face goes sympathetic. "Right."

"She's better at that stuff than I am."

"What, emotions?"

David lets out a bark of something that's almost laughter. "I meant, planning events. But yeah, probably emotions too."

"You need to tell her. You may be sitting on millions."

"Millions of what?" Debbie asks, walking over.

"Ants," David says quickly, brushing off the seat of his pants. "I think I sat on an anthill."

His wife wrinkles her nose. "Well, go inside and get cleaned up. We need to get into town."

"What for?" David follows her back to the house.

"You and I have a meeting at the funeral home," she says.

"Are you sure you need me there?" David asks.

"Yes, sweetie. They were your parents." Debbie says gently. She turns to Kevin. "Ellie and I were talking about the four of us going into Jackson for dinner tonight. No kids... what do you think?"

"Sounds great, we can get drinks," says Kevin.

David rolls his eyes. "You can... *I'll be the DD.*"

"Cool." Kevin gives David a goofy thumbs up that nearly makes him bust out laughing, but he's still too sour about Debbie's hawk-eye on his drinking habits.

"Are we sure we want Maddie watching Gracie?" David asks his wife.

"Maddie doesn't have her phone to distract her," says Debbie with a falsely sweet smile that actually does make David chuckle.

"Besides," says Kevin, "Joey will help... they'll be fine. We'll only be gone for a few hours."

* * *

Grace flops on the carpet in front of the TV, throwing her arms over her head with an enormous sigh.

"I'm sooo bored," she laments to Bethany.

The adults are long gone, out to a fancy dinner in Jackson to have loads of fun while she and Bethany are left to eat microwaved chicken nuggets with grouchy Maddie. Joey isn't so bad, but for a big kid, he can't seem to do much. When the movie ended an hour ago, Grace wanted to play a board game, but Joey had run upstairs saying he didn't feel good. Grace wasn't about to ask Maddie, and a board game is no fun with just two, so she and Bethany have been playing Barbies. But Bethany just wants Barbie and Theresa to keep going shopping. Grace wanted to get out her Ken doll to play boyfriends, but Bethany doesn't have a Ken.

"Well, what else can we do?" Bethany asks with a shrug.

Grace glances to the couch to find Maddie drooling onto the decorative pillow.

Grace's eyes light up as she pops upright. "Let's go on the raft."

Bethany hugs herself with a frown. "No, I'm not allowed."

"It's okay... I'm older than you." Grace pokes her chest with her thumb. "I'll make sure nothing happens. Come on."

Bethany presses her lips tight together, but when she glances over at Maddie, still sound asleep, she begins to grin. With a triumphant laugh, Grace pops up and races Bethany out the back and down to the dock.

Grace nearly slips on the wet wood, arms flailing in circles like a cartoon, and slows to a walk. The inflatable boat is bumping the dock with each little wave.

"Grace, we have to put these on," says Bethany, holding out an identical purple life jacket to the one she has already put on.

Grace sighs and hurries to get it, but her heel skids on the dock, and she screams as she flies backward over the side. A crack resounds in her head as the cold water splashes against her back, and then all she sees is black.

Grace sinks out of sight before Bethany's eyes. "Grace!" Bethany screams from the dock, watching crimson darken the water under the bright spotlight attached to the nearby shed. The inflatable boat's motor is sticking out of the water, the propeller dripping blood where Grace's head smacked against it.

Panic swells in Bethany's chest, and she shrieks all the way back to the house, flying barefoot through the grass and up the deck steps.

She bursts into the family room, screaming, "Help! It's Grace!"

Maddie jolts awake and her eyes grow big at the sight of Bethany in a life vest. "Where's Gracie?"

"She hit her head. She fell in the lake!"

Maddie sits frozen.

Bethany yanks on Maddie's arm, breathing so fast and hard her lungs hurt.

"I can't swim," says Maddie, ghost-white. "Where's Joey?"

"He's upstairs."

Maddie and Bethany run upstairs screaming Joey's name.

He comes out of the bathroom wiping his mouth. His already pale skin goes ashen. "What's wrong?!"

"Bethany said that Grace hit her head and fell in the lake," yells Maddie.

"What did she hit her head against?" Joey asks his sister.

"The boat," Bethany responds. "Hurry!"

Joey sprints past both girls, putting everything he has into his legs, ignoring the fire in his chest. Slowing only when he touches down on the dock to prevent slipping, he immediately spots the blood on the motor and leaps into a practiced dive, straight down into the dark.

Maddie watches his feet disappear and clings to the nearest dock post, leaning out over the water, her panicked tears splashing onto the surface. She tries not to look at the red smear on the boat, and instead holds her breath as she peers into the water, looking for Joey's shadow. Bethany drops to her hands and knees at the edge near Maddie, waiting and wideeyed.

No movement but the small waves rocking the boat. Maddie's streaming tears become raucous sobs. Joey's been too long. Grace has been down there even longer. *She's dead. She's dead and it's your fault*, a nasty voice whispers in Maddie's head.

Joey's head breaches, his mouth stretched wide as he sucks in a ragged breath. Maddie is reaching for him even before Grace's head pops up in his arms, her soaked hair plastered to her ghostly face. Maddie hauls Grace out, heaving with all her considerable strength against the dead weight. She falls backward with Grace limp on top of her, soaking her through her clothes.

"Oh my God!" She screams, wiping Grace's hair off her face. Her head rocks sideways, her eyes closed and chest still. "Is she dead?!" Maddie forces through a sob.

Joey climbs out and rolls Grace off Maddie onto the dock. Without a word, he tilts her head back and pinches her nose. The two quick breaths he forces into her mouth puff her cheeks and make her chest rise an inch. Then he presses both palms to her chest to begin compressions. He looks up at Maddie with wild eyes. "Go in the house and dial 911!"

Maddie reaches instinctively into her pocket, but her cell phone isn't there. With a loud wail of exasperation, she sprints to the house.

Joey yells at Bethany, "Go in the house with her. She may

not know our address… you do!" Bethany turns and runs after Maddie.

Joey focuses on his work, ignoring his own pain and the all the protests of his exhausted body. Two breaths, thirty compressions. Two breaths, thirty compressions. He mumbles "Staying Alive" under his breath to keep the rhythm.

Maddie's pounding feet on the dock make him look up. Bethany is right behind her.

"I called 911, they're on their way."

Joey takes two more breaths and on the fifteenth compression, a small fountain of water bubbles up from Grace's mouth. She sputters, her eyes still closed. Maddie's hands fly over her mouth as a hysterical laugh of relief spills between her fingers. Joey turns Grace onto her side and hits the center of her back with the heel of his hand. More water trickles out of Grace's mouth onto the dock, and Maddie hits her knees, her sobs comingling with soft, happy exclamations. She pulls her sister into her arms and rocks her. She coos Grace's name, but the little girl makes no sound other than soft breaths through her open mouth, her hands dangling to brush the wood of the dock.

When the sirens wail in the driveway and the ambulance casts a red backlight on the house, Maddie carefully lays Grace on the dock and runs to the front to direct the paramedics to the dock. As she waves the man and woman through the front door, a sheriff's patrol car zips up the driveway.

* * *

Debbie is choking on barely suppressed panic as she follows the nurse, who's moving much too slow, through the hospital halls. David, Ellie, and Kevin are on her heels, but she barely registers their presence.

The nurse ushers her into a waiting area where Maddie, Bethany, and Joey are sitting with hands in their laps, like punished schoolchildren. The deputy sitting beside them rises as Kevin enters, but Debbie blows past him and yanks Maddie into a hug. Maddie presses her face into Debbie's chest, and her sobs startle Debbie even more than the radio call that brought them all here.

Beside them, Kevin embraces his deputy and says, "Thanks for bringing the kids here and watching them. I really appreciate it."

The dark-haired man nods and says, "Anything for you, brother."

"Where is Grace," David asks the nurse, and she gestures for him to follow her to the nearby nurse's station.

Ellie takes her children in her arms and kisses the tops of their heads.

Debbie tips Maddie's chin up so she can look her in the eyes. "How did she fall in the lake?"

Maddie's eyes fill with a fresh glaze of tears. "It's all my—"

"It's my fault," Joey says loudly. "Maddie was sick to her stomach and asked me to watch the girls. I didn't see them walk down to the lake. Grace hit her head on the boat. I'm so sorry, Mrs. Schwarz."

Debbie looks between Joey and Maddie, utterly perplexed. Her mouth drops open, but no sound comes out. Her instincts are shot along with her nerves, and she's not sure what to think. Before she can decide if she's getting the truth, David taps her shoulder.

She turns to find him standing with a balding doctor in a white lab coat, a stethoscope hanging from his neck.

"How's Gracie?"

"She's going to be just fine," says the doctor with a soft smile, "despite a concussion and a few bruised ribs." He turns to Joey. "Are you the young man that performed CPR?"

Joey nods.

"You saved her life young man... or at the very least prevented her from having permanent brain damage. You're a hero." The doctor shakes Joey's hand.

Joey flushes pink, and a smile lights his face. Kevin nods his head at Joey, and Elli hugs him tight, saying, "I'm so proud of you."

Maddie offers Joey the smallest of smiles, wiping at her face.

"When can we see Gracie?" asks Debbie.

"Actually, you can see her now. She's talking to the nurses."

"Great, when will she be able to come home?" says Debbie, breathing much easier.

"We want to run a few more tests, then you can take her home."

The Schwarz's follow him to Grace's room. She spies them over the nurse's shoulder and pops a wide grin. Debbie's heart clenches at the sight of her in the white hospital gown, her name written on her plastic bracelet in marker. The nurse stands up from the end of the bed and says, "She's an amazing young lady," as she leaves the room.

Debbie takes the nurse's place and pulls Grace into a tight hug, covering her in wet, tearful kisses. "Thank God you're alright!"

David puts his hand on Grace's thin arm and says, "You're a Schwarz. We're built tough."

Debbie rolls her eyes at her husband then looks at Grace and says, "They have a few more tests to run and then you can come home with us." She smiles down at Grace and runs her hand over her soft cheek. "Thank God Bethany ran in the house as soon as you fell in the lake."

A knock on the open door signals the nurses' reentry. "I need to run an EEG," she says. "You can wait here if you want."

Debbie nods, folding her hands in her lap. She'll wait as long as it takes.

CHAPTER 8

July 7th, 2016 - 9:30am

Debbie pokes her head into Grace's bedroom for the fifth time this morning, her motherly anxiety pulling her back to check her breathing again and again, just in case. Grace's eyes are open this time. Debbie enters with a grin, sits on the edge of her bed, and checks her forehead, though she can summon no logical reason for doing so. "How are you feeling, Sweetie?"

"I'm fine, Mom."

"What you did..." Debbie shakes her head. "...you know better, you could have drowned."

Grace looks down at the covers, sheepish. "I'm sorry."

"You have to promise me... you won't do anything like that again. Promise?"

Grace nods.

"I don't know what I would do if I lost you." She pulls Grace in, savoring her warmth, the thrum of her pulse beneath Debbie's lips when she dips her head to kiss her neck. She is so small. A down-covered baby bird who only thinks she's ready to fly. She fell and Debbie was not there to catch her. There is no way to be there every minute. So many chances to lose her. Debbie squeezes her tight for as long as she possibly can, holding in the tears until she slips back into the hall.

* * *

10:30am

Joey makes swirling ripple patterns with the long stick he his holding, sitting at the end of the dock. The sound of footsteps makes him look over his shoulder, and with a jolt of surprise, he sees Maddie.

"Hey," Maddie says, sitting beside him. She tucks her knees to her chest to rest her chin atop them.

"Hi."

"Why did you lie to my parents?" she says, looking at the lake instead of him. "You took the blame even though it was my fault."

Joey shrugs. "I know what parents are like."

Maddie narrows her eyes, at last turning toward him. "What does that mean?"

"They're always looking for someone to blame when something goes wrong. I could see that your mom was upset and frustrated. She wanted someone to blame... someone to yell at." He offers a crooked half-grin that he hopes doesn't look as cynical as it feels. "I knew she wouldn't yell at me."

Maddie lets out a surprised chuckle. "You don't talk like a kid."

"Well... I am a freak... *remember*."

Maddie exhales sharply, picking at the hem of her fatigues. "I'm sorry I called you that. I was ... embarrassed, I guess."

"Why were you embarrassed?"

"I can't swim."

Joey scoffs. "So? You could have told me."

"Last year," she says, leaning back on her hands to talk to the sky, "I was at a birthday party when everyone decided to play 'Marco Polo'. I was the only one that couldn't..."

Joey waits patiently, observing the sheen of the sun on the hair around her face, wanting to give his full attention but not wanting to make her too uncomfortable by staring right at her.

"Julie Grey..." Maddie curls her lips in disgust. "What a bitch. She thought it was funny that I couldn't go in the water. She kept saying that I was afraid... *scared*. Everyone laughed."

"That sucks."

Maddie nods. "When she got out of the pool. I kind of, like... beat the crap out of her."

Joey snorts. "Really?"

"Really."

When she doesn't smile, he says, "How bad was it?"

She licks nervously at her bottom lip. "They had to rush her to the hospital."

Joey gawks. "Holy shit!"

"Yeah, my dad has been training me since I was six... but he didn't think swim lessons were very important."

His eyes travel over her arms, trim but much larger than most girls he knows. Her fingers are covered in tiny abrasions, her knuckles sporting bruises. "Is that why you wear fatigues all the time and not shorts or leggings?"

"I don't know... Maybe." She hugs her knees again. "After that day... everyone stopped talking to me. They're all afraid of me, I guess."

"You and I have something in common," he says, offering a smile.

To his surprise, she returns it. "What? Kids at your school are afraid you'll beat the shit out of them?" Her eyes travel over his arms now, spindly and mostly bone.

"No... but they're afraid they'll catch what I have."

Maddie scrunches her whole face as she snorts. "They think they can catch cancer?"

Joey nods.

"Idiots."

"It's true." Joey looks back at the house. His mother is in her usual post at the kitchen window, ever watchful and worried. "My mom always tells me, that it is so much easier to fool someone than it is to convince them that they've been fooled."

Maddie chuckles. "Is that what she tells you?"

"Yeah. Well... it's easy to fool an idiot into thinking they can catch leukemia by touching me, but nearly impossible to convince them that they can't."

"I guess."

A silence falls over them, but to Joey's delight, it feels natural rather than awkward. So ... normal. Just two people sitting beside each other, enjoying a nice view.

"You lied to protect me," Maddie says without warning, "but why did you tell your mom I called you a freak?"

Joey shakes his head fast enough to rattle his brain. "It wasn't me," he says, then flinches at how overeager he sounds. He looks away from her face, and the flipflopping in his gut eases. "It was Grace. She heard you say it and told my mom."

"God... she's always telling on me."

Joey chuckles. "Well... that's another thing we have in common. Bethany does the same thing to me."

Maddie smiles, and everything seems to sparkle. At long last, maybe he has a friend again.

* * *

Noon

David grins as he plants his feet to better brace himself against Maddie's blow, absorbing the punch with a square, padded bag attached to his palm. He grunts with the effort to keep himself upright as Maddie channels all her energy and momentum into her arms. Her strength is incredible for a thirteen-year old. Right hook, left jab, and then her leg shoots up without warning, her foot colliding with the very center of the bag, and David's arm flails to the side against his will.

"Good. Keep your elbow down," says David, correcting her stance. Maddie throws herself into a new round of punches, elbow tucked in obediently.

"What really happened last night, Maddie?" asks David.

"What do you mean?" she pants. "Gracie hit her head and fell in the lake." Maddie jukes him, throwing up her left but punching with her right, and David staggers back a step.

David signals a time out and grabs a water bottle for her. "That's not what I'm talking about. Why did Joey lie to us? Why did he take the blame for something that was your fault?"

Maddie stiffens. "What makes you think that?" she says too loudly.

"Don't lie to me!"

She flushes under his hard stare and looks at the ground, rubbing her right arm with her left hand.

"I've been a detective for ten years," he says, softening a

little as her stance reminds him of her age. "Don't you think I know when someone is lying?"

Maddie takes a sip of water and wipes her mouth. "Joey got sick and I was supposed to watch Gracie and Bethany, but I, like..." she heaves a huge sigh, "... fell asleep."

"I don't know what I am more disappointed in... the fact that you fell asleep or that you let someone take the blame for something that was your fault."

Maddie's lip trembles until she bites her cheek to steady it. "What are you going to do?"

David sighs, stares at her for a moment. "I'm not telling your mother... that's for sure. She'd overreact like she always does... but you have to promise me that you will never let someone take the blame for something that is your fault."

Maddie brightens a little, eyes shooting up to meet his. "Okay... I promise."

* * *

1:30pm

Maddie's freshly washed ponytail bounces around her shoulders, tickling her ears. Her baby hairs are already beginning to stick to her neck in the humidity as the Schumer and Schwarz families make their way into the heart of downtown Rindville.

"We're going to check out the boutique," says Ellie, making a circle with her finger to indicate herself, Debbie, and the younger girls.

Debbie thankfully doesn't try to get Maddie to come along as she leads Grace into the store by the hand. Grace "ooos" at the frilliest thing in the window display.

Maddie crosses her arms and looks both ways down the street. The entire downtown area is basically two short streets, and the buildings are all weird, like gingerbread houses with a ton of flower baskets on the fronts. Instead of a regular sidewalk, the walkways are made of wood. Nothing looks particularly interesting, based on what she can see of the thirty or so shops.

Kevin and David lead her and Joey to a hardware store. Joey's dad says something about a drill bit, and Maddie doesn't bother to suppress her yawn.

Joey smirks at her and pulls on his dad's sleeve. "Can Maddie and I go down the street and get an ice cream cone?"

"Sure," he says, and to Maddie's shock, he pulls out his wallet.

"Thanks, Dad," says Joey, as Kevin hands him two fives.

Maddie keeps pace with Joey as they head back onto the street. "That was lit," she says with a growing grin. "My dad would have said no."

"Well... there is one advantage to being sick all the time. When I ask for something to eat, they always say yes."

And as much as she's trying to push him away, she likes Joey.

Maddie isn't the same girl she was two years ago, when the Schumers visited Detroit. Of course, Joey is different too. She can hardly believe how different. He's like a ghost of his former self. But the changes he's gone through weren't his fault. He's a tragedy. Maddie is a cautionary tale.

They approach a tiny shop with a big blue sign that says, "Cedar Crest Ice Cream Factory." There's a line out the door. "It'll move fast," Joey says, getting in the line.

He's right. Within five minutes, they are inside. When it's their turn, they order one firecracker and one butter brittle cone. They lick their cones all the way to the nearest bench, set between two more flower displays, these grown in big barrels instead of baskets. Maddie is certain her pop-rock filled scoop is dyeing her lips blue and red, but she can't be bothered to care much.

It's not like she has anyone left in her life to impress.

As the thought crosses her mind, she sits up from the nonchalant slump she perfected at school this past year, after everything happened. If she doesn't have anyone to impress, she might as well try to talk to Joey the way they used to.

"You don't seem that sick today," she observes.

He startles and flinches, like he's anticipating a planned attack. "I feel okay," he says warily.

"You got sick not long after you visited us in Detroit, right?" Maddie twirls her cone to lick all the way around it. "You had hair then."

"I did. I started chemo and radiation a couple months later."

"Does it suck to be bald?"

Joey gives her a long, considering look, like he still doesn't trust her. Then he says, "Nah. What really sucks is losing my balance."

"Balance?" asks Maddie.

"I fall a lot. I used to—" Joey cuts himself off, and the tips of his ears go pink.

Maddie playfully pokes his arm. "What?"

"There's this cool place I like to go. It's on a cliff. It overlooks the town, but I haven't been there in over a year." He takes a huge bite with his lips to stop a large drip from falling on his hand. "I miss it."

"Why haven't you been there?"

"Well... for one thing... my mom won't let me out of her site... even for a few seconds. And, you have to cross this ledge that is only a foot wide to get to the cliff."

"So?"

"It's a long-ways down, and my balance sucks."

Maddie nods.

Joey's brings his cone close for another lick, and in the next blink, it flies out of his hand, swatted by a meaty hand. The cone crunches on the pavement. Laughter makes Maddie and Joey look behind them. Two tubby boys with the same weak jaw and button nose have Joey fixed in their sights, not even glancing at Maddie. She glowers at them all the same, figuring these are some of the idiots from Joey's school.

"Really, Jeb?! What did you do that for?" says Joey, standing up to face them head on. They tower over him by about half a foot.

"What's wrong... *skin head*?" asks Jeb.

Joey glares but says nothing. Maddie sees him swallow hard.

Jeb smirks. "Are you going to cry?" He looks to the slightly smaller boy who Maddie would bet money is his brother. "I think he's going to cry, Wilbur."

Wilbur's chortle sounds like a cartoon caveman, low, garbled, and vacant. "Be careful Jeb, don't let him touch you, or you'll lose your hair."

Both boys laugh so hard their dangling chins jiggle as they come around the bench to advance on Joey.

Maddie leaps up, a fire in her chest. "What the fuck?" She jabs a finger at Jeb and says through gritted teeth, "Give him five bucks to buy another cone... *and* say you're sorry!"

Jeb blinks at Maddie, his whole face drooping in confusion. Then he looks between her and Maddie, and he sprouts an oafish grin. He pulls a ten-dollar bill out of his pocket and dangles it in front of Joey. "Sorry..." When Joey reaches for the bill, Jeb pulls it away and shoves it back in his pocket. "Sorry you're such a freak!"

The boys guffaw again, and Maddie's ears ring.

Ice cream cone cracking in her right fist, she takes a step toward Jeb. "Give him your money and apologize."

Jeb raises himself to his full height and looks down his nose at her. "Fuck you. I'm not giving him anything."

Joey shakes his head and says, "It doesn't matter, Maddie. I didn't want it anyways."

Jeb smirks. "*Maddie*... your name is Maddie?" Wilbur laughs along with him.

Maddie scoffs. "You think that's funny... *Jeb!* What kind of name is Jeb anyways? It sounds like something a hick would name their kid."

"Fuck you!" Jeb thunders while Wilbur laughs on.

"You look like a dude in those fatigues."

In one stride, Maddie brings herself inches from Jeb and snarls up at him. "Give him your money or he'll give you leukemia."

"How's he going to give me leukemia?" says Jeb with a lackluster eye roll, but his scoffed laugh falters.

"You'll get it, after I make you *lick* his ice cream off the ground, " she hisses through her teeth, pointing at Joey's melting cone.

Jeb throws back his head and belly laughs. "Maybe I'll make you lick it off the ground."

Wilbur is in hysterics now, bent over double. Maddie rams her ice cream in his face, the cone shattering on his nose and choking off his laugh. The heel of her hand cuts off Jeb's protest, slamming into his Adam's apple. He doubles over, choking, and her knee cracks his nose, spurting blood into Joey's puddle of ice cream. Maddie sees Wilbur's clumsy swing a mile away. Ducking beneath it, she pops up in his face and throws an elbow across her body, snapping his head sideways. As his hands go for his face, her foot finds his groin. With a high cry, he bows in agony, and she breaks his nose with her knee, knocking him back onto his butt to writhe on the sidewalk.

The brothers groan together on the ground, but Maddie isn't done with them. She rolls Jeb over and twists his arm behind his back, making his shoulder joint bulge beneath his shirt. She forces him to his knees that way, and he props himself up on his left elbow, his right twisted toward the sky.

"Lick the ice cream!" Maddie roars.

"Fuck you!"

She pushes down on his arm, yelling "Lick it!" His high scream becomes a whimper, and he leans down to lick the blob of butter brittle.

Two pairs of sensible heels click closer, but Maddie doesn't bother looking up until one of the elderly women puts a hand to her chest and squawks, "My goodness, young lady! Stop that!"

Maddie releases Jeb and says, "Well... now you're going to get leukemia."

She backs off him, arms crossed, mostly ignoring the two women, who are shaking their heads.

"Who is raising these children," the second mutters.

"Now, the two of you—" the first woman says.

"You fucking bitch!" Jeb screams over her, rolling on his side to look up at Maddie. "I'm going to kill you!"

The two women shriek in unison and start clicking away, looking back over their shoulders as if the big bad teens might be chasing after them.

Maddie smirks down at Jeb, then turns a kinder smile on Joey. He is gaping at her, looking slightly green. Without looking down, Maddie swings her boot directly into Jeb's crotch. Bending over his moaning form, she rummages through his pocket and pulls out his ten-dollar bill.

Joey is rigid as she holds the bill out to him.

"Do you want another ice cream?" she asks, calming her breathing. She tilts a thumb toward the pavement. "It's on Jeb."

For a moment, fear seizes her chest. Perhaps Joey will be afraid of her now, just like everyone else her age. He isn't moving. His jaw still dangles.

Then, his mouth lifts in a flabbergasted smile as she shouts, "Oh my God, that was amazing! Holy shit!"

Maddie smiles. "Let's go." They walk around the two brothers. Wilbur keeps his head and eyes low, cowed as Maddie passes. Jeb spits blood and teeth on the pavement.

Running feet make Maddie look back at a middle-aged woman who crouches beside the boys. "Do you need help?"

Wilbur lifts his head, but before he can speak, Jeb shouts, "Fuck you!" Blood sprays from his mouth onto her dress and she gasps as she stumbles back.

"We should hurry," says Maddie, picking up the pace toward the hardware store. When David and Kevin aren't to be found, Joey and Maddie head to the parking lot and find both their parents and sisters packing bags into the car.

"Where were you two?" asks Debbie.

"We got some ice cream," says Maddie with a shrug.

She sees her father's eyes travel to the blood stains on the knees of her pants and the toe of her boot, and she fights to keep her face neutral.

"Everything okay?" he asks, raising one eyebrow.

Pulling her best Daddy's Girl smile, she says, "Yeah. Great!"

* * *

3:30pm

A booming on the front door makes Kevin jump in his seat on the couch. He makes a face at David, who shrugs and says, "Your house," as he holds out a hand toward the door.

Massaging a blossoming headache, Kevin opens the front door onto a giant of a man with a "protein shake" physique in the upper half of his torso but a pot belly below that dangles over his large belt buckle. His cleanshaven scalp is marked with an "okay" hand sign tattoo and the number 14. More ink loops around the straps of his muscle top.

Suppressing a weary sigh, Kevin nods and says, "Hey, Dan." Then he blinks hard, thinking his eyes are playing tricks. Dan's boys, Jeb and Wilbur are peeking their heads around their father with snarls that would be identical if Jeb had all his teeth.

"What happened to your boys?" he says through a grimace, looking closer at their blackened, taped noses and purpled eyes.

"Joey and that girl he was with, did this," thunders Dan, making Kevin's ears ring.

He holds up two hands, trying to keep from smirking his disbelief. "Are you saying that Joey and Maddie beat the crap out of your two boys?" asks Kevin.

"I want an apology," Dan says through his teeth.

In the living room, David hears aggressive shouts and hurries to the entryway. He narrows his eyes at the bloody and bruised boys, but he holds himself at his full height as he takes in their mountain of a father. "What happened here?" he says, using his no-nonsense cop voice.

"David, this is one of my neighbors, Dan. He said that Maddie and Joey are responsible for his sons' injuries," says Kevin, his eyes praying for David to say it can't be true.

Ignoring Kevin's silent plea, David lights up. "Really? Maddie!" he hollers back into the house.

She runs to the front door, standing at attention, and David smirks when he sees the two boys flinch under her stoic gaze.

David gestures to the two boys. "Is this your doing?"

She nods, standing like a soldier at attention and awaiting a verbal thrashing.

David smiles at her, basking in the glory of his pupil's victory. Thirteen and already a champ. Though he is not surprised (he's seen her humiliate grown men in sparing contests), the sense of pride does not dissipate with each new victory. This one was probably a piece of cake, though.

"What happened?" asks David.

"These idiots came up behind us and knocked Joey's ice cream out of his hand onto the sidewalk. Then they made fun of him. They called him a skin head."

David's chest swells. She was a regular samurai, in his opinion. A protector. He winks at her and whispers, "Nicely done."

"Are you going to make her apologize?!" Dan roars from the doorway.

David turns slowly. "Yeah, I should apologize." He meets Dan's eyes directly and tilts his head ever so slightly in a taunt. "I'm sorry your two boys are such pussies that they let a thirteen-year-old girl beat the shit out of them."

Dan lunges, but Kevin, steps between and shoves him back. "Back off, Dan."

"Let him in!" says David, throwing out his arms. "I would love to humiliate that fat fuck in front of his two morons!"

Dan's eyes bulge as he goes red. David only smirks at his

blustering. Kevin stands firm when Dan tries to shove him aside. Kevin backs Dan up a step and blocks the doorway with his arms. Looking over his shoulder at David while Dan throws wild arms over his shoulders, hands clutching at the air, Kevin yells, "You're not helping."

"I'm going to kill you," yells Dan.

Kevin pushes Dan backwards with his forearm and says, "Leave now! You're not getting an apology."

"I'm filing charges against that bitch!" Dan says, spitting everywhere as he thrusts a fat finger at Maddie. "She also stole ten bucks from Jeb!"

David storms the door, his ears whistling like a tea kettle with the mounting heat in his head. Kevin turns in the door and narrows his eyes, stopping David with a finger on his chest. "Stop, you'll just end up doing something you regret." Kevin swipes a hand through the air at Dan without turning, saying, "Leave now!"

Dan turns his boys by the shoulders and marches them back to his pick-up truck. Before he slams the driver side door, he bellows, "I'm suing!"

David knocks Kevin aside as he pulls a ten-dollar bill from his wallet. Walking into the lawn, he throws the bill into the grass. "There you go, you fat fuck!"

Dan rolls down his window and yells, "Fuck you!" The truck tires kick up dirt as he accelerates backward down the driveway.

Kevin just shakes his head slowly as he stares at David.

"What?"

* * *

5:00pm

David lets the sun warm his shins as its rays penetrate

between the thin porch rails, rolling his eyes at the "disappointed parent" tone in Kevin's voice as he rattles on. David isn't sure how long he's been talking, but it's something about Joey getting mixed up in a fight.

When Kevin pauses, David relaxes back into the chair.

"It's amazing you haven't gotten yourself suspended," says Kevin.

"What are you talking about?" says David, whipping his head toward Kevin.

"If I hadn't stopped you... you would have put Dan in the hospital."

David scoffs. "No doubt."

Kevin shakes his head. "God... you're so easily provoked. Nothing's changed."

"What do mean, nothing's changed?" asks David.

"You remember when we were fifteen and you put those three kids in the hospital?" asks Kevin.

Sour bile rises to the back of David's mouth. "That was different. They were making fun of my sister. They're lucky I didn't kill them."

"See... that's what I mean. You can't let guys like Dan provoke you. They're not worth it."

David rolls his eyes. "Whatever. I've managed to avoid suspension for fifteen years."

"It's a miracle," says Kevin, throwing up a hand. He sighs, frowning.

David has nothing to say. He does his best to focus on the lazily floating clouds.

"There's something I need to tell you," says Kevin, and David groans internally. "I talked with Janet this morning."

David perks up. "The coroner?"

"Yes... She said that the official cause of death is myocardial infarction."

David's lungs drop into his ass, and he struggles to find the air to speak. "Heart-attack?" he finally manages.

Kevin nods, jaw tight.

"That doesn't make any sense. Are you saying my mom and dad both died of a heart attack at the same time?" He snorts at the absurdity.

"Yes."

His fingers tighten around the arms of the chair. "What about the herd?"

"I don't know," says Kevin, sitting like his chair is lined with tacks. "The vet hasn't finished the necropsy."

David reminds himself to breath and then begins scrolling through his mental archives for a better answer. "You know. This sounds a lot like Monkshood."

"You mean wolfsbane," says Kevin.

"Yes, it is a poison that can look a lot like a heart attack. Remember, I told you, that's what Brad used to poison their dog with. We need to get a subpoena, and..."

Kevin throws up a hand. "Stop... let me finish. I listened when you said Brad used wolfsbane on the dog, and I had them test for it in the autopsy."

David feels a pang of guilt for not trusting Kevin to do his job, but the sadness on Kevin's face makes him hold his tongue, waiting for the bad news that's sure to follow.

"There was no trace of it in either of your parents," says Kevin. "They each had an enlarged heart with multiple aneurisms, *and* they had hardened arteries."

"Mom never had any heart issues," says David. "She was perfectly healthy."

"You don't understand. They had broken capillaries throughout their entire body. Janet used the term 'exploding capillaries'."

David smells a lead and jumps on it like a hound. "Is there a poison that would cause that?"

"No. She said it's as if their blood literally... *boiled*."

David's breath catches. "Boiled?" he says, hating the shape of the word on his lips.

"Yes," says Kevin with a nauseated grimace that matches David's sentiments exactly. "Janet is going to continue examining their bodies. Even though she gave the official cause of death as myocardial infarction, she's struggling to understand exactly what happened. She's officially bringing in WDHS, and she told me they've already contacted the CDC." He exhales sharply. "That might affect when you're able to hold the funeral. I don't know when the bodies will be released."

David rubs a hand down his face, wishing for some cold water to dunk his head. "What the hell?"

"I agree..." A burst of static from the radio on Kevin's hip makes them both flinch.

"Chief?!" a man's voice yells, distorted.

Kevin leaps up and walks out onto the driveway to take the call in private. David itches to follow, but hangs back. After barely five seconds in the yard, Kevin sprints to his car, yelling to David over his shoulder, "Get in!"

David is up in a blink. The moment he's in the passenger seat, Kevin turns on the siren and takes off.

"What happened?!" asks David, as Kevin turns out of the driveway toward the Schwarz farm.

Kevin guns it as he says, "Two of my deputies are down. They were checking on your parent's house. Luke radioed the station for an ambulance when he saw James fall to his knees, and a few seconds later our dispatcher heard Luke screaming."

"When did this happen?"

Kevin looks at his watch. "A few minutes ago."

They make the drive in under two minutes flat. Kevin turns onto the driveway, and then onto the access road. It doesn't take long to see the patrol car. A body lies in the dust by the driver door.

Kevin is out of his Jeep in a flash. He drops to his knees beside the body, rolling the man over. David is at his shoulder in an instant, but recoils from the sight. The deputy's eyes are red pools of blood. Kevin checks for a pulse that isn't there, then runs to another uniformed body, curled in a ball on the other side of the yellow caution tape line.

"Maybe we can get him back," he tells David, crouching beside the second body. Kevin's skin is deathly white, and David fears he might pass out, but Kevin begins chest compressions all the same.

David stands over him, watching the body bob and sway with the CPR rhythm. Eventually, he puts a hand on Kevin's shoulder. "Kevin, stop. Look at him."

Kevin's voice is gruff through the tears that begin spilling down his face. "He's got a wife... and a baby on the way. I'm not going to let him die."

"I'm sorry," David says, truly meaning it. "But you can't save him. He's gone."

* * *

David joins Kevin on the low bench on his parents' front porch. "How are you holding up?"

Kevin lifts his head out of his hands and fixes David with blood-shot eyes. "How do you think?"

David nods. He knows what it feels like to lose a man,

even though his own partner didn't die in the line of duty. "Well, I'm here if you need me. To talk, or whatever."

When Kevin doesn't respond, David stands to survey the scene. In addition to the multiple squad cars on site, there is now a Wisconsin Department of Health Services van parked in front of the farmhouse. *All this,* he thinks, *over an IOCG deposit at the property line...*

Then he shakes his head. As much as he hates to admit it—as much as he *knows* the Mullers want to get their grubby hands on whatever wealth is under that cliff at the border of their two lots—he's starting to think Kevin was right all along. This might not be a poisoning case, after all.

Being wrong galls him. It burns like an ulcer, deep in his gut. He lets out a little growl of frustration.

He tries following his original theory down the new path set by the deaths of the two deputies tonight. What would the motive be, for Bradley Muller to poison the officers? A cover-up? They got too close to... something? Even to David, it feels like a stretch.

No one knew that Kevin had sent deputies here for a random patrol this afternoon. Bradley would have had to have been lying in wait indefinitely. He would have had to have lucked out. And anyway, CSRU doesn't think anyone else was at the crime scene around the time of death. There were no fresh tire tracks, aside from the squad car's. No footprints, aside from the deputies'. There is nothing to indicate—

Kevin's radio crackles to life. "Chief Deputy Schumer, are you there?"

"Yeah," Kevin croaks, lifting the receiver to his mouth. "I'm here."

"This is Dispatch. I just got a call from Gordon Muller,"

the man says, and David snaps to attention. "He's got some dead cattle he thinks we should take a look at."

Kevin and David make eye contact. Kevin is the first to look away. "I'll send someone over."

"You should go yourself," David says. "I'll come with you."

Kevin ignores him, beckoning over a female deputy who's standing nearby. "Maura, can you and Rick head next door to Gordon Muller's? Take one of the forensics guys who examined the Schwarz cows."

"Yes, sir," Maura says, going off in search of her partner.

"David," Kevin says when they're alone again, "I think I need you to step back from this case for a bit."

"But—"

"I know they're your parents. That's why you need to let me handle things. You aren't objective. You aren't able to think clearly. You have a grudge—"

David tries to interrupt. "The papers in the lawyer's office—"

Kevin keeps talking over him. "—and it's pretty clear now that this isn't a poisoning case. So, unless you have another theory...?" He pauses long enough that David realizes he's waiting for an answer.

"I don't," David says reluctantly.

"Then we need to—"

Kevin breaks off as Terrance Wilkins, the lead epidemiologist with the Wisconsin Bureau of Communicable Diseases, walks up the porch steps in a full white hazmat suit. "I just got off the phone with the Centers for Disease Control in Atlanta," says Terrance, without preamble. "They are sending a team to investigate. They should be here early tomorrow. We've been told to issue an isolation and quarantine order for the entire town."

"Quarantine?" David says with alarm. "What does that mean?"

Terrance looks over at him, noting his lack of uniform and badge, and then begrudgingly says, "It's standard infectious disease response protocol. Whatever we're dealing with here, we don't want it leaving Rindville."

David blinks, shocked into silence.

"We'll meet with the CDC's on-site lead, Thomas Murphy, in the sheriff's office first thing in the morning. The sheriff's your father, right?" Terrance confirms with Kevin, who nods. "After that, we'll need to call a press conference to alert residents to the quarantine order. As chief deputy, you'll help us with enforcement."

Kevin nods. "Of course."

"We'll need to identify anyone who might've left town since the first deaths on July 2nd," Terrance goes on. "As well as anyone who may have hosted visitors in the past five days. And you'll need to station your deputies at the city limits to manage traffic."

"Wait," David says. "I'm supposed to be back at work in Detroit next week. How long will this quarantine last?"

Terrance gives him a grim shake of the head. "As long as it takes."

CHAPTER 9

July 8th, 2016

"Dan Jerkins wants to file charges," Jack says to his son as they rearrange the chairs in his office before the morning's big meeting. "He said Joey and Maddie kicked Jeb's teeth in. Did my skinny grandson really kick that boy's teeth in?"

"No…" Kevin says slowly. "That was all Maddie. She was defending him."

Jack shoots him a skeptical look. "Those boys are twice her size. How the hell did she beat the shit out of them? And without Joey as backup?"

"David's been training her since she was six."

"In what?!" Jack says with a jolt.

"Krav Maga."

Jack settles into the chair behind his desk and sighs. "Do I even need to ask why she did it? Knowing that asshole Dan, I'm sure his two boys…" He furrows his forehead. "What's that saying? 'The apple doesn't fall far from the tree.'"

"They were teasing Joey. Knocked his ice cream out of his hand and called him a skin head."

A murderous glint flashes in Jack's eyes, but it is quickly subdued. Still, Kevin can see the tightness of his father's jaw and knows he's just as furious as himself.

"You know... it takes true evil to tease a boy in Joey's condition," says Jack. "If you ask me, they got what was coming to them."

Kevin nods. "I agree."

"I'll have Inez at the front desk tell Dan to come into the station after the quarantine is lifted to give his statement. Maybe by then he will have cooled off."

Kevin scoffs. "Doubtful."

"A man can hope," the sheriff says with a shrug. "Anyway, we have bigger fish to fry right now." He pauses and says, a bit too casually, "By the way, how is my grandson doing?"

Kevin rubs at a stress headache behind his eyebrow, sitting in the chair closest to his father's right hand. "We were supposed to go into Jackson soon for a CBC and bone marrow biopsy, but with this quarantine..."

The sheriff nods. "What was his last blast count?"

"It..." Kevin clears his throat. "It just gets worse every time he's tested."

Jack grunts to himself. "Jesus... Maybe you need to have the boy see someone else... switch doctors."

Kevin feels his tear-ducts prickle. He bites the inside of his cheek hard to keep the tears inside. He can't sit in a meeting this important all misty-eyed. "No, Dad. He's been referred to one of the best oncologists in Wisconsin."

Jack slaps the desk with a throaty, unpleasant sound.

"What?" asks Kevin.

"If you had said one of the best in New York, I would understand, but Wisconsin?"

"He's getting the same treatments he would get anywhere in the country. We've tried everything."

The sheriff rubs his eyes. "I pray for him every day."

"Why don't you stop by tonight? Joey would love to see you."

Jack shakes his head. "You've got enough on your hands right now with David's family staying with you."

Kevin stiffens, gut sinking. "Whatever."

The sheriff narrows his eyes at his son. "What?"

"Nothing."

"No... it's something. I know that look. Out with it, before the CDC folks get here."

Kevin stares his father down as he says, "It's just that you haven't been by that much in the last six months."

Jack shrugs. "I've been busy. I'll stop by, I promise."

Kevin bites his tongue in favor of a nod. He's not sure whether he's angry or just sad and weary. Nothing about cancer is easy, for anybody, but it seems to Kevin that Joey's own family could bear some discomfort for him. Joey is the one who is truly suffering.

"What are we doing for my deputies? Have you planned the memorials?" asks the sheriff.

Kevin hangs his head. "Yes, I'm coordinating with their wives."

"Did you tell them that the department will pay for the services?"

"Yes." Kevin swallows hard, tearful conversations replaying in his head. James's mother's scream had echoed over the phone. Luke's pregnant wife, Judy, had fallen into Kevin's arms late last night with a wail that sliced into his bones. Kevin had finally made it to bed around 12:30 a.m., and he'd hardly slept. Too many phantom cries ringing in his ears.

There's a knock at the door. Jack's secretary, a white-haired woman named Doreen who's worked for the department since before Kevin was born, pokes her head inside. "Your guests are here," she says.

"Thanks. Send them on in," Jack says.

Terrance Wilkins leads the way, followed by a man with thinning brown hair that looks windswept, or else like he has a nervous habit of constantly running his hands through it. "I'm Thomas Murphy," the newcomer says, holding out his hand to first Jack, and then Kevin. "Lead epidemiologist for the CDC. I've been reading up on the situation here, but I want to hear the sequence of events in your words, if you don't mind."

"Sure," Jack says. "Take a seat."

Thomas, Terrance, and the three other specialists sent by the CDC get settled in their seats.

"Well," Kevin begins, "on July 2nd, David Schwarz and his family arrived to visit Stan and Margaret." He lays out the facts in an orderly, matter-of-fact manner, from David's discovery of his parents' bodies all the way to this morning. "And now you're here," he finishes.

"And now we're here," Thomas says, looking at his colleagues. "I know Terrance has warned you that we have to establish a quarantine to contain the contagion. Here's what that's going to entail."

"Wait, wait," the sheriff says, holding up his hand. "How do you even know a contagion, or whatever, is involved? My son and I were on that property. Our deputies, the crime scene team, the Schwarz family... no one else is exhibiting any symptoms."

"But the coroner from Marathon County—" Thomas

checks his notes. "—Janet Aguilar. She examined your two deputies' bodies overnight, and their presentations were identical to the farmer and his wife. Enlarged heart, broken capillaries, hardened arteries, aneurisms. I believe she used the phrase, 'it's like their blood boiled.'"

"So, you're saying, the rest of us are immune to this so-called contagion?" Jack asks.

"'Contagion' is our umbrella term for whatever this is: a virus, a parasite, a toxin," Thomas explains patiently. "And what we know as of now is that it seems to have originated on the Schwarz property."

"It's moved to the Muller lot," Kevin chimes in. "Gordon Muller lost a dozen cattle yesterday."

"Ah, yes. The neighbor." Thomas consults a printout of a map. "The dead cows were found in the pasture closest to the property line?"

"Yes." Kevin points out the approximate location.

"I'd like to get out into the field now, if that's all right with you," Thomas says. "We have a lot of equipment to unload, and then we need to establish a new perimeter. I understand you only had forensics in a radius around the Schwarz farmhouse?"

"That's correct," Kevin says.

"With the Muller cattle in the mix, that broadens the area under investigation," Thomas says. He nods at one of his colleagues, who hands Jack a thick packet of paper. "Here's some information on setting a quarantine. I'll leave the details to your department and check back in later. We need to make the announcement by the end of the day. I'm happy to stand beside you in order to lend some weight to the proceedings. Or not," he says as an afterthought. "Sometimes local populations don't respond well to an outsider telling them what to do."

Jack chuckles at that, but his face sobers again quickly as he looks at the handout about quarantine protocols. "I guess I'll get to reading," he says, standing to indicate the end of the meeting. "Kevin, will you escort our guests out to the farm?"

"Yes, sir," Kevin says to his dad, and then turns to Thomas, Terrance, and the others. "This way."

* * *

Joey clicks away from a cartoon to a superhero drama, leaning back into a comfier position on the couch. He hasn't watched for five minutes before Maddie appears, blocking the screen. She has a punching bag propped against her hip.

"Follow me," she says.

"Where?" he asks, standing up.

"You'll see."

She leads him to the timeless oak tree and stops beside the rope swing hanging from the thickest low branch. She holds up the pad, throws her other fist into it, and says, "I want you to teach me how to swim."

"With... a punching bag?" Joey asks, intrigued but not wanting to seem too eager.

"I'll teach you self-defense. We'll swim afterward. It's a trade."

"Okay." Really, it sounds great, not just okay. Since their trip into town two days ago, Joey has been nursing a... he hates to say "crush," but he supposes that's what it is. He thought Maddie was pretty even while she was blowing him off. Then she beat up his bullies and confessed her vulnerabilities... Now, looking at her makes his stomach flip-flop. "I guess it'd be good for me to learn to hold my own," he says, adding silently, *and it'll give us an excuse to hang out.*

Maddie looks pleased. "These should fit you," she says as she pulls her striking gloves over Joey's hands. "The first thing you need to know about Krav Maga is that this is not a martial art."

"Oh, okay," he says. It's a little hard to breathe with her face so close to his. "Um, then, what is it?"

"It's a self-defense system," she says, stepping back. "Let me show you the neutral stance and fighting stance. First... your legs and arms should be shoulder-width apart, arms down."

Joey looks at his dangling arms. "How am I supposed to protect myself?"

"Wait..." She glides her right leg back and raises her fists with thumbs at chin level, elbows tucked near her ribs. "This is the fighting stance."

Joey mimics her. "That makes more sense."

She walks behind him, crouches, and guides his right leg farther back with soft taps on his ankle. "You want to be more balanced. Are you right-handed or left-handed?"

"Right."

She nods, then moves his left arm up higher, a finger guiding his elbow. Even the soft touch of one fingertip lights up his skin.

She faces him again, holding up the punching pad. "Hit it as hard as you can."

Joey throws a punch, focused on hitting the target rather than hitting it as hard as he can. He strikes the center, but the bag doesn't even move.

"No," says Maddie with a stoic, sensei face. "Here." She hands him the bag. "You hold it, and I'll show you how it's done."

Joey straps his hand onto the bag while Maddie gets in

the fighting position. She snickers, eyes glancing down at his legs. "You better brace yourself."

"Why?"

"You'll see. Bend your knees. Turn slightly."

When he obeys, she throws a fake punch, slowly demonstrating the motion, saying, "You need to move your torso when you punch in order to get more force."

Her next strike comes full speed and before Joey realizes she's hit the bag, he is on the ground, feet completely knocked out from under him. The hard landing on his butt clacks his teeth and forces the air from his lungs.

She runs over to him. "You okay?"

He grins at her through his harsh breathing. "Can you teach me how to do that?!" he gasps.

Maddie chuckles, helping him up and taking back the punching bag. "It depends."

"On what?"

She punches him lightly in the shoulder. "On how long we're staying here. We're supposed to go home next week, remember?" Her face clouds. "I don't know when my grandparents' memorial service is going to happen. I think we'll probably leave right after that."

"Oh. Right." Joey feels a pinch of disappointment in his chest. She's going to leave. Of course she is. "Well, I can definitely teach you to swim before you go."

"And I can at least teach you the basics of self-defense, in case Jeb and Wilbur didn't learn their lesson the other day." She tilts her head. "Now, plant those feet."

Joey smiles at the raised pad and throws his shoulders into it this time.

* * *

An hour later, he's dripping in sweat and ready to dive into the lake. He knows he'll be sore in the morning—he's already feeling some of it now—but the thought can't tear the joy from his face. His cheeks are aching as he joins Maddie on the dock in his trunks. He tries not to let his gaze linger too long on her black suit.

"Now it's my turn to teach," he says.

Backing up a little, he does a running leap into a dive. He emerges doing a backstroke and goes in a wide circle back to the dock.

Maddie rolls her eyes. "Yeah, yeah. You're so amazing."

He chuckles. "Jump in."

She hugs herself. "I can't."

"Do you trust me?"

"Yes," she says, arms falling loose at her sides.

"You're safe. I'll make sure nothing happens to you."

She scoots up to the edge, her big toes jutting out over the edge. Joey treads water, waiting, but she makes no move to jump in.

"Do you want me to get my sister's arm floaties?"

She narrows her eyes at him, but her mouth is twitching. "Are you trying to be funny?"

"No. I thought it might help."

"That's never going to happen."

"Okay... just use the stairs then."

She nods and moves to the stairs. He sees her chest rise and fall with a steadying breath as she clutches the rails and makes her way down backward. When her torso is underwater, Joey says, "Okay, why don't you start by kicking your legs. Hold onto the railing and stretch out your body."

She cautiously follows his instruction. "Now what?"

"Now, kick."

Her feet make soft splashes on the surface.

Joey swims to the dock's edge to nab a forgotten pink donut float. Then he swims about six feet past Maddie and says, "Push off from the railing and swim to this floatie. All you have to do is kick your feet. That will propel you forward."

Maddie shakes her head. "Bring it closer."

He halves the distance and gives her a challenging look. She pushes off hard and basically glides to the float, arms outstretched as far as they will go. She throws her arms over the float and holds it tight to her chest.

"I did it," she says through a heavy breath.

"That's awesome. Now go back to the railing."

She pushes from the floatie, but its squishy sides provide little force, and she sinks before her fingers touch the stairs. Her arms flail, and Joey swims toward her, but she grabs the railing. Her head emerges, mouth gaping like a fish as she wipes her hair out of her eyes.

"Are you all right?" Joey asks.

"Yes," she chokes out.

"Let's try something else. We need to teach you how to float first. I'll hold you up while you float on your back."

"What?" Her voice rises an octave.

"Lie on your back, and I'll hold you up," repeats Joey.

She shakes her head. "I don't think so."

"We'll be right by the stairs," he says, drifting closer. "You need to learn how to float in order to learn how to swim."

She looks down at his hand when he lightly brushes her arm. "Okay." Maddie lets go of the railing and tilts onto her back. Joey catches her, praying his fingers won't tremble, and keeps her afloat, directing her posture.

"You're doing it!"

She smiles up at him, her ponytail bobbing in the water

and caressing his shoulder. "Well... not really. You're helping."

He slowly pulls his hands away, and she doesn't sink.

"I'm doing it! I'm floating on my own!" she shouts to the clouds above.

"You are!" says Joey, smiling along with her.

She floats for a few more seconds and then grabs the railing. "Thanks," she says, and Joey notes the blush on her cheeks. "What's next?"

* * *

Eventually, they climb onto the dock to dry out in the sun. When they go inside, the TV is on in the kitchen. "Can you turn that up for me?" Ellie asks, wrist-deep in a mixing bowl. She's making homemade meatballs for tonight's spaghetti dinner. "There's going to be a press conference. Your dad texted me."

"Sure, Mom." Joey goes over and raises the volume, and then he and Maddie sit at the kitchen table.

When the commercials end, the news cameras are showing the front steps of the sheriff's department. Jack Schumer walks out, flanked by two men Ellie doesn't recognize. Kevin is also visible, but off to the side. His face wears a worried scowl.

"Good afternoon, folks," the sheriff greets the press and the public. "I have an unfortunate announcement to make. Starting at sundown tonight, Rindville is under quarantine by the Wisconsin Department of Health Services, in partnership with the Centers for Disease Control. This quarantine is in relation to the recent deaths at the Schwarz and now Muller properties."

The reporters erupt in shouts, but Jack holds up a hand.

"Let me finish," he says. "I have up here with me Terrance Wilkins from the Wisconsin Bureau of Communicable Diseases and Thomas Murphy from the CDC. They're going to give you a few more details about their investigation. But before I turn over the podium—"

"What's going on?" Debbie asks. She and David enter the kitchen, David carrying Grace in his arms. She had a follow-up appointment at the hospital this afternoon.

"Shh," Ellie hushes her friend, pointing at the TV.

"—no one will be allowed to enter or exit the quarantine zone," the sheriff is saying. "If you work across the Rindville city line, you can get in touch with our office for an official notice to share with your employer about your absence until this matter is resolved. I will have deputies posted along the main roads to remind travelers of the need to stay put during the quarantine."

"Quarantine?!" Debbie yelps, looking at her husband. "Did you know about this?"

"Sort of," he mumbles guiltily, and she punches him in the arm.

"We'll also be following up with folks who may have visited or have hosted visitors since the start of the month," Jack continues. "If you receive a call from the sheriff's office, or if our deputies stop by your door, please cooperate with us. We're trying to resolve this situation as soon as we can, so you can return to your normal lives safely. Now, I'll take a couple questions."

The reporters all start talking over one another.

Jack points at a woman in the front row. "Yes, Cheryl."

"How long will this quarantine be in place?" she asks.

"I can't tell you that just yet. But when you hear from Thomas and Terrance, you'll get a better sense of the timeline. Yes, Leland," he says, pointing out another reporter.

"What are we dealing with here? Is it a new virus? How worried should local residents be?"

"Again, Thomas and Terrance will explain that part of the investigation. But what I can say is, so far, the effects have been confined to the two farms."

"Then why does the whole town have to be quarantined?" a woman shouts from the back of the crowd.

"If I may," Thomas says, stepping forward with a hand on the sheriff's shoulder, "quarantines are about containment. We need to rule out the idea that this thing is communicable, or that it's capable of traveling. That means keeping the whole community isolated for a *hopefully* brief window of time."

"What are the symptoms?" a reporter calls out.

"Do you know how it's transmitted?" another yells.

"Is it in our food?" a third bellows.

Thomas holds up both hands. "I'll start going through what we know now, if that's all right with you, Sheriff Schumer."

Jack steps back with a nod.

"Mommy, what's a kwarra... a kwarra-tee?" Grace asks, stumbling over the unfamiliar word.

Her tiny voice is like a jolt of adrenaline to the three adults in the room.

"Let's turn this off," Ellie says, forcing a false cheer into her voice. "Kevin can give us the rest of the details when he gets home. "Maddie, Joey, can you set the table?" She looks at them, realizing they're in their swimsuits. "Go get changed for dinner first." The teens are still staring at the TV, pale and wide-eyed, so Ellie uses her elbow to hit the "power" button. "Go on."

They stand without argument and head for the stairs.

"Hey, let's go find Bethany," David says, carrying Grace

out of the kitchen. "I bet she'd love to play a board game with you."

The two women stay in the kitchen. "Um," Ellie says, looking helplessly at Debbie. "How was Grace's doctor appointment?"

"Good. No after effects from the near drowning," Debbie answers, just as dazed by the new development.

"But it sounds like we're stuck here," Debbie says, stating the obvious.

"Well, you're welcome to stay with us as long as you need to."

"Thank you." Debbie sets down her purse on the counter. "Do you need help getting dinner ready?"

"Can you put together the salad? I've already cut the vegetables."

"Sure." Debbie goes to the refrigerator.

Together, Ellie and Debbie finish preparing the meal that will nourish their families. They don't try to make small talk. That scary word, "quarantine," is still ringing too loudly in their ears.

CHAPTER 10

July 10th, 2016

Thomas Murphy begins his third day on site at the Schwarz dairy farm by donning his white hazmat suit at the property line. The motions are familiar: step in feet-first, pull the jumpsuit up to his waist, snap on a pair of gloves, shrug his arms and shoulders into the suit, zip it up, add another pair of gloves, and finish with the hood that includes the large plastic shield to protect his face. His assistant at the entry tent gives him a once-over to make sure there are no breaches in the suit and then dismisses him with a thumbs-up.

"Thanks," Thomas says, voice slightly muffled by all the gear. "Is Terrance here yet?"

"He's at the farmhouse."

"Great."

Thomas begins the long walk up the driveway. Although they have vehicles at their disposal, when he's not in a rush, he actually prefers to go on foot. He feels like it lets him take in his surroundings in a different way than when he's viewing them through a car window. He sees more details. And for an epidemiologist, details are key.

The details of this case are puzzling. No recognizable foreign substances in any of the victims' toxicology reports. No telltale residues anywhere near where the bodies were found. So far, nothing unusual has come up with the water or soil sampling. Which leaves open the possibility of an infectious disease... a new one. Nothing Thomas has ever studied kills in quite this way.

But where did it come from?

H1N1 jumped from pigs to humans. Ebola most likely incubates in bats. Zika is mosquito-borne. Were the Schwarzes' cows the carriers for this novel disease? Or was it the mice or the birds that were discovered dead in the barn?

Of course, this could be something else entirely. A gene mutation, perhaps, that made the victims susceptible in a way that others who visited this property weren't. Or maybe the victims had a trauma response to an event that the others didn't experience.

Thomas's job, as a scientist, is to rule things out. The more he can learn about what *didn't* kill the Schwarzes and their animals, the closer he'll home in on what *did.*

He crests a small hill and sees the main tent next to the farmhouse. Inside the white vinyl walls, several people in hazmat suits mill around, running experiments and logging data. Thomas brought along three specialists from his own department in Atlanta, while Terrance supplied a team of local experts. All in all, there are almost twenty personnel on site, not counting law enforcement.

"Morning," Thomas says, lifting a hand in greeting as he passes two sheriff's deputies wearing hazmat suits with their badges on lanyards around their necks. The men mumble their replies. They seem uncomfortable in the unfamiliar jumpsuits. And of course, two of their colleagues died on this farm only three days ago. Thomas doesn't blame them for not being in the mood for small talk.

He enters the tent, looking for Terrance. It's impossible to distinguish one person from another in the baggy hazmat suits, but Terrance is taller than most, which helps. Thomas finds the man studying a map of the property that's hanging on a freestanding bulletin board.

"Have your people been over here yet?" Terrance says, instead of "good morning." He stabs at a spot on the map near where the Schwarz and Muller lots align.

"Not there, exactly." Thomas indicates a nearby area. "We did some sampling here, since this is the closest to the Schwarz farm where Muller's animals were found dead. Why, do you have a theory?"

Terrance makes a thoughtful noise. "One of the forensic techs from Wausau noted that the two dead deputies' footprints indicated that they were returning from this direction." He points at the corner of the Schwarz farm again, near the cliff. "Their chief deputy says he'd sent them on a patrol, but without any clear instructions of where to go or what they were looking for. Just some recon."

Thomas nods. "So, they were in that quadrant of the property right before they died."

"Might've been."

"Let's send a couple people that way this afternoon. This morning, I want all hands on the well water and groundwater tests. The sooner we can cross that off our list as a causal factor, the better. Contaminated water could affect the whole town."

"You got it." Terrance marches over to his subordinates and begins barking out orders.

Thomas stares at the map a moment longer, willing it to relinquish its secrets.

* * *

Joey treads water, staring at the sheen of the sun on Maddie's hair. She's clutching the rail like a lifeline even after two days of practice, because this time, Joey is ten feet away from the dock.

"You can do it, Maddie. You know how to dog paddle, so even if you get out of rhythm, you won't sink."

"I'm scared."

Joey shakes his head. "You're fearless. You took on Jeb and Wilbur without blinking."

"That's different."

"It's not." He lifts his arms out of the water and beckons her to him. "You can do it. I'll make sure nothing happens to you."

Maddie closes her eyes and takes a deep breath. She furrows her brow, fixing her gaze on him, and then pushes off as hard as she can, extending her arms and then sweeping them around to her sides, kicking her feet close together. She keeps her nose above water, her eyes wide but not panicking. The moment she tags his hand, she lights up like a star. "I did it!" She throws her arms around him, but quickly draws back when they start to dip underwater together.

Joey's cheeks are hot despite the dunk in the cool water. "I knew you could do it."

They swim back toward the dock together. Maddie does the dog paddle this time because it makes her feel safer. Braced on the railing, she turns back and draws him into a tight, one-armed hug. Her mouth is so close he can feel her breath on his cheek as she says, "Thank you."

Joey swallows hard, blushing but unable to pull his eyes away. "You did it all on your own, Maddie."

"I couldn't have done it without you." She lets go, and instantly he misses her touch.

She climbs onto the dock and then looks back down at him. "Aren't you getting out?"

Joey clears his throat, trying to adjust his trunks without tugging on them too noticeably. "I'm going to stay in here for a few more minutes."

She dangles her toes into the water while he swims in a wide circle in front of her. "I can't wait to tell my mom I can swim now."

"You know what's next?" asks Joey.

"What?"

"You need to learn how to dive."

Maddie laughs, tipping back her head. "No."

"I can teach you," he says, watching sparkling droplets of water from her dripping hair roll over her lips.

She shrugs. "I don't know."

"You can do it. You can do anything, Maddie."

She rewards him with a smile that warms his gut. Joey can now get out of the water without being embarrassed, so he climbs out and sits next to her, their pinkies almost touching.

"You can do anything too, you know," she says, after a moment of quiet.

He deflates like a balloon stuck with a pin. "No, I can't."

"Why, because you're sick?"

"You know that's why." He wraps his arms around his knees and stares down into the water. "I feel awful all the time. Even my good days aren't really good—not like they used to be. And I don't know if I'll get to graduate from high school and go to college."

Maddie startles. "Why wouldn't you?"

He can't look directly at her. "It's getting worse. Every time I'm tested... it gets worse."

"I'm so sorry," she says softly.

"Every time we go into Jackson for my test results, it's the same thing. My mom cries, and then says, 'We're going to beat this thing. We'll just try another treatment.'" He shakes his head. "Like she's the one that has to take a drug that will make her lose her hair and throw up all the time. But you know what really sucks?"

"What?"

"The look on everyone's face when they see me. My friends, my parents... *everyone*."

"What look?"

"It's a lot of things all together. They're scared of me, or they feel sorry for me, or they're freaked out and don't want to be around me, but they don't want me to notice..." He shrugs. "I always notice."

"Oh."

"You looked at me like that, when you first got here."

Maddie winces, and her eyes well up. "I really am sorry."

"At least you don't look at me like that now. You look at me like I'm normal."

"You *are* normal."

Joey makes a face. "I wish..." He scrunches his eyes closed, feeling stupid and embarrassed.

"What? What do you wish for?"

He looks over at her and finds only kindness in her face. No pity. No awkwardness. The shock of it unhinges his jaw and lets the thought fly free. "I want to have a day... just one day where I don't have cancer… where people don't treat me differently."

Maddie nods, looking thoughtful. "That gives me an idea. Let's get away from all of this."

"All of what?"

"The quarantine. Our parents are losing their minds—you can see that, right? And with my dad still upset about my grandparents, but not wanting to show that he's upset—"

"Sounds like someone else I know," Joey mutters, giving Maddie a meaningful smirk.

She playfully smacks him on the arm. "*Anyway…* let's go to that place you talked about, with the cliff and the ledge."

Joey glances over his shoulder, toward the house. "My mom would never let me. I told you, she won't let me out of her sight. Besides, my balance sucks. I wouldn't be able to cross the ledge."

"You can cross with my help."

"How?"

Maddie gets up and holds out a hand to him. "I'll show you."

Joey is reluctant to release her hand after she rises, but she turns him around by the shoulders, not giving him much choice. "Put your arms straight out."

With his back to her, he obeys, trying to remember how to breathe with her so close.

"Pretend that board you're standing on is the cliff and walk across it."

He puts his hands down and faces her. "Why?"

She spins him back around. "Just do it."

He obliges and is rewarded by her hands under his armpits.

"I'll make sure you don't lose your balance," she says, as if it's that simple.

And maybe, just maybe... it is.

Joey takes a step, and then another, lining up his feet heel to toe. He tips to the right, but Maddie's hand gently nudges him back upright. Grinning, he keeps moving forward.

* * *

Debbie takes a wet plate from Ellie, relishing the comfortable silence and mind-mellowing monotony of swirling the drying rag across the surface of the ceramic. By focusing on the movement, she can push her worries aside for a moment.

A dish clangs against the side of the sink, making Debbie jump. She looks over to see Ellie with her hands dangling in the sink, water running over her wrists and the chipped plate as she stares out the bay window.

"What is it?" asks Debbie, all her anxieties rushing back to drown her from the inside. Is Maddie acting out again? Are David and Kevin arguing?

Ellie points. "Look."

Debbie moves closer to Ellie for a better view, and relief sweeps through her. Maddie is walking behind Joey, holding him up in some strange, synchronized balancing act on the dock. Odd, sure, but nothing to worry about.

"What in the world are they doing?" Debbie asks, turning to Ellie with a budding smile that vanishes when she sees a tear fall off Ellie's chin. "El, what's wrong?" She rests a hand on Ellie's back.

Debbie offers her the dish cloth, and she wipes the tears

away as she says, "I can't tell you the last time Joey had someone his own age... *that wasn't afraid to be around him.*"

Debbie's breath hitches, and she has to try not to cry as she says, "It's great seeing the two of them spending so much time together. They've been inseparable these last two days."

Ellie throws her arms around Debbie and says, "Your daughter is amazing."

Debbie's heart lifts, ready to fly out of her chest. She hugs Ellie back tightly. "You know... it's been awhile since Maddie has had a friend. I happen to think Joey is pretty special too."

"Yeah, I guess we have amazing kids, don't we?" says Ellie, pulling back with a smile.

"We do."

Ellie claps her hands together once like an excited teenager. "We should make them a treat, for after lunch. *Brownies.*"

Debbie laughs. "Great idea."

For a few seconds, it's like the quarantine doesn't exist. Joey's cancer doesn't exist. Stan and Margaret's deaths never happened. Debbie and Ellie are just two old friends enjoying each other's company.

But then Ellie sags, gaze lost in the suds. "We were supposed to go to Jackson in two days for tests."

"What tests?"

"A CBC and bone marrow aspiration."

"David mentioned a blast count?"

"That's what the bone marrow aspiration is for... to test his blast count," says Ellie. "It measures the number of immature cells, or Myeloblasts."

Debbie nods. "David said Joey's count was high."

"Yeah... a normal count would be five percent, but Joey's

is over sixty percent. It keeps rising each time we test it."

"I'm so sorry," says Debbie, feeling like the sentiment falls flat but unable to think of anything that would truly hold all of her sympathy.

"None of it has been working," says Ellie, turning off the water. "We've tried cytarabine, cladribine, fludarabine, mitoxantrone, etoposide... you name it. None of the chemo drugs have worked. We've tried radiation with chemo. TBI and a stem cell transplant." She puts her finger to her lips a moment, as if to hold in a sob. "I just don't understand why he's not responding to any of the treatments." She braces herself over the sink like she might vomit all her grief into it.

Debbie rubs her back, hoping to provide more comfort with a touch than with words.

"We've been fighting this for over two years," Ellie gasps. "He was diagnosed on June 17th, 2014. That was the day my heart broke."

Debbie thinks of her little Gracie, still resting and recovering after her fall in town. She thinks of Maddie—how fierce she is, and yet how vulnerable. If anything happened to one of her girls...

And now they're stuck here, living through a government quarantine. Debbie's normal life, back in Detroit, seems as far-off and fuzzy as a half-remembered dream.

How long have they been here, in Rindville? Just over a week? It honestly feels like forever.

* * *

It's late afternoon, and Terrance has gathered his team near the location where the deputies' bodies were found. "We're going to fan out from here," he says, "working in pairs. You've each got a radio. Don't hesitate to use it if you find anything interesting... or threatening." He pauses. "I hear there's a mountain lion around these parts. Obviously, that's not what we're looking for as far as the case is concerned, but that doesn't mean it's not a danger."

"What are we looking for, sir?" a woman asks.

"Anything that seems unusual," Terrance says, remembering what the chief deputy, Kevin Schumer, said after the deaths of his men. "Anything that jumps out at you."

"Except a mountain lion," one of the lab techs pipes up. It's a macabre joke, given the circumstances, and only a few people laugh.

"If a mountain lion jumps out at you, son," Terrance says wryly, "I recommend you run." He consults his clipboard. "Okay, first two: Jackson and Pesselle." Two hazmat-suited people step forward, and Terrance points them in a northerly direction. "Next up: Simmons and Gutierrez." They get sent slightly northeast. The routes are divvied up until only Terrance himself remains, along with Thomas, who is approaching from the direction of the main tent by the house.

"Can I join you?" Thomas asks.

"That's what I was waiting for," Terrance says, tapping his wrist in mock-indignance.

Over the past couple days, the men have formed a good working rapport. Thomas was a bit nervous, to be honest. He hasn't always found state and city officials to be welcoming to federal agents such as himself. Then again, he and Terrance are both scientists first, and government officials second.

"I've plotted each pair's course so that there's a bit of overlap," says Terrance, showing Thomas his hand-drawn map with various serpentine routes drawn in colored ink.

"Nice." Thomas studies the map with a grin. "Is this standard protocol in Wisconsin?"

"Huh?"

"Are all of the state's communicable disease experts also amateur cartographers?"

Terrance chuckles. "I dabble."

"Well, we're lucky you do." Thomas looks out toward the far corner of the Schwarz farm. "Lead the way, mapmaker."

They walk and walk, Terrance guiding their path with a compass so that they wind their way gently through the rolling hills of the pasture. Hiking in a hazmat suit in mid-July is hard, hot work, and it's not long before both men are huffing and puffing, sweat rolling down their cheeks and dampening their necks, armpits, and lower backs.

"What I wouldn't do for a cold beer right about now," Terrance says.

"Mmm," Thomas agrees, as the cliff comes into view.

"At least we're almost there."

Something catches Thomas's eye. It's like there's a blue light embedded in the cliffside. He squints, wishing he could rub the sweat from his eyes but knowing he can't break the seal of his hazmat suit. "Do you see that?" he asks.

"I see it," Terrance confirms.

They move closer. Neither man says another word until the cliff rises up in front of them, steep and imposing. In front of the cliff is...

"What the hell...?" Thomas asks.

"You said it," Terrance murmurs.

"Get the rest of your people over here," Thomas orders. "Now."

CHAPTER 11

July 12th, 2016

Joey is pulled from sleep by someone jiggling his shoulder. He blinks through the dark, expecting his mother, but it is Maddie's face hovering over his. He sits up slowly, still groggy. She is dressed in her fatigues and boots, and a backpack strap is slung over one shoulder.

"Get dressed," she says.

He looks at the alarm clock on his nightstand. "It's five in the morning. What the hell, Maddie?"

"We're going on an epic adventure."

"What?" Joey rubs his eyes.

"We're going to the cliff."

A little thrill races through Joey's veins—a sensation of hope he hasn't experienced in so long he's nearly forgotten what it feels like. It puffs him up like one of Bethany's donut rings, but he tries to deflate it and put on a skeptical face. He's not yet sure if Maddie is serious.

He rolls out of bed, and she chuckles.

"Nice pajamas."

He looks down at the Star Wars set, the bottoms covered in stars and the yellow logo, the shirt emblazoned with Vader offering cookies as a lure to the Dark Side. "What? They're comfortable."

"I'm sure they are." She can't hide her smile behind her fingers.

"Whatever."

She slides the backpack off her shoulder and holds it up like a peace offering. "I packed us some snacks and water."

Joey unzips it and looks in. "Leftover pizza, cool."

He extracts a pair of jeans from his drawer. "Can you turn around?" he asks Maddie.

"I've seen you in your bathing suit. I doubt your underwear is any different. But if it makes you feel better..." She crosses her arms as she turns.

He swaps his pants as fast as he can, then grabs his flashlight.

"What's that for?"

Joey smiles. "It's a surprise. You'll see when we get there."

Maddie smiles back. "Fine. Keep your secrets. Let's go before anyone else wakes up."

They sneak out the back and walk alongside the lake for a bit. Then Joey turns, heading through the green pastures toward the river. The sun peeks its bald yellow pate over the horizon line, casting a warm glow over the dewy grass. The world feels... magical.

Joey chuckles, feeling giddy. "Our parents are going to kill us."

Maddie shrugs. "Oh, well... what are they going to do? Ground us? It's not like we can go anywhere right now, anyway."

They laugh together, and Joey glances sidelong to watch

the way Maddie's ponytail bounces around her bare, lightly freckled shoulders.

"You're going to love the surprise," he says.

"Is it cooler than the cliff?"

"I don't know," Joey says, considering. "They're cool in different ways. I mean... wait. Are you making fun of me?"

Her mouth twists to try and hold back a smile. "Maybe. But if you're excited, I'm excited."

"I'm excited," Joey says, too eager for an adventure to play it cool.

"How far is the cliff?"

"Not sure... maybe two miles. I used to ride my bike there, with my friend Tom. Walking's a lot slower."

"The scenic route," Maddie jokes.

They walk side by side as the sun rises, seemingly lifting itself out of the earth, and the day warms rapidly. After forty minutes of walking, they're both sweating. When the fields become dotted with tall plants topped with showy, purple flowers, Maddie veers off the trail.

Joey rushes after her and swats her hand before she can caress the petals. "Stop!"

"What the hell?"

"It's poisonous."

"Really?" says Maddie, doing a double-take.

"Haven't you ever heard of wolfsbane?" asks Joey.

She gives him a look he's come to associate with frazzled mothers. "Clearly I haven't."

"The poison can absorb into your skin, so if you touch it, you can get really sick. And... if you swallow it, you'll die."

She steps back, as if respecting the plant's personal space. "Why is it called wolfsbane?"

"I'm not sure. Tom always said it has something to do with werewolves... but I think he's full of shit."

"Look at you," she says around a smile.

"What?"

"You said... *'full of shit.'*" She chuckles.

Joey rolls his eyes, but the back of his neck heats with embarrassment. When they return to the trail, his mind wanders, trying to dissect her teasing. Did he sound lame when he cursed? Or did she just not expect him to? Does she like rougher boys who say things like that all the time? He is certain he is overthinking, but the questions still pop into his head. Too bad his brain doesn't provide any answers. When he manages to pull himself back to reality, he stops in his tracks.

"Do you see those rocks up ahead?" Joey points. The blurred, dark green rise in the distance seems to greet him like an old friend, and he has to fight to keep tears from materializing.

"Yeah."

"We're close."

"How did you find this place?" asks Maddie as they shift their course.

"Exploring."

"Let me guess: with your friend Tom."

"He used to be my best friend," Joey says. The "used to" part of that sentence feels like a sledgehammer to the guts.

"What happened? Was he one of the kids who..." Maddie's hand clenches into an involuntary fist.

"He didn't drop me right away, if that's what you're asking. He was one of the last..." Joey has to clear his throat to continue. "One of the last people to still hang out with me. But I think his dad eventually told him to stop."

Maddie makes a sound like she's got a wad of something vile caught in her throat. "What?! Why would he do that?!"

"I don't know."

Maddie crosses her arms in a huff. "That is so ridiculous."

The cliff begins to take shape, a dark rock dotted with shades of green. The top is a lush miniature forest, but even on the rocky sides, resilient plants grow right out of the cracks and crawl their way up toward the sun.

"You said you stopped coming here because of your balance?" says Maddie.

"Well… that and it's not as much fun alone."

"Lucky you're not alone anymore."

"Yeah. Lucky."

They reach the base a few minutes later. The cliff itself is a sheer climb. No way up without gear. So, Joey leads Maddie to the sloping hill covered in a blanket of grass that sits next to it. The uphill climb is pretty easy going, just a few large boulders to dodge. Although, once upon a time, Joey would have climbed those, too, just for the fun of it. Now, he has to conserve his energy.

After thirty minutes of trekking ever upward, their legs on fire, they make it to the top.

Maddie hands Joey a water bottle. As he starts to chug eagerly, she walks to the edge and whistles at the rock walkway bridging the cliff and the hill. It's barely a foot wide, but nine feet long. No railings. She makes fists at her sides and does the breathing exercise her father taught her for steadying her mind before combat.

Maddie puts one foot on the walkway and looks down into the chasm. Her stomach leaps into her throat, and she pulls her foot back. "Damn… that's a long way down."

"You see what I mean?" says Joey, coming to her side.

"I wouldn't want to cross it if I was struggling with balance." She chews on her cheek as she takes another look. "How far down do you think that is?"

Joey shrugs. "a hundred feet? Maybe."

Blowing out a long, calming exhale, she smiles for him, not wanting him to know she's nervous at all. He might back out, worried about her, and she isn't going to let him miss this. "Are you ready?"

Joey nods.

"We can do this," she says, hoping to convince herself.

Joey turns and puts his arms out. Maddie steps behind him and positions her hands under his armpits. She feels his skin jump beneath her touch.

"Did I hurt you?" she asks.

"No, no. I'm fine."

He takes the first step onto the walkway faster than she expected, and she sucks in a harsh breath. He waits for her on the next step, and they move together, both edging out over empty space.

Three steps in, Joey pauses, head bent.

"Don't look down," says Maddie, keeping her gaze fixed on the back of his head, focusing with all her might on his torso beneath her hands so that she is ready if he starts to lean.

He nods and lifts his gaze.

She's seriously starting to question her sanity, bringing him out here. She had been so convinced she could keep him safe, give him something nice to remember… if he was stuck in a hospital soon. But hovering over empty space on a rock tightrope makes her toned muscles feel pretty useless.

She's lost in thought when he takes the next step, and as she hurries to move with him, he starts to sway left. Maddie stops breathing as her whole arm goes rigid, pushing him ever so lightly with her left hand to straighten him out without tilting him too far right.

Joey stops. "Thanks." She hears his shaking breath, and

then he takes another step, swaying to the right. She's ready this time, but too focused on him. As her right hand steadies him, she tips to the right, her left foot lifting off, just the toe touching the rock. With a sharp gasp, she flings her hands out to regain her balance.

Joey goes stiff when her hands leave him, and his voice trembles as he asks, "Are you okay?"

"Yeah… I'm good," she says, swallowing hard. She puts her hands back under his arms.

He takes the next two steps slowly, and she can adjust his weight before it really starts to shift. Just as she begins to relax, and her heart begins to slow a bit, her shoes touch dirt.

"We did it!" Joey pumps two fists over his head. Maddie staggers past him, away from the edge, and puts her hands on her knees, breathing long and hard. Her muscles ache from clenching, but it's her brain that's really screaming at her for a rest. Realizing her toes are curled up in her boots, she releases them with a wince.

The farther up the slight incline they go, the looser her stride becomes, the anxiety eased by the beauty of the pink and yellow morning sky. At the top of the cliff, Maddie braves the edge to admire the amazing view. Her eyes follow the nearby Rindriver past downtown Rindville. Though the landscape is dotted with farms and a few clusters of houses, green pastures and flourishing trees dominate the view, swathing everything in soft, green edges.

"This view is amazing," she murmurs.

Joey grins back, flashing a cute dimple in his right cheek. "Told you. Thanks."

"For what?"

"Bringing me here. I've missed it."

Happiness swells in Maddie's chest, but all she says is, "Yeah, it's pretty cool."

Nestled in the valley directly below the cliff is her grandparents' farm. She recognizes the old red barn, and the newer open-stall barn. The white house's large porch is distinctive even from this angle. The miniaturized buildings summon memories of summers gone by, back when life was easier. She had convinced herself she didn't miss the place over the past five years, but seeing it like this, bathed in fresh sunlight, she realizes she was wrong.

"Do you miss them?" Joey asks quietly.

"My grandparents?" she asks. At his nod, she says, "Yeah. I do. It's weird... we hadn't seen them in five years, and Dad and Grandpa didn't get along at all."

Maddie remembers her dad shouting into his phone, stomping around the kitchen while her mom tried to get him to take it outside. *I won't end up like you! That place is a shithole, and I refuse to live there!* he'd screamed. But back then, he'd gotten angry about everything. He always smelled like beer, and when the scent was strong enough to drift between rooms, anger and shouts came with it. Now the smell of beer makes her sick.

"I wish I'd known them better," she confesses. "I guess I always thought I'd have the chance to, one day. And now I never will." She goes quiet, and Joey doesn't push her further. Maddie likes how they can drift into comfortable silence together. It feels nice, like being wrapped in a big blanket.

"What time is it?" asks Maddie after a while.

"9:00 a.m.," says Joey, checking his watch. Maddie doesn't know anyone else her age who wears a watch. It makes him seem older.

"Think our parents have realized we're not at home?" she asks.

"If they haven't yet, they will soon."

Maddie tilts back her head to admire the drifting clouds. When she looks down again, she sees a bunch of tiny figures in white making their way across her grandparents' pasture, toward the cliff. "Who's that?" she asks. "And what are they wearing?"

"Hazmat suits," Joey says. "Those are the people here with the CDC and the WBCD—the ones who set the quarantine. Dad says they're trying to figure out if a virus killed your grandparents."

"Oh. Right. Why aren't they over there, by the farmhouse?" Maddie points toward the large white tent set up next to the driveway.

"I don't know. Do you think they found something?"

"I hope so," Maddie says. "I'm ready for this quarantine to be over."

Next to her, Joey makes a barely perceptible flinch. *I'm not ready,* he thinks guiltily. But out loud, he makes an *mm-hmm* noise of agreement. "Yeah. It's about time things get back to normal around here."

Debbie sets the last fork on the checkered blue tablecloth and looks to Ellie at the stove. She raises the spatula in a little salute, and Debbie yells to the house, "Breakfast is ready!"

David and Kevin are the first to appear. Kevin snatches a piece of bacon off the paper-towel-lined serving plate as Ellie passes.

"Can you wait until we sit down?" asks Ellie, swatting at him with the spatula.

"Sorry."

"Smells good, ladies," says David.

"Thanks," Ellie says.

Grace walks into the kitchen with one side of her hair mussed by her pillow. Bethany trails in on her heels, arms dangling like a sleepy ape.

"Can you go wake your sister and tell her breakfast is ready?" Debbie asks Grace.

Grace perks up at the prospect of bossing her sister and runs off toward the stairs.

"Joey should be up by now too," says Ellie, eying the stove clock with a frown. "I'm going to check on him." She sets the platter of hash browns on the table and follows Grace.

"So, our follow-up appointment with the funeral home is at 11:00," Debbie says to her husband.

He grunts in response, his mood seeming to sour in an instant.

But she soldiers on. "Then we have to stop by the florist. Because of the quarantine, all of the arrangements will have to be made with businesses within the city limits, but I think everyone here in Rindville will want the service to do Stan and Margaret justice."

Another grunt from David. "Mom was well-liked," he says.

"She was." Debbie sets a bowl of scrambled eggs on the table. "Since we don't know when the bodies will be released, we don't have to pick out urns right away, unless we want them there at the memorial—"

Grace flies back into the kitchen. "Maddie's not in her room!"

"Maybe she's outside." Debbie gets Grace settled with a helping of eggs and bacon and then checks out back. No sign of Maddie on the dock.

As she turns to go back inside, Ellie comes out, face pale. "Joey's not in his room either."

Debbie and Ellie start up a call for the teens, and soon Kevin and David join them, walking the perimeter of the large yard. Ellie frantically runs back inside to check the house again, hoping they just missed them. When all efforts turn up nothing, they reconvene in the living room.

"Do you think they went for walk to the river?" asks Debbie.

"Joey knows better than to leave the house without asking for permission," says Ellie, wringing her hands.

Kevin scoffs. "Well, clearly that's what he did."

Debbie pops her head into the kitchen, where Grace and Bethany are scarfing their breakfast. "Gracie, did your sister tell you where she was going this morning?"

Grace shakes her head, cheeks full of egg.

Ellie looks around Debbie to ask Bethany, "Do you know where your brother is?"

"No, Mommy."

"They couldn't have gone far," says Kevin, thumbs in his belt loops. "I'll call the station and have my deputies start looking for them."

When he leaves in search of his radio, Ellie asks Debbie, "Can you call Maddie's cell phone?"

"No… I took it away from her last week."

David rubs his chin. "Would they go into town?"

"I doubt it," Ellie says. "That's too far for Joey to walk, and his bike is still here."

"Okay, what about something within walking distance?

Is there a place nearby that Joey likes to hike? Somewhere he went with his friends, before...?"

Ellie thinks for a moment, the dry skin on her hands making swooshing sounds as she continues to wring them. "Maybe the river," she says just as Kevin returns.

"I hope not," says Kevin. "There's a mountain lion on the loose."

What little color Ellie has left drains from her face, and Debbie takes a step toward her, worried she might faint. "We'll find them," Debbie says reassuringly. "They're probably fine. Just being teenagers."

Kevin gestures to David. "Get dressed. Let's take my Jeep. We'll drive to the river."

"But—our appointments—" Debbie cuts off as she sees the determined look on her husband's face. "I'll reschedule."

He nods crisply. "This is more important."

* * *

Maddie isn't really looking at the view anymore. All her concentration is fixed on Joey's hands on the rock. She wages a silent battle with herself on whether she should close the two-inch gap between their fingers. What if it makes things weird? But... what if it doesn't?

"I'm sure they're looking for us by now," says Joey, and Maddie jerks her hand away.

"What time is it?" she asks as casually as she can.

"Eleven."

"Oh, definitely. They're probably losing their minds."

Joey reaches for Maddie's backpack and sets it between them. "I'm hungry for some pizza."

"Me too." Maddie pulls out a big baggie of pizza slices.

As the clouds cast sporadic, shifting shade overhead,

they dig in, scarfing a piece each and then slowing down to savor their seconds.

Just as he stuffs the last piece of crust into his mouth, Joey spots something. Movement, down below. "Did you see that?" he asks, mouth full.

"See what?"

"Look, by the river." Joey points to his right.

Maddie shakes her head, ripping off another bite. "I don't see anything."

"It looks like a dog or something," says Joey.

Maddie spies a beige shape moving lithely downstream along the bank. Looking down on it from this distance, she cannot be certain of its exact form. "I see it. I don't think it's a dog. That thing is way too big to be a dog."

"Then what is it?" asks Joey.

Maddie chuckles. "Maybe it's a werewolf. You should've let me pick that wolfsbane, after all."

"Funny."

Maddie peers at the creature and observes the way the tail adjusts like a rudder with each leap the animal takes to a new boulder, escaping the muddy sides of the river. "It looks like a cat..." she says. "Maybe a mountain lion?"

"My dad said that a mountain lion was spotted a few days ago by the river," says Joey, getting to his feet. "I guess it was feeding on your grandparents' dead cows."

Maddie scrunches her nose in disgust. "Ew. I'm glad we're not going to the river."

Joey dissolves into silence again, his eyes on the sky. Maddie finishes her slice and lounges back, watching Joey watch a bird circling in front of them and then whizzing past the lip of the cliff, black wings flashing a spot of red. Joey walks toward the edge. Maddie sits up, her muscles tensing.

When he steps to within three feet of the drop-off, she coils her whole body like a spring and says, “What are you doing?”

“Thinking.”

“Do you have to think that close to the edge?”

He doesn’t even glance back, just watches the sky with an odd look on his face that makes her heart beat an uneasy rhythm.

“You ever wonder what it’s like to fly?” he asks.

“I was on a plane once. I was pretty young, but my family flew to Florida.”

“No, that’s not what I mean. What it’s like to fly... *like a bird*.”

“That would be dope. Can you back away from the edge now, please?”

Joey puts his arms out, but she is not there to support him. Her brain screams at her to jump up and grab him, but a calmer voice in her head (a voice that sounds like her father) says that lunging for him might startle him over the edge. He’s not even a whole shoe length away from open air.

Maddie stands slowly, saying, “Stop... you’re scaring me.”

Joey at last looks over his shoulder. “Don’t worry. I’m not gonna fall.”

Maddie dares a step toward him. “What about your balance?”

Joey turns back to the scenery. “It’s funny,” he says, voice distant and flat. “Even though I’ve been fighting to stay alive these last two years, I am literally just one step away from not having to fight anymore. Not having people feel sorry for me. Not having to be in constant pain.”

“Step back, Joey!” Maddie says, voice squeaking on his name as she takes a bigger step.

Joey scoots even closer, the toe of his shoe perfectly aligned with the edge of the cliff. “How many times in your life can you say that you’ve been a moment from death? A step away?”

“Is that why you wanted to come here?” Maddie asks, tears suddenly blinding her. She rubs them away violently, desperate to keep him in her sights.

Joey looks over his shoulder. He lets out a heavy sigh and takes a step back. “No, I’m not going to... I just wanted to... I don’t know...” His brows rise as he gazes back over the edge. Far below, the people in the white hazmat suits mill around like busy ants. They go toward the cliff, then away from it, then toward it, and then away again.

What are they...?

He leans toward the chasm, trying to see what’s got their attention. If he just... leans... a little... further...

Maddie pounces, wrapping her arms around Joey’s midsection and yanking him backward so hard they both land on their butts.

Joey looks around so that his cheek touches her forehead. “I wasn’t going to jump.”

“You still could have lost your balance,” she says, heart hammering.

“Well, I didn’t.” He shirks her off and stands. “I think I saw something weird from the edge.” He inches closer, and then thinks better of it and lies on his stomach, crawling toward the drop. “Straight down.”

Maddie joins him, so they’re lying side by side. "I see it! What is that?”

The slender structure looks small from up here, but based on the trees surrounding it, it’s pretty tall. Something blue catches the sun at the top.

“Is it a radio tower?” Maddie asks.

Joey shrugs. "I don't think so. It doesn't look like anything I've ever seen. What's that blue bit?"

"Search me."

"It's on your grandparents' lot. You've never seen it before?"

"We only were ever around the farmhouse and the barn," Maddie says, "and anyway, I haven't been here in five years."

Joey moves forward one more inch. "Let's go down and check it out."

"How do we get to it without being seen by those guys in hazmat suits?" asks Maddie as Joey crawls backward, not sitting up until he's well away from the edge. She follows his lead. "Plus, they're in *hazmat suits.* Doesn't that mean it's dangerous to get too close?"

"Where's your sense of adventure?" Joey asks teasingly.

Maddie raises her eyebrows at him. "Someone's feeling brave today," she says.

"It's all thanks to you." Joey smiles, and she knows she'll do whatever he says next. "Anyway, there's a cave. That's the other cool thing I wanted to show you. We can enter on this side and come out on your grandparents' back acres without anyone seeing us. We'll scope out the tower thing from a safe distance and get out of there before they spot us."

He gets to his feet and starts packing the remaining pizza and their water bottles into Maddie's bag. When she holds out her hand, he passes the backpack over. Together, they head back to the narrow walkway across the chasm.

After their second balancing act goes off without a hitch, and they reach the other side, Joey turns to Maddie with a smile. "I can't believe it!"

"I know, right?" Maddie says, dropping her hands from his sides.

"Maybe my balance is getting better."

Maddie nods, offering an encouraging smile.

The trek down is a whole lot faster. Instead of burning thighs, they have sore toes, their feet jammed to the fronts of their shoes by the downward slope. At the very base of the hill, Joey veers left and leads Maddie around a pile of boulders to show her the small mouth of a cave.

Maddie bends to peer inside. "It's so dark."

"Good thing I brought *this*." Joey unzips Maddie's pack and pulls out the flashlight with a big smile. "Follow me."

Maddie chuckles. "You're such a dork."

Bending at the waist, they squeeze through the entrance, shoulders brushing the rock. The narrow passage soon becomes a larger tunnel, where they brush off the dirt and roll their shoulders as they stand upright. The walls are damp and smell of mold, and they can hear the sound of dripping water. After a ten-minute walk, they come to a fork. Joey stops.

"Which way?" asks Maddie.

"Right."

Maddie narrows her eyes. "You don't seem sure."

"I am." He takes a big stride down the right-side path, and with no other choice, Maddie follows.

This dark passage is not uniform, and Maddie's arm bumps the stone where the wall bulges inward unexpectedly. Rubbing what is sure to become a bruise, she feels a chalky substance stuck to her shirt. "Stop."

Joey turns around. "What is it?"

"Let me see your flashlight." She grabs it from his hand and examines the wall. She trails her fingertips over a soft gray substance that shifts and crumbles off the wall beneath her touch, staining her fingers. "What is this stuff?"

"I don't know. I don't remember seeing it before, when Tom and I came here."

Maddie lifts a little chunk of it to her nose to smell, but Joey knocks it out of her hand. "Don't do that. What if it's dangerous?"

Maddie snorts. "Dangerous... *to smell*?"

"Or to touch. What if it's like... wolfsbane?"

"Seriously? It's not like wolfsbane. It's more like soot."

"Let's go," says Joey, eyes shifting nervously around the walls.

When they come to another fork in the path, Joey stares at it even longer than he did at the one before.

"You don't know where we are, do you?" says Maddie.

"I only remember one fork in the path." Joey shakes his head. "I think we need to go back."

Maddie drops her head with a groan.

Joey gives an apologetic grimace as he skirts around her to head back to the first fork.

They're only about halfway back when Joey pauses and crouches, shining the light on a small, two-by-two-foot hole about a foot off the cave floor. "Look."

"Uh, that thing looks like an animal hole," says Maddie, remembering the large cat they'd seen from the cliff earlier.

Joey gets on his hands and knees to stick the flashlight in the hole as far as his arm will go. Then he crawls forward on his elbows, keeping the beam in front of him, until his shoulders disappear through the entrance.

"What are you doing?" asks Maddie, feeling a ripple of unease.

Joey just crawls deeper, and Maddie crouches in the deepening darkness to watch him shimmy all the way inside. "Check it out," he says, and she is relieved to see he has made it to the end of the narrow tunnel and has turned around to wave her forward. "It's empty. Come see."

She takes off her backpack and sticks her arm inside to hand it to him. The crawl is an anxiety-inducing squeeze, but it's over in less than a minute thanks to Joey, who grabs her wrists and helps pull her waist and legs out. She stands up in a small chamber the size of her bedroom back in Detroit.

"This is so cool," says Joey as he spins to shine his flashlight all around.

"I guess." Maddie shrugs. "It's a dead end," she says, spying no exits other than the way they came.

"Check out the walls." Joey angles his flashlight in all directions. "They're covered with that same gray stuff. What the heck?"

"This is so weird," says Maddie, swiping more of the strange, powdery substance off with a finger. "Seriously, you have to touch this."

After a beat, Joey nods and runs his fingers over the wall. "Huh," he says, rubbing his thumb across his fingertips.

"You ready?"

Joey nods.

"Okay. I'll crawl back out first, and then I'll pull you through." Maddie takes the lead and gets them back to the first fork in the path. "This way, right?" she says, pointing to the path they haven't already tried. Before Joey takes a step forward, he doubles over the waist with a sharp gasp. "Do you feel that?!"

CHAPTER 12

Kevin's legs are dripping sweat in his jeans, and he wishes he had pulled on some shorts like David. He takes a desperate swig of water, then bends to drag his hand through the cold, flowing river. He flicks the crystalline water on his face and the back of his neck.

"Well, they clearly didn't go to the river," he says through a sigh, surveying the surrounding trees. "So, where are they?"

David grits his teeth. "I'm going to kill her when I see her."

Kevin only raises his eyebrows at his old friend.

David looks up at the cliff towering over the treetops nearby. "Can you think of anywhere else that Joey might have taken Maddie?"

Kevin racks his brain and finally says, "I once heard him talk about a place where he could see the town and river."

"When was that?"

Kevin rubs away sweat about to drip in his eye. "About a year ago."

His cell phone rings, and he whips it out. "It's El." He

turns from David as he answers. "No, not yet. They're not at the river." Her voice rises an octave on the other end of the line, and he quickly tries to divert her mind. "Hey, do you remember Joey talking about a place where he could see the town?" He nods. "Thanks."

David is waiting with thumbs through his belt loops.

Kevin gestures upward. "She remembers him talking about that cliff."

"Let's check it out."

They hop back in Kevin's Jeep and take off as fast as the terrain allows.

"How in the world would they be able to climb that thing?" David says as they get closer and the sheer rock wall comes into plainer view.

"Don't you remember when we were kids? We used to climb the hill on the other side, with Ben Muller. It's on their lot."

"Oh, yeah."

The Jeep takes them halfway up the grassy hill, but when the slope steepens and the wheels start spinning, they throw on the parking brake.

"This sucks," says David, not three minutes into the hike.

"If the kids can do it, so can we," says Kevin, resisting the urge to ask David what all those muscles are for, exactly, if this hill is giving him so much trouble.

At the summit, David tosses up his hands with an impatient groan as he spins in a circle. "Where's the cliff?"

Kevin shrugs. He walks the perimeter of the hill's top, and just past a pile of boulders, he finds a short, narrow walkway over a deadly drop.

David is at his side in an instant, scratching his head. "I don't remember this... do you?"

"No." Kevin approaches the edge and looks down. His

stomach does a somersault. "Do you think they crossed this?"

David takes a peek and says, "No... they wouldn't be that stupid." He flashes his teeth like an angry dog and groans. "Although we probably would have crossed it when we were their age."

"Well, Joey shouldn't have. Not with his balance."

"What do you mean?" asks David.

"His balance has been off since he started the chemo. He knows he shouldn't be walking across this thing."

David shrugs. "If you don't think he'd try it..."

Kevin puffs his cheeks before letting out his breath. "There's only one way to find out." Thinking of Ellie and knowing he cannot possibly come back to her without their son, he straightens his back and walks onto the rock bridge. He speeds up when he reaches the halfway point and instantly regrets it. The outer portion of his right foot misses the stone, and he lifts it too quickly, trying to readjust. As his center of gravity tilts right, the air leaves his chest and he lunges forward, tilting himself almost horizontal as he leaps the last two steps in a full, wobbly sprint. He flies through the air on the last spring and slams into the grass on the other side, blood rushing in his ears.

He rolls over to see David smirking at him from the hilltop. "Looks like Joey's not the only Schumer with balance issues," he calls over.

Kevin glares back. "Fuck you."

David, of course, makes the crossing look easy. He smiles like a winning Olympian just off the balance beam as he reaches Kevin's side. They split up to search the area, and Kevin is the first to spot signs of life. Near the edge, he finds a small piece of bread crust nestled beside a rock and smells it. "Pizza." He looks over at David. "They were here."

David walks to the edge of the cliff and looks all around. There are men and women in white hazmat suits criss-crossing his parents' pastures. A few of them seem to be having a conference, and one of them points directly at the cliff. All of the heads turn. David follows their gaze and sees...something.

"Hey, Kevin," he says, trying to lean further over the edge without sacrificing his stability. "There's something over here."

"What is it?"

"Do you see that blue light?" David points down slightly to the left as Kevin comes as close as he dares to the edge.

Kevin shields his eyes from the blue ray that shoots up at him from the odd beige tower below as the sun peeks from behind a cloud. "Whoa, what is that?"

"I have no idea."

"Do you think it has to do with the IOCG deposit Gordon Muller was trying to get his hands on?"

David startles. "What, like it's some kind of... drill?"

"I don't know. How do people get that stuff out of the ground these days?"

David shrugs, still staring down at the strange tower. "But it's on my parent's property."

Kevin shrugs.

"We should go check it out."

"You're right. I bet the kids saw it and thought the same thing."

"We'll catch up to them for sure," David says, scanning the ground. "Look, there are cordons around the entire perimeter of my parents' land. If Maddie and Joey try to cross the property line, they'll get caught by your deputies."

Kevin's face softens with relief. "You're right."

Feeling renewed purpose, the two men begin their trek back down to the Jeep.

* * *

"Joey!" Maddie is by Joey's side in an instant. She reaches out, and then pulls her hand back, afraid to touch him. After a moment, she changes her mind again and starts to rub his back. "Are you having a..." She doesn't know how to finish that sentence. Are seizures a side effect of chemo? What about fainting? And acute pain? She settles on, "What's wrong? What can I do?"

"Tingling... all over..." Joey stands upright.

"Don't try to stand up," Maddie says. "Not if it hurts—"

"It doesn't hurt," Joey says, shaking his head. "It actually feels kind of... good."

"But you're in pain!"

"It surprised me. It was like..." Joey holds a hand in front of his face, turning it this way and that. "You know when you walk around on a carpet in wool socks, and then you touch a doorknob, and you get shocked?"

Maddie nods, still numb with fear.

"It was like that, but bigger. And now it's like... the pins and needles after your foot goes to sleep. But all over my body." He gives her a piercing look. "You don't feel anything?"

"No."

"This way to that weird tower," Joey confirms.

"Are you sure you want to keep going to that thing?"

"I'm fine now. Look." Joey stands straighter. He takes stock of his limbs. The tingle is still very much there, like little vibrating wavelengths running out from his chest to the tips of his fingers and toes and the top of his head. But it's pleasant, now that he's gotten used to it. "Let's go."

It's not long before they see the light at the end of the tunnel. Joey wishes he could take Maddie's hand and lead her out into the sun in true movie fashion. Instead, he walks ahead of her, stepping out alone into the blinding sunlight. The fresh air tastes sweet after being in the cave for so long. He rolls his shoulders, and the muscles in his back feel warm and energized.

Then he turns his head, and he sees it. "Oh," he says.

"Oh, my God," Maddie whispers beside him.

Joey's skin is prickling, the few hairs on his arm standing on end. They're close to the tower now—closer than the scientists and deputies in their hazmat suits. Even better, they're hidden from view behind a couple large boulders. "I want a closer look," Joey murmurs.

He walks to the hundred-foot-tall beige structure. It's like a fat, smooth pole most of the way up, but at the base, it spirals just before digging into the earth. As he moves toward it, it shifts from a soft tan to the color of sand with each step. He touches the side and finds it is made of what feels like a metal of some kind, almost too hot to touch. He tilts back his head. At the top of the tower is a wide pole, and at the top of *that* is a blue diamond crystal.

A low hum fills his brain. He closes his eyes as his whole body warms and the tingling becomes a vibration in his bones. It ought to be frightening, some part of his brain tells him, but it is actually soothing, like nestling back under the covers after a bathroom trip in the middle of the night.

He can sense Maddie hovering right behind him.

"This is the source," he tells her. "I can feel it."

"This… *thing* is what is making your body tingle?"

"Yes. You really don't feel it?" He opens his eyes and looks over his shoulder at her.

"I really don't." Maddie steps forward and slides her hand along the metallic structure. "It's warm. I can hear a low vibrating sound."

Joey nods. "I can hear it, too, but I can also feel it. It is so much stronger when I touch it."

"Maybe you shouldn't. What if it's, like… dangerous?" Maddie rises onto her tiptoes to peer over the rocks that comprise their hiding place. The CDC team is still hard at work in the pasture beyond. "If this is what killed my grandparents and the others…"

Joey stares at his reflection in the metal and feels as though it is talking to him without moving its mouth, telepathically whispering reassurances. "It won't hurt me."

"You don't know that." Maddie crouches to inspect the base. "Do you think my grandparents built it?"

"I don't know. What would it even be for? Maybe they didn't know it was here."

"Dad always said Grandpa would know if someone clipped a piece of grass on his land," Maddie counters, standing with a hand on her hip. "You think somebody came on their property and built it without their knowledge?"

"I doubt it."

"This farm has been in the Schwarz family for like... two hundred years or something," Maddie muses. "This thing wasn't built two hundred years ago. It doesn't even look like something you'd build *now.*"

"Maybe you were right the first time—maybe it is some kind of radio tower. And that blue diamond up top—" Joey points. "That's the transmitter. What do you think?"

"I got a C in Science last year," Maddie mutters. She reaches into her back pocket and then pulls her hand right back out with a groan. "I hate not having my cell. What time is it?"

Joey checks his watch. "2:30 p.m."

Her eyes widen. "We should get back soon. Before our parents call in the National Guard."

"Can we stay a little longer?" Joey runs his hand along the tower again, feeling its vibration travel from his fingertips up his arm to his spine and out the crown of his head.

"I don't know..."

He smiles at her. "This has been the best day ever. *Thanks.*"

Maddie smiles back, her deep brown eyes sparking, and Joey can't tear his gaze away. His body is a live-wire, and it's only in part from the odd tingling. This feeling goes deeper, all the way to the bone, all the way to parts of him that have nothing to do with anatomy... his soul... his inner core...

He's not sure what to call it, but he knows she has set it ablaze.

* * *

Kevin brakes in front of the checkpoint at the end of the Schwarz driveway. Two men in white hazmat suits walk around the large CDC tent, waving their arms like they're greeting space aliens.

When Kevin rolls down his window, the taller man says, "You're going to have to turn around."

Kevin pulls out his badge. "I'm the chief deputy for this county. Is Thomas Murphy here? We need to access the property."

The man steps back from the Jeep and gets on his radio. A few minutes later, a new hazmat-suited figure exits the tent. "Kevin," Thomas says. "What can I do for you?"

"Our kids are missing," Kevin says, gesturing to himself and David. "We have reason to believe they're on the north side of the property, near the cliff."

Thomas jolts at the mention of the cliff, but he covers it well. "Our people haven't seen any kids over there," he says, carefully avoiding mention of the tower. "We've got the property pretty well secured."

"Can we go take a look?" Kevin asks, also not mentioning that he knows what they're hiding. "We won't interfere with your investigation."

"I'm afraid this site is currently closed," Thomas says. "I could let you through, as chief deputy, but not Mr. Schwarz here."

"I'm the heir to the property," David huffs, claiming ownership for the first time. The words feel strange coming out of his mouth, after so many years vowing he'd never come back. "This is *my* land."

"Right now," Thomas says, "it's under government purview." He turns back to Kevin. "If you want to come through, you can suit up. Mr. Schwarz could wait here. Or I could see if any of your deputies are near the cliff. They could take a look around and report back."

Kevin looks at David. "I should go myself," he says, almost apologetically. "Ellie will have my hide if I don't bring Joey back soon."

"Understood," David says gruffly, still smarting from the perceived slight. "I'll wait here." He crosses his arms and settles back into the passenger seat.

It takes several minutes for Kevin to get dressed in all of the requisite protective gear, and several more for one of the WBCD vans to show up to drive them to the northern property line. Two of Kevin's deputies exit the vehicle to take over guarding the checkpoint, while the two CDC personnel who were at the tent board the van. Thomas drives and Kevin sits beside him, eyes peeled for the wayward teens.

When the tower comes into view, Kevin leans forward in the seat. "Do you know what it is?" he asks.

Thomas glances at him sideways. "You don't seem that surprised to see it," he comments. "Do *you* know what it is?"

"Not a clue." Kevin points at the cliff, knowing the jig is up. "David and I were up there this morning, looking for the kids. That's when we spotted... that."

"Well, we have no idea what it is, or if it's responsible for... all of this," Thomas says. "But we're moving forward as if it's the cause." His voice lowers with concern. "Are you sure your kids are here? It may not be safe for them to be anywhere near that thing, especially unprotected."

Kevin lets out a worried breath. "Pretty sure, and yeah,

that's what I'm afraid of."

* * *

At the back of the lot, Joey has just edged closer to Maddie, with their fingers an inch apart on the beige tower's side, when movement in the distance catches his eye. He jerks back his hand to point with a groan. "Look. Another van's here."

Maddie shields her eyes, following his finger to the white van kicking up dirt as it bumps toward them over a mild rise in the field. It parks and two people in hazmat suits get out, pointing toward the tower.

No, pointing toward *them*.

"Oh, shit. Let's run." Maddie bolts toward the cave, but quickly skids to a halt when she realizes Joey is not following her. She waves at him. "Come on! They've spotted us!"

"What's the point?" asks Joey.

"We can hide from them, that's the point! We're obviously not supposed to be here. What if they're going to arrest us for trespassing, or something?"

"Or our parents told them to look for us," Joey says. He squints as the two people come closer, spotting familiar features through a face shield. "Actually, I think one of those guys is my dad."

Maddie sags. "Are you ready to be yelled at?"

Joey smiles. "It was worth it."

"If you say so," she says, but she's smiling too.

Kevin yelps and breaks into a run. He reaches for his son, but then pulls up short, hampered by the bulky protective suit. "We've been looking all over for you!" he shouts.

"Looks like you found us," Joey says.

Kevin shakes his head, thinking that Maddie's smart mouth is rubbing off on his son. "Get in the van. Both of you. Now."

The teens exchange smiles and walk off toward the van.

Kevin lingers, staring up at the tower. He has to crane his neck to take in the whole thing. The color of it is subtly shifting, from beige to something slightly darker. And there's another odd thing... He crouches and rests a hand on the ground.

"The vibration," Thomas says from beside him. "You feel it?"

"Just barely. It's so slight..."

"It's stronger the closer you get to the tower," Thomas says.

"It's like a generator," Kevin says. "But where's the energy coming from?" He takes a step toward the tower, and Thomas stops him with a hand on his arm. Kevin shakes him off. "The kids were over there. I just need to go see what they were looking at."

After a moment, Thomas steps back.

"Thanks." Kevin jogs to the base of the tower. He rests a hand on its side. It's warm to the touch. He squats to look at the mounds of freshly stirred dirt around the spiral. He paws at the earth, creating a small hole that reveals more of the beige metal underground. "How far down does it go?" he murmurs to himself.

"Kevin!" Thomas shouts from the van. "We need to go."

The chief deputy returns to the WBCD vehicle and is quiet for the ride back to his Jeep at the end of the driveway. The two teens are quiet as well, probably waiting for their dressing-down to start. Well, let them wait. Kevin knows David will jump right in as soon as he sees Maddie and Joey safe and in one piece. He can't stop thinking about that glimpse of metal underground. Exactly how big is that tower?

What the hell is it?

As they approach the checkpoint, Thomas says, "I need to talk with the sheriff. Is he in town?"

"Yes, but he leaves the office at five," says Kevin.

"Thanks. What time is it?"

"Four," Joey pipes up from the back seat, holding out the wrist with his watch.

"Do you want us to give you a ride?" Kevin asks.

Thomas looks at the Jeep, no doubt considering the cramped seating and the high probability of yelling, and shakes his head. "No, I'll drive the van. But thanks."

They park and Thomas shows Kevin how to get out of his gear. Maddie and Joey stand awkwardly to one side, clearly in no hurry to join David, whose fuming is visible even from a distance. Eventually, Kevin tells them, "Just go. Peel off the Band-Aid. Get it over with."

Maddie leans in to Joey and whispers, too quiet for the grown-ups to hear, "Totally worth it."

He smiles, and together they head to the Jeep.

Kevin moves to follow, but Thomas says, "Wait. If they show any symptoms..."

"What kind of symptoms?" Kevin asks, throat clenching.

"Who knows? Fatigue, nausea, nosebleeds, heart palpitations... You name it. We still don't really know what we're dealing with here."

"My son..." Kevin begins, and then coughs to clear the emotion from his body. "My son has leukemia."

Thomas's eyes go wide. "I'm sorry. I didn't know."

"We'll be in touch if anything changes."

"Anything," Thomas stresses, though with more kindness than urgency now. "I'm just a phone call away."

* * *

"What the hell were you thinking, young lady?!" David barks the moment all of the Jeep's doors are closed.

"We just went for a hike. We left early. I didn't want to wake you and Mom," says Maddie, her voice higher and sweeter than usual.

Joey smiles at the way she tilts her head, playing the part of Daddy's innocent angel.

David's face turns crimson. "Are you kidding me?!"

Apparently, he knows the act well already and has grown immune.

"What are you smiling about?" Kevin says, meeting his son's eyes in the rear-view mirror.

Joey wipes the grin off his face and adopts a somber, humble look.

Kevin shakes his head. "You actually crossed that narrow walkway on the cliff? You could have lost your balance and..." Kevin rubs a hand over his mouth instead of finishing that thought.

"It's okay, Dad. Maddie helped me cross. I'm fine. Nothing happened."

"That doesn't make it okay!" Kevin yelps. "Not to mention..." His chest constricts as the terror he feels for Joey threatens to overwhelm him. He needs to get control of himself. Maybe he should let David drive.

Then he looks over at David's flushed face and narrowed eyes. Maybe Kevin is still the calm one.

"Did you see the cordons around the property?" he asks. "Did you see all the people in hazmat suits?"

"Yes," Joey begins, "but—"

"Did it not occur to you that perhaps that meant you two shouldn't be there?"

In the back seat, Maddie and Joey exchange a look.

"We thought..." Maddie starts.

"You thought wrong!" David bellows. "Jesus, like this trip hasn't been hard enough, without you two running away from home."

Joey objects, "That's not—"

"You're grounded," Kevin says flatly. "You will not leave the house or yard unless accompanied by an adult, for a necessary activity. Is that clear?"

"You too, Maddie!" says David, arms crossed in true cop fashion, chest puffed.

"*Is. That. Clear*?" Kevin repeats, when neither teen speaks.

"Yes," Joey and Maddie chorus together.

And then they're home.

The mothers' lectures are almost as bad as the fathers' were, except with more shrieking. Also, no one mentions the people in hazmat suits. When Joey sees how distraught his mother is, he realizes that his dad is trying to hold back any details that might make her more scared. That gives Joey a twinge of guilt. He didn't pause to think about how today's grand adventure might make his worried mom feel.

But then he feels annoyed and even a little angry. Why should he have to sneak out to go hiking in the first place? Why should his illness make him a little kid again?

It's after 5:00 p.m. by the time Maddie and Joey are dismissed. They can't watch TV and Maddie's phone is still confiscated indefinitely, so they head out to sit at the end of the dock.

"Parents are so predictable," Maddie says, flopping back to stare up at the sky.

"Being grounded is... honestly not that different than my usual life," Joey says with a snort. "Some punishment."

"Yeah, but the chores," Maddie points out. "Those will really suck."

Joey thinks, *I don't care as long as I am with you*. But what he says aloud is, "The work will go faster since we're doing it together."

Up on the deck, Kevin cracks open the first beer of the night and hands it to Ellie. David watches her take the can with envy, wishing for the cool condensation on his hand in the heat. As Kevin bends down for two more, Debbie asks, "Do you think we were too hard on the kids?"

Ellie shakes her head, licking foam from her lip. "Not hard enough, if you ask me."

Kevin nods as he hands Debbie a can. "I agree. They could have fallen from the cliff. That was careless."

David laughs. "Oh my God. Do you hear yourself?"

Kevin glares. "What?"

"Do you remember all the shit we did as kids? We did way more stupid shit than that."

"That was different."

David sees the trajectory of that statement and doesn't want to dip into those waters. Not without a beer anyway. He changes the subject. "I wonder if that tower you saw today is the cause of the deaths."

"What tower?" asks Ellie.

Kevin glares at David. He didn't want Ellie to know about the tower. "There is this strange tower on the north side of the lot."

"Strange how?" asks Debbie.

"It's this long tower with a blue diamond shaped thing at the top," says Kevin.

"Did your mom ever mention your dad building something on the farm?" asks Debbie.

"No," says David with a scoff. "You know my dad, there is

no way he would have spent money on something that wasn't directly related to farming. That thing had to be expensive to build."

"True, but what purpose does it serve?" asks Ellie.

David shrugs. "I can't think of anything."

"I wonder if it's related to the IOCG deposit," says Kevin as he sits on the end of Ellie's lounge chair.

Debbie asks, "What's an IOCG deposit?"

Kevin snickers at David. "You didn't tell Deb about the Survey?"

David shoots Kevin a deadly look and then turns to smile sunnily at Debbie.

"What survey?" Debbie says, warning him against lies with the mere intonation of her voice.

"I was going to tell you, but I got distracted looking for the kids. Honestly, I didn't think it was a big deal."

"What isn't a big deal, David?!"

"I happen to come across a geological survey that showed an IOCG deposit on the Muller's… and my parent's property. But looking at the map, it's mostly on the Muller's property."

Debbie pulls out her cell phone with a huff. "What's an IOCG deposit?"

"IOCG stands for Iron, Oxide Copper, and Gold," he says hastily, before she can google.

"Gold?!" Debbie leans forward with enormous eyes. "Why wouldn't you tell me about this?"

David sinks in his chair, feeling like a thirteen-year-old about to get grounded for life. "Like I said, I was distracted."

"I get today, but were you distracted… *yesterday*?"

Kevin is wearing a big, satisfied grin that makes David want to knock him off his chair.

David pulls out his phone and puts a photo between

himself and Debbie's wrath. "See... I was able to take a picture of a geological survey."

She grabs it from him and widens the photo.

"Yeah, David," says Kevin, smirking behind his can, "why don't you tell Deb how you were able to *somehow* take a picture of it."

David bores holes through Kevin's forehead, but the dumbass just keeps grinning. He grits his teeth audibly in a predatory threat, promising death if Kevin spills another word through that cocky grin. He smooths his expression as he turns to face Debbie and says, "I got it from the Muller's attorney."

Debbie glances up from the phone with narrowed eyes. "How did you get it from the Muller's attorney?"

"He broke into his office," says Kevin.

David nearly decks him but knows that will only make Debbie angrier. She's already got her hackles up, shrieking at him like a cornered cat.

"You're in this town for... *not even ten days* and your breaking the law?!"

David puts on his poker face and waves her off. "We're getting side-tracked here. That's not important. Look at the survey."

Kevin is still grinning ear to ear, but it's David's turn for a malicious smirk when Ellie kicks Kevin in the shin.

"Ouch... what the hell?" Kevin rubs his leg while Ellie hisses at him under her breath.

To David's relief, Debbie's attention is back on the survey for a few minutes. "Are you sure about the location?" she says, squinting at the tiny writing. "It says there's an estimated 50,000 tonnes of IOCG at these coordinates." She taps the screen. "That looks like your parent's property not the Mullers."

David takes back the phone for closer inspection of the map, saying, "No, that can't be right."

Debbie stands up and moves behind him to point at the markings. "That's the cliff and the deposit is on the south side of the cliff… not north side."

"No that is north and that is south."

Debbie shakes her head. "David… isn't that the river?" Her painted nail traces a line that snakes around to the right of the cliff.

David nods.

She slaps his shoulder, raising her brows as if to say, duh. "Then it has to be south."

David gawks at her. "You're right. It is mostly on my parent's lot."

Kevin laughs. "Geography wasn't your strong suit," he says, earning himself another shin kick from Ellie.

While Kevin pouts, Ellie asks, "How much do you think fifty-thousand tonnes of IOCG are worth?"

Debbie is already on the case, researching on her cell phone. "This website says that it can be worth up to seven-thousand per tonne, depending on the coper and gold concentration. I guess copper is also really valuable."

"How much would that be?" asks David.

Debbie opens her calculator app, expression taut as she punches in some numbers. She nearly drops the phone and her breath whooshes out of her lungs. She turns the screen toward David.

"What the…!"

"What is it?" Kevin asks.

"Three hundred and fifty million!" says David, letting out a wild, bark-like laugh. "We need to hire a geologist, right away!"

"No shit!" says Kevin.

Debbie lets out a weird, garbled giggle, like a drunken hiccup laugh, and grabs for David's hand. "I can't believe that a day that started out so wrong… ends up with us being… millionaires?"

"Talk about a turnaround," Ellie says, smiling warmly. "Congratulations."

"Imagine what we can do with that money," Debbie says. "Oh! We could pay off Joey's medical bills!"

"We could never let you do that," Ellie says, even as her eyes widen with hope.

"You let us stay with you during this crazy time. You've taken such good care of us. We can take care of you, in return. Right, David?"

Feeling magnanimous, David squeezes his wife's hand. "Right."

"Well, let's wait and see how much your land is *actually* worth," Kevin says practically, "before we—"

Kevin's police radio crackles, as usual, he leaps up and heads out of earshot down the deck steps as he answers.

David strains to catch the deputy's words, but there's no need.

Kevin comes sprinting back up the steps, pale as death. "Oh my God!"

"What is it, Kevin?" asks Ellie breathlessly, jumpy as a mouse.

"You're not going to believe it," says Kevin, fixing David with defeated eyes that fill him with dread, "*The entire CDC team is dead.*"

David chokes on his own saliva. "Dead?" he sputters, clutching his burning throat. "But how? They were wearing hazmat suits."

CHAPTER 13

July 13th, 2016 - Washington, D.C.

Catherine Harris walks quickly toward the private plane, dragging her rolling suitcase behind her. With her other hand, she presses her phone to her ear. "Yes, sir. I understand." A pause. "I'm boarding now. We're due to land around 9:00 a.m. local time."

She tucks the phone between her shoulder and cheek as she digs out her government identification to show the pilot and flight attendant.

"Yes, I'll check in as soon as I'm on site," she says, nodding as she's waved onto the plane. "Speak to you then." She hangs up, tucks the phone into her purse, and ascends the small jet's fold-out stairs.

Inside, she takes a moment to get herself situated at one of the tables. She sets out her dossier on the Rindville case, as well as the long list of federal agencies that want to be kept in the loop. Catherine is officially going to Wisconsin on behalf of the Federal Bureau of Investigation, but as the on-scene commander for a joint task force comprised of personnel from the FBI, Homeland Security (FEMA), Department of Defense, Department of Energy, and other agencies, she'll be managing a lot of people—and opinions. She wants to walk off this plane ready to lead, and that means knowing exactly who and what she'll be dealing with on that deadly dairy farm.

The plane's engines rumble to life. They taxi out onto the runway and take off.

* * *

Rindville, Wisconsin

Thomas Murphy paces the sheriff's office with a cell phone pressed to his ear. "Yes, sir, thank you," he says before hanging up. He collapses into the chair across from Jack's desk. "The Schwarz farm is going to get awfully crowded in the next few hours."

"What do you mean?" Jack asks.

"After reading my report last night, the Director of the CDC called the Secretary of Defense. The DOD and the Justice Department believe that the tower could be a WMD."

"A weapon of mass destruction?!" Jack exclaims. "You've got to be kidding me."

"I wish I were." Thomas rubs at his eyes. "They're also assuming that the deaths could be the result of a terrorist attack."

The words themselves are terrifying, but they don't match up with the images in Jack's head of his town and his neighbors. Stuff like that doesn't happen here in small-town America.

"Whatever that tower is," Thomas goes on, "and no matter why Stan Schwarz built it—"

"Old man Schwarz was not a terrorist," Jack says firmly. "He may have been a lot of things, but terrorist was not one of them. That man bled red, white, and blue."

"That may be, but they are going to treat this as a serious threat."

In the silence that follows, Jack studies the younger man. Thomas looks even more haggard than Jack feels. He wonders how many of the men on his hazmat team Thomas knew personally. He looks like he's taken several punches to the gut, his body bent inward, as if trying to curl into the fetal position. His eyes are red-rimmed with sorrow.

"You said it was about to get crowded," Jack says. "Who exactly is about to show up?"

"Agents from the FBI, Homeland Security, the DOD, Health and Human Services... oh, and the Department of Energy."

Jack rubs at the beginnings of a migraine. "Why in the world would the Department of Energy get involved?"

"They provide technical support to the LFA. Basically, diagnostic and device assessment, and possibly... *radiological assessment*."

"What the hell is the LFA?" Jack grumbles.

"Lead federal agency," Thomas says. "In this case, the DOJ or the FBI."

"You government employees sure like your acronyms."

"Aren't you a government employee?"

"Not a federal one." Jack resists the urge to add, *Thank God.* He knows that right now he needs to be the model of professionalism. He doesn't want to be taken off this case. With two of his own deputies now dead, this is personal. "What happens when they determine this isn't a terrorist attack?"

"Homeland Security goes home. Everyone else stays until this gets sorted out."

"Right." Jack sighs heavily. "When will everyone start to arrive?"

"The OSC is already in the air." Thomas pauses. "Sorry, that's the on-scene commander, Catherine Harris. She'll coordinate everyone from the various agencies, and she'll be your liaison for the duration of the federal investigation. She's due to land in about half an hour."

"Wow, they don't waste any time."

"No, they don't."

"What about you? Do you still think we're dealing with some kind of pandemic?"

Thomas looks up at the ceiling. "Honestly? No. We haven't found any evidence that points to a communicable disease or an infectious microorganism. It's not bacterium, protozoan, prion, viroid, or fungus."

"Is it a parasite?" Jack asks.

"There are still more tests to run, but in my personal opinion..." Thomas shakes his head. "I truly think this has to do with that tower. And that's what I'll tell Catherine when she gets here."

Jack nods, digesting everything Thomas is telling him. "You know," he says thoughtfully, "it's a good thing you drove into town yesterday to meet with me. Seems like, had you stuck around on the Schwarz farm, you would be dead too."

Thomas hangs his head.

"I am sorry about your team," Jack says quietly.

Thomas closes his eyes long enough to breathe once through his nose. "Thanks. I just met most of them on the 8th, but still... it's so hard to believe. Terrance Wilkins is the only one who survived, and he is in critical condition."

"Thank God for small blessings," Jack says. "I hope he pulls through. Then maybe he can shed some light onto this thing."

* * *

Maddie's lower back feels hot, and it has nothing to do with the morning sun overhead. She rolls her shoulders as she frees another weed from the soil and straightens up, arching her back to stretch herself out. She tosses the scraggly plant into the bucket at her feet with a groan. "Have I mentioned how much I hate pulling weeds?"

Joey chuckles. "Only about a hundred times."

Maddie wipes sweat off her forehead. "This really sucks!"

"You know what sucks even more?" Joey tosses another weed in on top of hers.

Maddie shrugs.

"Having a bone marrow sample."

"What's that?" She wrinkles her nose, already expecting something gnarly.

Joey stretches his thumb and forefinger as far apart as they'll go. "They use a long needle and take a sample of marrow from my hip."

Maddie cringes, curling her lip like a dog. "Damn. That really sucks. You're right, I would rather pull weeds." She takes a swig from her water bottle, surveying the white picket fence and the rows of pansies and petunias trapped inside around a dirty-looking green pond. "Why does your mom have such a big garden?"

"I know, right?"

They work in silence for several minutes, until Maddie

gets up the nerve to ask, "Why do they do a bone marrow sample?"

"To test my blast count. That's the percentage of Myeloblasts... which are the bad cells. My last count was over sixty percent."

Maddie watches Joey bend for another weed, his movements far more careful than her own. He looks like a war veteran grandpa trying not to tweak an old injury. Yesterday's hiking and climbing clearly took a toll on him. "What's normal?"

"Five percent."

Maddie looks at the ground. "Oh." For some reason, the numbers put it in perspective better than his bald head and horrible muscle tone. They feel more... finite.

"I actually have to go to the clinic in Jackson tomorrow for that and a CBC," he says, tossing her that grin that begs, *Don't look at me like you feel bad for me.*

"What's a CBC?" asks Maddie, doing her best to keep her tone light.

"Complete blood count. They measure my white blood cells and platelet count."

Maddie gets back to weed-pulling to hide the worry tugging at her guts. "They're going to let you break the quarantine?"

"My dad got special permission for me to go to my appointment," Joey says. "But he also thinks the town won't be under quarantine that much longer anyway."

"Did they figure out what's going on?"

"No, but I guess they don't think it's a virus or whatever." Joey stares at his dirty hands, wondering whether he should tell Maddie the other thing he overheard this morning, when his dad was on the phone with his grandpa, the sheriff.

"What is it?" she asks, visibly bracing for bad news.

"Those hazmat dudes we saw yesterday... they all died, not too long after we left the farm."

"What?!"

"Yeah, and the guy who didn't die, the epidemiologist from the CDC... he thinks that tower is the cause."

"But... we were standing next to it," Maddie says, her breath quickening. "I touched it. We both did."

"I know." Joey's eyebrows draw together with concern. "I don't know what to think. It definitely made me feel different. I don't feel... sicker. Do you?"

Maddie looks down at her arms, half-expecting to find lesions popping up all over her body. Everything looks normal. But what about on the inside?

Are they both dying now?

* * *

Thomas Murphy's teeth ache from clenching his jaw. It's already been a long day, and it's barely 10:00 a.m. He stayed up late drafting his report and checking for news on Terrance's condition and the other victims' autopsies. After a few hours of restless sleep, he was up again and taking phone calls from various concerned government agencies. Then he had to stop in at the sheriff's office to brief local law enforcement on next steps. Now, all he wants is to curl up in a ball, close his eyes, and rest.

Of course, he can't do that, he thinks as he pulls his borrowed van into the makeshift parking lot at the base of the Schwarzes' driveway. There is a deadly force on the farm, and no one is sure what it is, how it strikes, or when it will decide to deal out death next.

He dons hazmat gear, even though these plastic suits

couldn't help his colleagues yesterday. Then he walks up the driveway toward the farm. The land is dotted with enormous white tents, billowing from the fans inside, powered by the best generators money can buy. In addition to the tent his people previously put up by the farmhouse and the one at the property's main entrance, there's now one in the west field and one in the east. Farther in the distance, dozens of agents are setting up two more. All personnel are wearing hazmat suits, which makes Thomas glad he put his on. He supposes this means Catherine Harris is a stickler for rules and regulations.

He heads for the main tent, knowing the drill. The federal OSC will be planted at a desk there—probably the desk that used to be Thomas's. Sure enough, he finds a woman bent over the white fold-out desk, her short brown ponytail cocked to the left as she writes in a black notebook. Her hazmat helmet is propped on the floor beside her uncomfortable metal desk chair.

Hm. Maybe not such a stickler after all.

When Thomas gets close, she notices him and stands up to extend a hand. "Thomas Murphy?"

"Yes. Catherine Harris?"

Her thin lips form a tight, sympathetic smile. "Yes, that's me. As I'm sure you know by now, I'll be taking the lead on this joint task force."

"Yes. Nice to meet you."

"You as well. Take a seat." She gestures to an equally rickety chair across from her desk.

Thomas sits, trying to ease the tension in his back by rolling his shoulders.

"Do you want to take that off?" she asks, gesturing toward his bulky helmet. "I appreciate the formality, but I think we both know that whatever this is doesn't care whether or not you're wearing a suit."

He removes his helmet, gulping in a breath of fresh air. "Are you going to make an announcement?" he asks, nodding back toward the rest of the white-suited agents.

"Soon. The suits make them feel safe, for now. I..." Catherine pauses, seeming to carefully consider her next words. "I read up on the case on my way here, and I have some... thoughts. But before I weigh in, I'd like you to tell me what you've experienced." Something in her tone makes Thomas very interested to hear those thoughts, and he almost presses her further, but then she says, "Also, my condolences."

He blanches. "Thanks," he says stiffly, thinking the condolences ought to go to those men and women's families, not him. Along with... well, actually, he's not sure any gift or speech could ease their pain in the slightest.

Her dark, close-set eyes probe him for a moment. "I don't mean to sound insensitive, but it's a good thing you drove into town to meet the sheriff when you did."

Thomas's nod is more like a muscle spasm.

Catherine pulls a folder from the chestnut satchel hanging off her chair. "So, why don't you start from the beginning."

Thomas sits straighter, unhitching his locked jaw. "My team and I arrived here in Rindville on July 8th. We issued an isolation and quarantine order because we suspected that the deaths were caused by a contagion. The property's owners, Stan and Margaret Schwarz, were found dead in their upstairs bedroom on July 2nd. The county coroner determined the time of death to be approximately 5:00 p.m. We examined the bodies and concurred." His mouth is dry, but he's not sure water would help; he needs a stiff drink. "The autopsy report indicated heart attacks. Both Stan and Margaret had enlarged hearts, hardened arteries, aneurisms, and over ninety percent of their capillaries had… literally ruptured."

Catherine shakes her head, rubbing her lips against her forefinger. "According to the toxicology report, there was no trace of poison in the victims... at least, nothing widely known."

"Yes, that's correct." Thomas pulls out his phone to check the digital, abridged record of his own notes. "Stan and Margaret's entire herd also died on the 2nd."

"How many in the herd?" asks Catherine.

"Three hundred and twenty-five. They were located approximately two thousand feet from the residence."

Catherine flips deeper into the file. "I read the necropsy report."

"Yes, the vet couldn't determine a cause of death. However, they had the same symptoms as Stan and Margaret, as did an assortment of small vermin found dead in the barn. Mice, birds, and the like."

Catherine nods at her papers and then gives him her undivided attention again.

He powers on. The faster he talks, the sooner this is over. He can speed back down that driveway.

"On July 7th, two men with the local county sheriff's office were found dead by the main residence. The coroner's office confirmed that they each had an enlarged heart, hardened arteries, and ruptured capillaries. The same as Stan and Margaret. The coroner's office contacted the Wisconsin Bureau of Communicable Diseases through the electronic disease surveillance system. The WBCD then contacted our office, and I packed my bags."

"Time of death for the deputies?" Catherine asks.

"Between 5:00 and 5:15 p.m. They called for help and were dead by the time their chief deputy arrived."

"Hm."

"My team arrived in Rindville on July 8th and started our investigation. I brought three specialists from Atlanta, and Terrance Wilkins at WBCD brought a team of twelve. We examined the bodies and the surrounding area, and did not find any evidence of an infectious microorganism. In my opinion, there is no deadly bacterium, protozoan, prion, viroid, or fungus present on this property."

"But there is... something *else* here," Catherine says slowly. "Can you tell me about it?"

Thomas nods. "The tower was discovered by our team on July 10th. It's a spiroid structure embedded at the base of a natural cliff formation. It appears to give off some sort of soft vibration. It has a blue stone of some sort at the top."

"How was this tower not found sooner?"

"Because the first two bodies were found inside the house, initial investigations were focused on the immediate surrounding area, as well as the barns."

"But, after the two deputies died you expanded your search."

"Exactly. So, once we'd run our planned array of tests, and had come up empty, Terrance had the idea to—well, he thought there might be something we'd missed. The deputies had been patrolling the north pastures before they died."

"Terrance is the survivor of the most recent incident?"

Thomas gulps. "Yes. He's in critical condition at the local hospital in Jackson."

"The other..." Catherine runs her finger down the page in front of her, counting silently. "...fifteen victims yesterday were all wearing hazmat suits, correct?"

Thomas feels like the farm itself is growing spiny tendrils that have wrapped around his throat, preventing him from speaking. He shifts in his chair, moving to loosen his tie only to realize he's not wearing one. Instead, he tugs at the collar of his plastic suit. "Yes."

"Why do you suppose Terrance survived?" Catherine leans forward, fingertips pressed together.

Thomas shakes his head. "I have no idea."

"From the moment you arrived in Rindville, your team was located here at the Schwarz farm, correct?"

"Yes."

Catherine glances at her notes. "And over the past two days, you'd been in proximity to this strange tower?"

"Yes, along with several civilians," says Thomas.

At that, her eyebrows go up. "Civilians?"

"Two teenagers snuck onto the property yesterday. They were removed by their parents."

"What time was this?" Catherine asks quickly.

"Around 4:00, maybe?" Thomas thinks back. "They were off the property by 4:00, because that's when I went into town to meet with the sheriff."

"And the deaths yesterday occurred around 5:15 p.m."

Thomas checks his own bullet points. "Yes."

"Do you think the tower is somehow linked to the deaths?"

Thomas shrugs, weariness pressing down on him. He sags, defeated, in his chair. "It sure seems like it."

"Any unusual deaths in Rindville in the last year or so?"

"No… nothing out of the ordinary."

Catherine leans back and looks up at the tent's ceiling. She's quiet for several moments. Then she stands up suddenly. "Where exactly was Terrance located when the medic found him?"

Thomas heaves himself out of his chair and follows her out of the tent. He leads her to the place Terrance was found, twitching and groaning, his eyes full of blood, his skin purple and swollen with blood freed from his decimated capillaries. "It was about here." He focuses on the tire tracks from the WBCD van Terrance had been trying to escape into, avoiding looking at the orange flags that mark where the bodies of his team had lain.

"South of the house," Catherine notes. "Were any of the cattle in these fields—" She motions toward the south side of the farm. "—when they died?"

"Not that I know of."

"What about the other team members?"

"Everyone was, to my knowledge, north of Terrance."

"We need to relocate," Catherine says, gesturing at the main tent.

The puzzle pieces click together in Thomas's mind. "We're too close to the tower."

Catherine nods. "If that tower somehow caused the deaths, then we need to maintain a safe distance from it. Based on the fact that Terrance survived, I'm assuming that anything past this point may be safe. Terrance was the farthest from the tower at the time of the—well, I hate to call it an attack, but that's the theory we're operating under at the moment."

"So, anything within this radius—" Thomas draws an imaginary line on the ground with his toe. "—will die if there is another attack. That makes sense, and it would explain the cattle that died on the neighbor's lot as well. But how will you examine the tower if you can't be within this radius? And what about the civilians? They were in closer contact with the tower than my people yesterday."

"Look at the times of death." Catherine stares past his

left shoulder, out at the rolling hills. "The first deaths were on the 2nd at approximately 5:00 p.m. The deputies died on the 7th between 5:00 and 5:15 p.m. Your team died on the 12th at around 5:15 p.m. It would seem that every five days, there's an attack of some kind. Possibly originating from that tower." She points in the direction of the tower nestled below the cliff. "Anyone within a certain radius of it will die during the attack. But based on the pattern, I think we have four days before there is another attack, around 5:00 p.m."

"You may be right," Thomas says, praying it's true. The logic is sound, and he can already feel his body relaxing a little.

"It's just a theory, so I don't want to take any chances. My agents are taking samples of the tower this morning, but as soon as that's done, we'll focus all our efforts on pulling back. I don't want any tents within the unsafe radius." She pauses for a moment. "We need to test my theory."

"How?" asks Thomas.

"We'll place mice in cages at certain distances from the tower. If the ones placed beyond this point survive, then we'll know."

Thomas admires her confident stance, elbows splayed with hands on her slender hips. He's more than willing to let her take charge of this operation; they'll be in good hands. Better hands, probably. "We'll know for sure on the 17th if your theory is correct," he says. "In the meantime, what can I do to help?"

* * *

The lake surrounds Maddie, cradling her back and leaching all the heat and sweat from her skin as it gently laps over her shoulders and stomach. She closes her eyes against the soft breeze on her face and sighs. "It feels good to be in the water after weeding for five hours straight."

Joey is floating in a pink innertube beside her. "No kidding. It's nice to be done with our punishment."

"Well, not technically. We're still not supposed to leave the premises," says Maddie, adopting a deeper voice that sounds nothing like her father's baritone.

"I wish I didn't have to go to my appointment tomorrow. I wish I didn't have to get tested."

It's the second time he's brought up the tests today, and Maddie can hear the dread in his voice. She moves from floating to treading water. "Does the bone marrow sample hurt that bad?"

"It's not that..." He fades off, looking away.

Maddie's stomach dips. She can tell he expects his results to be worse than ever. If his numbers keep rising, how long does he have? She doesn't want to think about it, so she swims to the ladder. When she steps onto the dock, she turns to find Joey watching her with a slack-jawed stare. She flushes with a mixture of embarrassment and excitement, while he snaps his face back into its usual genial grin.

"You said you could teach me how to dive," she says with what she hopes is a flirtatious smile. She doesn't have much practice with things like that, though she wouldn't admit it aloud.

"I can. I think it will be easiest if you stand on the top step of the ladder."

Maddie tilts her head. "Why?"

"I'll show you."

She shrugs and takes his advice, balancing on the hard metal step. "Now what?"

"It's better if I show you first." He swims over and taps her foot. "Let me get out." She turns to climb down as he reaches to grab the sides of the ladder, and his arms go around her, his chest brushing her back. She can feel goosebumps rise on his arm as it accidentally touches her side. She smiles in secret as she ducks under his arm to get back in the water. He clambers onto the dock and poises himself on the edge. "You want to put your arms out like this. Then bend over and kick your feet up and extend your entire body." He dives, all ten fingers breaking the water first so that his body slips in with barely a ripple.

Maddie gets back on the top step and extends her arms as Joey pops to the surface. "You make it look so easy, but it's not."

"It is easy."

She adjusts her stance, preparing to spring. "Like this?"

"Yes, your biceps should cover your ears."

She moves her arms a little higher.

"Good... now bend down and kick your feet up."

She dives, her body nearly bent in half when she hits the water. It definitely wasn't the graceful, subtle curve of grass bending in a breeze, as she'd envisioned. When she reemerges, she fixes him with a sheepish grin. "How was that?"

"Close. But you didn't extend your legs. Your entire body needs to be a straight line. Yours was more of a V. If you had jumped from the dock, it would have been a belly flop."

"Good thing I didn't dive from the dock."

After practicing for about thirty minutes, straightening her spine a little more each time she strikes the surface, Maddie is convinced she can dive from the dock. She braces herself on the edge, conscious of how slippery the wet wood has become and curling her toes to compensate.

She looks down and says, "I'm scared."

"Do you want to practice some more from the step?" asks Joey.

Maddie shakes her head, but her legs don't bend. She hears giggles and looks around to see Grace and Bethany heading down the deck steps. If she doesn't jump now, she'll have an audience. She bends her knees and leaps, but her right foot jerks back on the wet wood and her whole body tenses, ruining her form. The loud pop of her skin slapping the water precedes a sharp, stinging pain. She flails to the surface and screams, "Fuck, that hurt!"

"You said the f-word! I'm telling Mom!" Grace yells from the dock.

Maddie karate chops the water, trying to splash Grace, but she and Bethany dodge the spray. "Go ahead, you little brat!"

Grace and Bethany run hand in hand back into the house.

Maddie winces and rubs her stomach as she faces Joey. "That was a belly flop, wasn't it?"

Joey nods, doing a horrible job of concealing his grin. "You didn't kick out your feet and extend your legs."

Maddie looks up at the house and chuckles. She can see her little sister talking to her parents on the deck. "I may be pulling more weeds tomorrow," she says ruefully.

Joey laughs. "Maybe... but if you have to, I'll help you."

Maddie splashes him, and his lashes drip shimmering droplets. "Thanks, but you have to go into town tomorrow, so I'll be on my own."

"Yeah, but it shouldn't take all day." He splashes her back.

Then they're splashing each other, howling and laughing, and for a few minutes, it's like nothing bad in the world can touch them. They're invincible.

* * *

David and Debbie watch the splash-fight from the deck, glasses of cold iced tea in hand. As soon as Grace and Bethany go back inside, they resume their conversation.

"It just feels strange to talk about something like this at a time like this," Debbie murmurs. "It's like we're... taking advantage of a tragedy."

"We aren't," David assures her. "The IOCG deposit was there already. And we have to discuss it now, before the government gets any more entrenched on my land."

Debbie purses her lips at how her husband is now calling the farm *his* land, but she doesn't comment. "Did Kevin say who all is there now?"

"FBI, Homeland Security, a bunch of other feds..."

"So how will a geologist be able to do an assessment?"

"There's the problem," David says. "Also, Kevin mentioned the possibility of eminent domain."

Debbie's eyes widen. "What? The government could take your parents' farm from you?"

"I guess, if it meets the requirement for 'public necessity.'" He makes quote fingers around that last part, grimacing.

"Don't they have to pay you for the land?"

"Yeah, but I doubt they're going to pay me a hundred million."

Her jaw drops. "Is that what it's worth?" she whispers, as if saying it too loud will scare the possibility away.

David had spent the morning calling around, trying to find someone who would take a look at the map he'd... *procured* from the Mullers' attorney's office. He'd finally gotten through to the head of the geology department at a big university. "The woman I talked to earlier said that they would need to determine the gold and copper content in order to properly value the land, but she did say that if the total tonnage is over 50,000… it would be worth at least a hundred million."

Debbie's eyes pop out of their sockets. "Oh, my God."

David nods, still a little shell-shocked. "I can't believe my parents were sitting on that much money."

"Well, if the government does take your property, they'd better pay you what it's worth."

"Yeah… no shit."

Debbie looks over her shoulder. Through the bay window, she can see Ellie in the kitchen, staring out at the teens. "How's Kevin doing?" she asks.

"Not great," David admits. "The loss of his deputies..."

"It's so sad," Debbie says. "And to think that all of this started with your parents…"

David looks over at her sharply, as if to shut her up.

But Debbie will not be cowed. "No," she says. "We need to deal with this. We haven't even finished planning your parents' memorial service! And now, all you can talk about is becoming a millionaire."

"Don't *you* want to be a millionaire?" David shoots back.

"That's not the point! You're avoiding your feelings again. You went straight from one investigation to the next—"

"It was important to rule out the Mullers as murderers," David says with a stubborn scowl. "And like I said, we need to handle this IOCG thing the right way."

"That day in your mom's garden," Debbie says. "You broke down and cried."

"Yeah, because this all feels awful!" David hisses. "I hate that everything was left unfinished between me and my parents. And now the government is marching around, probably trampling Mom's edelweiss…" He growls a little. "They wouldn't even let me on the property yesterday. I could've checked that they were taking care of the place. So, excuse me for focusing on the one good thing to happen—"

He breaks off abruptly as Ellie comes outside. "Everything okay?" she asks.

"Yeah," Debbie says, trying for lightness. "How about you?"

"Good, good," Ellie says vaguely, her eyes on her son. "Now that the quarantine's being lifted soon, do you think you'll head back to Detroit?"

"I don't want to leave until I know what killed my parents," David says bluntly. He gives his wife a look, like, *See? I do care about something besides the money.*

"What about work?" Ellie asks.

"I already talked to my boss. He said to take all the time I need."

"Mine too," Debbie adds.

"Well." Ellie breathes out a sigh. "I can't say I'm upset about that." She keeps staring at the two teens. "At least something good is coming from all this. I haven't seen Joey this happy in a long time."

CHAPTER 14

July 15th, 2016

Catherine Harris mutters under her breath as the video conferencing software stutters again. The FBI Director's face freezes with lips puckered. The Deputy Secretary of Defense squints at his screen while pushing up his wire-framed glasses, suggesting his monitor is showing the FBI Director frozen, too. The Secretary of Homeland Security is so still and solemn, his video could glitch and no one would notice.

"Is he—" Catherine starts to say, and then the Director's video feed catches back up to reality just in time for everyone to see him smack the living shit out of his monitor.

"Am I back?" he asks, the web cam shaking from the blow.

Catherine nods, suppressing an inappropriate laugh. She relaxes back in her chair and continues where she was cut off. "The DOE agents have finished their assessment of the tower. They weren't able to identify the source elements."

The FBI Director smooths his gray hair, which is always pushed back with some cheap product that makes it look crunchy. "What are you saying, Catherine?"

"Whatever this thing is made of, it doesn't exist on our periodic table, sir."

He frowns, as if his glitchy video equipment has messed up the words. "I thought you said that the tower was metallic."

"No, I said it *looked* metallic. But it's not."

"So… are you saying this tower consists of materials or elements that are not found on Earth?"

Catherine nods. "It appears so, sir."

The Director's frown deepens into a scowl. She can't tell if he's worried or if he thinks she's yanking his chain. "How did it get there? Isn't it over a hundred feet tall?"

"That's just the part we can see. We haven't yet been able to dig around the tower, but our best guess is that it goes underground another hundred feet, at least."

The Director leans over to whisper in the ear of the dark-suited man sitting half out of the frame, then says, "I don't understand. Why haven't you begun excavation?"

Catherine takes a deep breath at his tone. She knows he wouldn't be questioning her decisions nearly as much if she weren't a woman. But she says, calmly, "I ordered an evacuation of the site."

"Why would you do that?!" he blusters, another egomaniac in a suit who thinks every situation requires slamming your head against the problem until it breaks.

Catherine fights to keep her face neutral. "It's just for another two days, sir. I believe the tower is releasing… *something deadly…* every five days. I need to test my theory before we venture any closer. In the meantime, we're going over all the work the CDC and WBCD did last week. I've kept in touch with Thomas Murphy, who's now back in his CDC office in Atlanta—"

"Can't you measure the tower's depth with GPR or EML?"

"The electromagnetic signals haven't detected anything."

"What about ASTER?"

She shakes her head. "That won't help."

"Well... assuming it is two hundred feet in length... how the hell did it get there?"

"The soil surrounding the tower had been recently disturbed."

"Are you saying it was... built?"

"Not necessarily. We need to study the tower's foundation in order to determine if it recently penetrated the surface."

The Director's eyes bulge. "You mean... it was buried, and on July 2nd, it... broke through?"

"Possibly... we don't know."

The Director whispers to his friend again, but the man in black offers no advice, only nods like a good little robot. The Director clears his throat, addressing his screen again. "We should see if this tower is somehow related to Cheyenne."

"I agree," says the Deputy Secretary of Defense, finally adding his reedy voice to the conversation.

Catherine waits for Mr. Homeland Security to chime in, but he just folds his hands over his stomach and ponders his screen like it's a riveting crossword puzzle.

"Cheyenne?" she prompts, when the men don't elaborate. "There's nothing with that code-name in my briefing materials."

"It's not a code-name. It's a place," the Director says. "And what happened there is need-to-know."

"I'm the OSC for this task force," Catherine points out. "I'd say I need to know."

"You'll receive the dossier if it turns out to be relevant to what's going on in Rindville."

"Thank you, sir," Catherine says tightly, not liking the feeling of being left out of the loop.

"I'll have two of my agents investigate the connection," says the Director. "Thanks for the update, Catherine. We'll be in touch."

The three squares go black before she can do much more than nod.

* * *

San Francisco, California

Though she's a San Francisco gal, born and raised, Professor Solheim is already aching for the crisper air, less crowded streets, and cooler weather of Sweden. The classrooms of UC Berkeley are absolutely frigid, but the powerful A/C units don't remove the sweat from the nape of her red braid. Instead, they only chill the moisture and give her a dreadful shiver in her light, linen suit.

She crosses the front of the classroom and drops her bag on the desk. When she turns and scans the room, she spots two familiar faces in the back of the auditorium. An auditorium that seats one hundred and fifty students. She smiles at them and then clears her throat to begin the lecture. After a brief recap that allows her more attentive students to shake off any early morning brain fog, she launches into today's lesson.

"All objects have a property known as their resonant frequency. It involves the reinforcement of vibrations of a receiving system due to a similarity to the frequencies of the source. If the frequency of excitation coincides with the natural frequency of the system, resonance occurs. The result is large oscillations within the structure, creating potentially harmful stress."

She stops her pacing to assess the many faces in the room. Most appear blank. A fair few look like they're nursing horrible headaches. Time for the visual aid.

"What is an example of resonant frequency?" she asks.

All eyes dip to keyboards and textbooks in perfect sync.

Professor Solheim digs in her bag with all the flourish of a Vegas magician and pulls out a crystal glass. "Have you ever seen a cartoon or movie where an opera singer shatters glass using only their voice?" She next extracts a clear plastic case, puts the glass inside, and sets a portable sound system next to it.

Eyes all over the room are rising to the front once more.

"Now, I'm not an opera singer," Professor Solheim jokes, "but this should have the same result." She turns the dial, and a high ringing makes some of the students clutch their aching heads or slap hands over their ears. With a shrill crash, the crystal glass shatters as if struck with a hammer.

The professor taps the container. "*This* is an example of resonant frequency."

The room fills with excited whispers.

Professor Solheim resumes her pacing. "Did you know that sound with a frequency of less than 16 Hz is inaudible to humans? It's called infrasound, and its effect on human beings is not completely understood. We do know, however, that high-intensity infrasound causes headache, fatigue, and anxiety. Our internal organs are attached to the bones by elastic connective tissue, and at low frequencies may be considered simple oscillators. The natural frequencies of most of them are below 12 Hz, which is in the infrasonic range. As a result, the organs may resonate."

She surveys the students, hoping for a raised hand. Most are too busy typing notes. Others just look baffled.

"Can anyone tell me what would happen if you were exposed to sound waves that were at the 7 to 10 Hz frequency range… and the decibel level was greater than 150?"

At last, a hand rises in the front row, hesitant at first but then shooting toward the ceiling.

Professor Solheim points to the young lady. "Yes."

"It would kill them."

"Very good. More than likely, their internal organs would simply rupture." She flicks her fingers wide with a little pop sound, and a few jaws around the room drop in horror. "And, since the sound is below 16 Hz, it is considered infrasound, so you wouldn't even hear it."

Now that she has their attention, Professor Solheim heads to her desk to begin the slideshow that will act as the meat of today's lecture. When she next glances at the clock, she's right on time. She clicks out of the slideshow and says, "Please review chapter 13 before Friday's test."

While the students cram their laptops and books into their backpacks in a race for the door, Professor Solheim puts away her own materials, side-eyeing the two dark-haired men as they walk down the aisles toward her.

When they reach the podium, she embraces the taller man and says, "Hi, Jared." She turns to the shorter man and embraces him as well. "Hey, Evan." She steps back to take the brothers in, hands on her hips. Evan is younger by a year, but they look like twins. They could be identical, if not for a few inches and the differences in their glasses. Jared has gone for the sophisticated, expensive horn-rimmed, wayfarer style while Evan has gone for a quirkier, rounded style with basic silver frames. "It's good to see you both."

"It's good to see you too, Sarah," Evan says.

"So, what did you guys think?" she asks them.

"I understood most of what you said," says Jared with a smirk.

"I loved how you shattered that crystal," says Evan.

"Now you both know how resonant frequency works."

"Yeah, whatever." Jared laughs. "Let's get something to eat. I'm starving."

"Sarah, you know the area better than us. Where do you want to go?" asks Evan.

"Gypsy's," Sarah says without hesitation.

Being with the two brothers brings back a love for California summers she thought she'd lost. Walking with them to the parking lot conjures memories of cruising in Jared's beat-up sedan with no real plan for their day, just cold sodas, good music, and the prospect of maybe sneaking some beer when the sun went down.

The car ride to Gypsy's is a little less glamorous, but she smiles the whole way.

After they're seated in the little bistro with their drinks ordered, Jared says, "Can we talk about it now, or what?"

"Yeah, why couldn't we do this on the phone?" Evan asks.

"Because I wanted to see the two of you, for a start," Sarah says. "But also… you don't talk about these kinds of things on the phone." She looks around furtively, which makes the brothers laugh.

"Right, these kinds of things… like the FBI investigating our parents," Jared says. "Because that's a normal thing a person says."

"My dad and your mom aren't being investigated, exactly," Sarah says. "They didn't do anything wrong. They're just being questioned about their trip."

"Their... *epic adventure*," Evan says, rolling his eyes as he unrolls his silverware.

It's part of their shared family lore: in the summer of 1969, Sarah's father Mitchell Solheim and Jared and Evan's mother Mary Jacobs (now Mary Miller) took the bus cross-country from their hometown of Potosi, Missouri, all the way to San Francisco. They traveled with Mary's best friend, Sarah Wade—Sarah Solheim's namesake. Their goal was to help Sarah show her homemade computer microprocessor to someone at the Stanford Research Institute.

Sarah's dream had come true. She'd actually landed a job at Intel.

Then she'd disappeared.

"Maybe now that the FBI is involved," Sarah Solheim says to the boys, "you'll actually believe the whole thing happened."

"Oh... I believe they went on their trip," Jared says. "I even believe they met John Lennon. I just don't believe there was this mysterious white-haired man that followed them the whole way."

Sarah crosses her arms in a mild challenge. This is a years-old argument that's now just Sarah and Jared's way of poking fun at each other. "I've never known your mom to lie."

Jared scoffs. "She does like to exaggerate."

Evan nods. "Yeah, and funny how Uncle Mitch never saw the white-haired man."

Jared snickers. "You still call him Uncle Mitch. We're not six anymore. Besides, he's not actually our uncle."

Sarah pats Evan's arm. "I think it's sweet."

"Thanks," says Evan, shooting Jared a triumphant, cheesy grin.

"Well, I don't hear you calling our mom *Aunt Mary* anymore," Jared says to Sarah.

"Who cares?" She rolls her eyes. Jared and Evan's presence always revives some of her teenage self's energy. "Look, just because my dad didn't see the white-haired man, doesn't mean he didn't exist. They all saw the strange light. And then Sarah vanished, along with her parents."

"Actually," Jared says thoughtfully, "I wonder if the FBI is interviewing our parents because they have new information about the Wades' disappearance? The FBI handles missing persons cases, right?"

Before anyone can answer, the curly-haired waitress drops off their drinks and gives them more time to peruse the menu.

"When is your dad's interview scheduled?" Jared asks Sarah, peeling his eyes from the woman's retreating back.

"They are coming to our house at noon. He had to cancel his trip to Salt Lake."

Evan clucks his tongue. "I was planning to go with Uncle... sorry, with Mr. Mitchell Solheim."

Jared and Sarah laugh together.

"I'm just saying, he's your boss, so you can't call him Uncle Mitch," Jared says.

Evan looks ready to stick out his tongue. "Whatever."

"He said you're going to manage the new restaurant," says Sarah, nudging Evan with a smile.

"Yeah, that's the plan." Evan tries to wave it off as nothing, but she sees his pride in the way he holds his chin higher.

"Funny, when I was a kid, he so badly wanted me to follow in his footsteps and manage his restaurants," Sarah says. "Now, you're the one picking up that baton, and I am more like your mother. A doctor."

"It's not quite the same," says Jared. "Mom's a medical doctor. You're a PhD."

Sarah points the corner of her menu at him. "Still, we are both scientists and doctors."

The waitress returns. This time, they're ready to order.

"Are you still planning to return to Stockholm in three weeks?" Jared asks when the woman leaves again.

"Yes, I have to be back before the fall semester."

"We'll miss you," says Evan. "I'm so glad you decided to come home for the summer. I miss hanging out with you."

Sarah stretches herself to pat both their hands. "I miss you guys too. You're still my best friends, after all these years. I hope you know that."

As they catch up on each other's lives, Sarah thinks more about what she was told about that fateful trip in 1969. Everything that happened to their parents back then bonded them for life. For that, she feels nothing but gratitude.

But she's always been curious, more so than Jared and Evan. She believes in things that other people find unbelievable. The white-haired man, the beam of light... and then there's what Mary once told her about Sarah Wade's... abilities. After that conversation, Mary swore her to secrecy. She made her promise never to tell anyone—not even the two men sitting across the table from her now.

But the FBI is in town, asking questions. Sarah can't help but feel something is about to come to light.

* * *

A knock on the door forces Mitchell Solheim out of his easy

chair. He hitches up his pants, cursing the belly that hangs over his belt loops. Scratching his mostly grayed red hair through a yawn, he ambles toward the door, wondering what time it is. He didn't mean to doze off while he was waiting, but on a hot summer day like today, naps can sneak up on a person.

He opens the door to find two men in dark suits standing on the narrow porch of his old South San Francisco home. So, it's noon, then.

The larger man with a comically square jaw holds out his badge. "My name is Agent Thompson, and this is Agent Anderson."

The shorter agent, whose angular, boyish features make him look more suited for one of those goofy teenage vampire flicks than detective work, nods at Mitchell.

Mitchell welcomes them by stepping aside. "Come on in."

He leads them to the living room and falls back into his easy chair, letting the agents take the sofa.

"Thank you for agreeing to meet with us today," says Agent Thompson.

"Sure." Mitchell eyes the fidgeting, smaller agent. "Can I ask what this is about?"

"As we said when we contacted you," says Thompson, redirecting Mitchell's attention, "we are following up on a report that you and your friends filed with the Cheyenne, Wyoming police department in 1969."

"Right, but why does the FBI care about something that took place in Cheyenne over forty years ago?"

"Forty-seven years, to be exact," says Agent Anderson, holding up a finger like a cartoon teacher's pet. His eyes flick to Thompson, and Mitchell half expects the senior agent to toss his partner a dog treat and pat his head.

Mitchell chuckles. "Fuck me. When you say it out loud... forty-seven fucking years ago. It's so hard to believe. But still. Why contact me now?"

Thompson leans forward and clasps his hands between his knees. "We're investigating an incident that took place recently. We believe it may be connected to Cheyenne."

"No shit. What happened?" Mitchell rocks the easy chair forward and his feet hit the hardwood with a loud thump.

"We can't say," says Agent Thompson, perfectly stoic.

Mitchell holds back his frown. "Okay, well, fire away."

"According to the police report filed on July 19th, 1969, you and two young women, Mary Jacobs and Sarah Wade, saw a blue beam emanating from an alley off of Main Street. When you entered the alley, you found two men dressed in black leather jackets lying on the asphalt."

"I know how it sounds," says Mitchell, heart clenching at the mention of Sarah Wade, even after all this time. "Crazy, right?"

"I know it was a long time ago," says Agent Thompson, his poker face still glued on, "but is there anything else that you can remember? Anything that wouldn't be in the police report?"

Mitchell huffs, sick of not being believed. "No, we were just walking down the street looking for a place to eat before we had to be back on the bus. That's when we saw what looked like a blue laser beam. Sarah saw it first and ran toward the alley. I ran after her. She screamed when she saw the two men lying unconscious on the ground."

Agent Anderson licks his lips in a nervous tic. "Did you notice anything else by the bodies?"

"No, nothing unusual. When Mary caught up with us, I went across the street to call the police." The younger agent's twitching is making Mitchell uneasy. "By the way... it was my idea to call the police."

Agent Anderson nods, but his smile isn't at all comforting.

"Anyway," says Mitchell, choosing his words carefully, "as soon as I hung up the phone, the police arrived and took our statements."

"Did you notice anything strange... about the two men?" asks Agent Anderson, voice breathy.

Mitchell chuckles. "Besides the fact that they were wearing matching leather jackets, no. Sarah mentioned that she didn't see any injuries, so we were wondering why they were unconscious."

"You didn't see any objects in the alley?" asks Agent Thompson.

"You mean, like needles?" Mitchell forces a chuckle. *What are they fishing for?* he wonders.

"No. Something that you wouldn't normally see... something that looked out of place?"

"No... nothing."

Agent Thompson's gaze sweeps the living room, lingering on the wall-mounted pictures. "Is that your wife and daughter?"

Mitchell nods. "I lost my wife a few years back."

"Sorry for your loss."

"Thanks."

"Does your daughter live here?" asks Agent Anderson, noting the pair of women's sneakers in the shoe rack by the front door.

Mitchell stiffens. "Just for the summer," he says, narrowing his eyes at the young agent, who shrinks back a little. "She's teaching at Berkeley. She actually lives in Sweden. She's a professor at Stockholm University."

"Impressive," says Agent Anderson cheerily.

Agent Thompson clears his throat. "According to our records, your daughter's name is Sarah Wade Solheim. You named her after the woman that was with you in Cheyenne?"

Mitchell doesn't miss a beat, staring evenly back at the agent. "Yes, the whole trip was actually Sarah's idea. She'd built a microprocessor that she wanted to show to someone in San Francisco. My life in Potosi was shit, so... I decided to go with her." He chuckles, remembering meeting Mary and Sarah at the bus stop, all three of them toting heavy bags and wide-eyed in disbelief of their own actions. "I didn't have a plan. Just wanted any excuse to get out of town... out of my dad's house."

The agents share an unsmiling glance.

Mitchell clears his throat and wipes the grin off his face. "Wait a minute. Does this have something to do with Sarah's disappearance?"

"No." Agent Thompson looks down at his notes. "In 2014, your daughter worked at the SETI Institute, correct?"

"Yeah... that's my Sarah. She's a true believer."

Agent Anderson gives him a keen look. "A believer in *what?*" he asks.

"Searching for extra-terrestrial life," Mitchell says with a shrug. "But she also believes that using the electromagnetic spectrum, radio waves—are a waste of time. That intelligent life outside this solar system would use something different to communicate, like gravitational waves." Though it mostly sounds like a crock of shit to him, he says it with a fond smile playing at his mouth. Sarah is far smarter than him, just like her namesake, and if she says there's other life out there... maybe it's not just science fiction. He'd just as soon not know the answer himself, though.

"Your daughter wrote a paper on... *gravitons*. I must admit, I didn't do well in physics, so..." Agent Anderson's voice trails off when he catches Agent Thompson's glare.

Mitchell nods. "I hear you, brother. I didn't go to college and I certainly didn't study physics in high school, but my daughter has made it her goal in life to teach me about this shit. It's because of her that I know what the hell the electromagnetic spectrum is."

"She believes that gravitons can be used as a form of communication?" asks Agent Thompson, in a tone that gives Mitchell the distinct impression he already knows the answer.

"Yes, but don't ask me to explain how it works."

Agent Thompson stands up and extends his hand. "Thank you, Mr. Solheim, for taking time out of your day to meet with us."

Mitchell grunts as he rises to take the offered hand. "No problem. Sorry I couldn't be more help," he says, walking them back to the door.

"Actually, this was very helpful. By the way, when will your daughter return to Stockholm?"

"Not for another three weeks."

"Thanks."

Mitchell holds the door open and watches them head down the porch. Before he shuts the door, he asks, "Have you already interviewed Mary?"

"No," says Agent Anderson. "We are headed there next."

* * *

"She's withholding something," Agent Thompson says two hours later, as they make their brisk exit from Mary Miller's house.

"Her story was pretty much the same as Mitchell Solheim's," Agent Anderson observes. "Do you think they rehearsed it?"

"No... I think she saw something back then that he didn't."

"Should we go back and press her?"

Agent Thompson scowls at his partner. Anderson is too eager. In the interviews, he's agitated, twitchy. This is supposed to look routine, and the kid keeps acting like a bomb might go off at any moment. "No, not yet," he says stiffly. "Let's check in first."

Thompson dials the FBI Director as he gets into the driver's seat. The Director doesn't even greet him before demanding a report.

"We talked with Mitchell Solheim and Mary Jacobs Miller," Thompson says. "As you know, the third person who was present in Cheyenne, Sarah Wade, disappeared not long after they arrived in San Francisco. Her parents disappeared from their home in Potosi, Missouri, about the same time."

"Their disappearances must be related," says the Director, even more gruff than usual. Thompson suspects he hasn't been sleeping. "Did you learn anything new that isn't already in the police report?"

"No... nothing new about the Cheyenne incident. Neither Mr. Solheim nor Mrs. Miller seemed to be aware of the objects."

"I'm not surprised. They weren't found until the men arrived at the hospital. Is there anything else that could be helpful?"

"Yes," Thompson says slowly. "It's only a hunch, but..."

"Spit it out, agent," the Director barks.

"Mrs. Miller got a bit cagey when we asked about Mr. Solheim's daughter."

"What about her?"

"Mr. Solheim named his daughter after the missing girl. Sarah Wade Solheim worked for SETI in 2014, and she published a paper last year that addresses the use of gravitons as a form of communication. She's now a leader in the field of resonant frequency."

"What does all that have to do with—"

"It's a pretty big coincidence that her father had the encounter that he had, and that she's in the scientific field she's in, and that she believes in extraterrestrial life. There might be a link. Or maybe Mrs. Miller told her something she wouldn't tell us." He pauses. "No stone unturned, and all that."

"I agree," the Director says after a beat. "I'll fly out tomorrow to handle Sarah Solheim's interview myself. Please make the arrangements."

"Will do." Agent Thompson hangs up with a heavy sigh. He hasn't been after a trail this cold in a while, and he certainly hasn't missed the frustration. "What the hell?" he says, mostly to himself.

"None of this makes any sense," says Agent Anderson.

Agent Thompson snorts his agreement. "Yeah, but the boss is convinced there's a connection between Cheyenne and Rindville, so here we are." He turns the key in the ignition. "In the meantime, looks like we're off the clock for the day. Want to check out Ghirardelli's?"

CHAPTER 15

July 16th, 2016

Sarah shuts her laptop and shoves a memo into her drawer as the Director of the FBI enters her temporary office at UC Berkeley. As the door shuts behind him, she catches a glimpse of a solemn agent in a dark gray suit waiting outside. Trying not to seem nervous or suspicious, she stands and holds out her hand. "Good morning, sir."

The man shakes her hand and then sets his leather bag next to the chair she offers. "Thank you for taking the time to meet with me, and on such short notice."

What Sarah wants to say is, *I couldn't exactly say no to the head of the Federal Bureau of Investigation.*

What she actually says is, "Of course. Anything to help. I have to say, I'm intrigued."

The Director's eyebrows raise. "By what?"

Sarah smiles, even though the man's whole visage is as intimidating as his title. "Why would the Director of the FBI travel to the Bay Area to meet with a professor of physics?

Does it have to do with my work, or with my dad's trip in 1969?"

"The latter."

"But I wasn't there. I hadn't even been born. And besides, yesterday Dad spoke to two agents. Why would you make the extra effort to speak to me, instead of having one of your agents do it?"

"What did your father tell you about Cheyenne?" the Director asks.

Sarah dutifully recounts the story. A blue light, two unconscious men in black leather, blah blah blah.

"What about Mary Jacobs Miller?" the man asks next. "What did *she* tell you?"

Sarah opens her mouth and closes it again, unsure how to respond. A moment too late, she realizes that her hesitation was response enough.

"There is something Mary didn't share with us," the Director says with satisfaction. "Something that will help us make sense of all this. Agent Thompson was correct."

"Um." Sarah hesitates. If Mary thought it unwise to share certain details, who is Sarah to deny her wishes or go against her judgment?

But this is the Director of the FBI. He'll get the information he wants, one way or another.

"Ms. Solheim?" the Director prompts.

After another long moment, Sarah begins, "Did Mary tell your agents about the white-haired man?"

The Director leans forward in his seat. "No. She did not."

"She told me that the three of them were followed on that trip by a strange-looking man with long, white hair. He saved their lives."

The Director perks up like a dog on a scent. "How? From what or from whom?"

"Two men dressed in black leather tried to kidnap Sarah. Mary said they fired lasers from a square device. The white-haired man stopped them."

"What did they want with Sarah Wade?"

"Mary told me that Sarah had certain... *gifts*."

"You mean abilities?"

Sarah narrows her eyes. How much of this does he already know... or suspect?

"She could cause neurological pain telepathically," says Sarah. "Mary saw Sarah use her ability several times. Sarah brought grown men to their knees without even touching them."

The Director shakes his head. "Remarkable. And you believed all this?"

"Mary doesn't lie," Sarah says simply.

The Director looks back at the door, as if to double-check that it's closed. "What I'm about to share with you is classified." He pulls out a small device from his leather bag and sets it on her desk.

She points at it. "Can I?"

He nods.

She picks up the long, sleek device and turns it in her hands. It's rectangular, and bigger than her palm. It looks sort of like a retro cell phone—one of the enormous ones, with an antenna as long as the user's face—except it's incredibly thin, thinner than any smart phone she's ever seen. The edges are raised slightly, but overall, it is smooth and flawless. She's unsure of the material. A metal of some kind?

"What is it?" she asks.

"On July 19th, 1969, this—" The Director nods at the device. "—was found in the possession of one of the two unconscious men in Cheyenne, after your father, Mary Jacobs, and Sarah Wade continued on their journey."

Sarah holds up the light device, incredulous. "This was found in 1969?"

"Yes."

Sarah shakes her head. "I don't understand. Technology like this didn't exist back then."

The Director nods. "You're right. It didn't."

"Is this part of some secret government project?"

He scoffs. "No." He gives her a meaningful look. "This technology didn't exist... *on Earth* in 1969."

Sarah quickly sets the device back on the desk. She feels like she had the wind knocked out of her. The Director of the FBI just acknowledged the existence of advanced extraterrestrial life. Out loud.

"So," she says carefully, trying not to betray her excitement, "why show this to me?"

"An object was recently discovered in northern Wisconsin. A tower of unknown origin. Our investigators on site have concluded that it was made from elements that do not exist on our periodic table."

Sarah's next breath shakes, but she keeps her hands folded tight in her lap, out of the Director's view. "I take it this device—" She motions with her chin. "—is also made from elements that do not exist on Earth?"

The Director nods, his eyes wary. "Yes."

"Do you think this thing and the object in Wisconsin were created by the same people? Are they responsible for Sarah's disappearance?"

At that, the Director sighs. "I have no idea."

"You said the one in Wisconsin is a tower?"

"Yes. It rises about one hundred feet aboveground, and

our joint task force believes there may be another hundred feet still buried."

Sarah gawks. "How did it get there?"

"We don't know." The Director fidgets, then says, "We believe the tower is responsible for the deaths of almost two dozen individuals."

"Oh, my God! How?"

"Each of the victims had an aneurism, hardened arteries, an enlarged heart, and ruptured capillaries. We believe the object is sending out some sort of deadly signal."

Sarah taps her chin, her brain racing with half-formed theories. "Incredible." She pauses to make sense of her jumbled trails of thought. "What kind of signal?"

"We haven't been able to identify electromagnetic signals. The device is warm to the touch, and there's a slight vibration, so we know it has an energy source, but we haven't been able to locate it."

"Have you tested for infrasound?" Sarah asks.

The Director smiles like she just confirmed something for him. "It is not emitting sound waves. We were hoping you could help us identify the signal."

"Ah, so you do want more from me than just family secrets."

He tilts his head. "It seems that way."

"What else do you know about the tower?"

"The surrounding area has a large IOCG deposit."

"Iron Oxide Copper Gold?" Sarah asks. The Director nods. "Is that unusual for northern Wisconsin?"

"Yes."

"Any idea how long the tower has been there?"

"The first deaths occurred on July 2nd, and the object is not exactly inconspicuous. The soil around the tower had been recently disrupted when we were alerted to its presence. Either someone dug around the base, or..."

Sarah drums her desk with her fingertips. "Or it recently breached the surface."

"Right." The Director scratches his head, and for the first time, Sarah sees the exhaustion in his square face. "Look, your knowledge in this area is... *unrivaled.* I'm hoping you will agree to come with me to Rindville, to join the research team. We need to know what that tower is and if it has a purpose. And of course, we need to stop any further loss of life."

Sarah nods, already thinking about emailing a substitute to handle her classes in her absence. "When do we leave?"

The Director smiles. "I was hoping I wouldn't have to convince you." He places a business card on the desk, collects the unknown object, and stands. "We'll fly out tomorrow morning. Go home and pack."

* * *

July 17th, 2016

Mary bends one window blind to peek out at the black, unmarked FBI SUV at the end of her driveway. She is a soft, curvy, huggable woman, and the worry on her rounded, amiable face makes Sarah fidget with guilt.

"I'm sorry for the surprise visit," Sarah says, "but I didn't want to leave town without talking to you."

Mary waves off the concern. "It's my day off. I don't have plans. I just wish you could stay for lunch."

"Me too, but I'm on a tight schedule. There's a plane to catch."

Mary lets the blinds drop. "The Director of the FBI is actually out there in that car?"

"Yes."

"And he wants you to travel with him to Wisconsin, to join an investigation."

"Yes. Did the agents you spoke to the other day mention that something was going on in Wisconsin?"

Mary shakes her head. "They didn't do anything but ask me questions about 1969. I thought that maybe..." Her voice hitches with emotion. "I assumed they'd found... remains. Either Sarah or her parents. Why else would they be asking about Cheyenne? It was so long ago."

Sarah's cringe squints her eyes. "I'm not supposed to tell you, but there is something that I think you should know... that you have a right to know."

Mary hurries over on her tiny, slippered feet and puts a comforting hand on Sarah's arm. "What is it, sweetie?"

Sarah swallows hard and her gaze drifts to the window. If the FBI is listening in, she could land in hot water before her trip even starts. But Mary has a right to know the truth about Cheyenne.

"You were right all along," she says.

"Right about what?" asks Mary.

"You always said that you thought that the man that was following you in 1969—him, and the people that were after Sarah—were not from Earth."

Mary pales, but Sarah presses on, needing to spill it now. "You were right."

"Sarah, I never doubted it, but... what makes you so certain now?"

"The FBI Director showed me something. A device was discovered on one of the two men you guys found in that alley in Cheyenne forty-seven years ago. They analyzed it, and it turns out it was made from elements not found on Earth."

Despite her assurances that she had no doubts, Mary falls back onto the couch so suddenly that Sarah jerks forward, thinking for a second that she fainted. Mary closes her eyes, and Sarah can see the older woman's pulse pounding in her neck as she steadies her breathing.

"Wow... it really is true," says Mary. When she opens her eyes again, they are full of wonder rather than fear. "Those people that were after Sarah were not from Earth. I knew it, but at the same time..." She shakes her head.

Sarah sits beside Mary. "You mentioned that your friend Sarah had special gifts. Maybe she's related to those people."

"Considering her parents went missing at the same time, you're probably right."

"Then Sarah could still be alive."

Mary smiles, her large eyes sparkling. "I would give anything to see my friend one more time." Mary pats Sarah's hand. "It's so appropriate that you're named after her. You two are so much alike. Both of you are so... *fearless.*"

"Really?"

Mary nods. "I know I've told you this story before, but Sarah and I met in kindergarten. We were playing on the jungle gym when the meanest boy in school told us to stop. He said it was his jungle gym. Well, being the scared little girl I was, I ran up to the classroom, but Sarah didn't budge. She stood her ground."

"She was brave, even then." Sarah smiles, knowing exactly how this tale unfolds.

"When I came back with the teacher, I saw Sarah bring that boy to his knees. He was curled up in a ball, screaming in pain."

"She used her ability that day."

"She sure did. She used it on that bully, who happened to be your father."

Sarah laughs, trying to imagine her dad as a mean child. "It's amazing that they became friends."

Mary smiles wistfully toward the picture frames on her mantle. "Sarah was the one that reached out to your father when he was in pain. It was after Mitchell's father beat him. She knew he was suffering, and she helped him. It didn't matter that he bullied us throughout our school years. She knew there was good in him. She saw it long before I did."

"I wish I could have met her," Sarah says.

"She saved your father's life. If it wasn't for her, he would never have left Potosi. He would have stayed there and worked in the mines with his alcoholic father." Mary smiles at Sarah, but it is not as bright as usual. "She saved my life too. I would never have realized that there was a whole world outside of Potosi—much less traveled to see any of it. And... I wouldn't have had the courage to become a medical doctor if it hadn't been for Sarah." She wipes a tear that leaves a track down her plump cheek. "I miss my friend. I think about her all the time."

"So does Dad," says Sarah quietly. "He feels the same way. He said he would never have achieved his dream of owning a restaurant if it wasn't for Sarah. The way he talks about her... I think she was the love of his life."

"I always thought so," says Mary, voice distant, and then she jerks with realization, looking to Sarah with an apology hidden in the creases around her eyes. "But he loved your mother. So much."

Sarah hugs her. She knows her father loved her mother with all he had. Losing Sarah Wade had marked him indelibly, but he'd never withheld his love from the family he'd built without her. "I am so glad you stayed friends with my dad," Sarah tells Mary. "I'm so glad you're in my life. I'm so grateful for everything you've done for me."

"When I was younger, I hated your father... *so much...* and yet here we are... best friends. If you had told me in high school that your father and I would end up living in San Francisco and becoming best friends, I would have thought you were crazy. We owe it all to Sarah Wade."

There's a knock at the door. Sarah knows, without having to answer, that it's her FBI escort, letting her know her time is up.

She stands. "I might have to go straight back to Stockholm from Wisconsin," she says, "so if I don't see you again this summer..."

"Promise to stop by the moment you're back in town," Mary says firmly.

"I will."

The women hug.

While Mary has Sarah pressed to her chest, she whispers into her ear, "If you see any aliens in Wisconsin, I want to be the first to know."

Sarah laughs out loud. "Love you, Aunt Mary." She's still chuckling to herself as she follows the FBI agent back to the SUV.

* * *

Rindville, Wisconsin

Seven hours later, Sarah is in another black SUV, driving through downtown Rindville. She finds herself charmed by the small-town leisure and the adorable architectural style. The rolling fields that amble by once they leave downtown lull her with their calming greens. But the moment they turn onto the Schwarz driveway, Sarah sits rigid, taking in the apocalyptic scene of white vans, dark sedans, and military Humvees parked alongside CDC white tents buzzing with hazmat-suited worker bees.

The Director drives them through the grass of the outer, eastern field to the smallest tent. Sarah exits the vehicle into the balmy air. The setting sun makes the white tent a little more ethereal and less imposing, but as a group of workers peer at her from behind plastic shields in their helmets, Sarah wonders anxiously if she's safe here in plain clothes.

When they enter through the tent's rolled-back flap, Sarah is relieved to see that the woman who stands from her fold-out desk to greet them is in khakis and a button down, her brown ponytail bouncing free of a helmet.

"Sir," she says to the Director.

"Catherine." The Director nods to Sarah. "This is Sarah Solheim. She'll be working with the DOE."

"Catherine Harris," Catherine says, shaking Sarah's hand. "Nice to meet you."

"Nice to meet you too."

"As I explained on the plane, Catherine is the federal OSC," says the Director.

"On-scene commander," Catherine inserts, "in case he didn't explain that part. I'm coordinating all of the various agencies, as well as liaising with local law enforcement."

"Big job," Sarah observes.

"Yes, but my background is in science, not military or law enforcement, so we'll have a lot to talk about. Speaking of which..." She leads Sarah and the Director over to the next tent. "We've just been gathering the cages."

"Ah," the Director says. "Your experiment. Were the results conclusive?"

"Yes."

The second tent is filled with scientists with clipboards. They peer through the bars of small metal cages, scribbling rapidly as they mutter to one another. Sarah takes a peek in the nearest stack of cages and startles when she sees little, fuzzy gray mice lying dead on their sides.

"All of the mice placed within three thousand feet of the tower in any direction died," says Catherine, leading them down the rows. "Same cause of death as the other victims." She pauses at the last stack of three cages. "The mice outside of that radius survived." She points inside where lively mice snuggle down in their provided bedding or tug at the water bottles attached to their cages.

"Amazing," says the Director. "You were right." He looks at his watch. "What time was the attack?"

"5:12 p.m.," says Catherine.

Sarah looks at her own watch. It's just past 6:00 p.m. "You're sure it's safe to be on the property now?"

"The strikes only occur every five days," says Catherine. "And it's always around the same time of afternoon. Also, we placed these tents out of the radius, as a safety precaution."

"So, the next attack will take place on July 22nd," says the Director. "Until then, we can proceed full-steam ahead with assessing the tower."

"I believe so, sir," Catherine says.

The remainder of Sarah's anxiety leaks out with a soft sigh. Now she can focus on the work at hand. She supposes the hazmat suits just make the CDC workers feel better. They are a familiar security blanket while studying an object that brings all they knew of the universe into question.

"Wonderful," the Director says. "I'm heading back to D.C. tonight, so I will leave this site in your capable hands."

"Thank you, sir," Catherine says, her smile tired but proud.

The Director puts a hand on Sarah's shoulder. "Professor Solheim here will help determine the purpose of that tower." He heads back to his SUV, followed by his protective detail.

CHAPTER 16

July 19th, 2016

Ellie has her brave face on, and the sunny smile is hurting her cheeks. As she knocks on Joey's bedroom door, it nearly falters. She's more certain every day he sees through her fake smiles in an instant, and she's just putting on this show for herself.

"Yeah," his voice comes through the door.

She opens it, the smile resilient, and says, "We need to leave here in fifteen."

Joey sighs. "Okay."

Ellie knows why he's sluggish. Follow-up appointments are even worse than the ones with the actual tests. They always involve bad news.

But then Joey perks up, eyes sparking. "Can Maddie come with us?"

Ellie slumps. "I don't know, sweetie. I doubt she would be comfortable going to the hospital... waiting while we get your test results. And anyway, her parents might need her help getting ready for the memorial tomorrow..."

"I really want her to go with us," he says, the plea overtaking his features and bringing on memories of him as a bouncy toddler with a head full of soft waves.

Ellie contemplates him. She is thrilled that someone his age wants to hang out with him, but she's certain no thirteen-year-old wants to spend a nice summer day in a hospital waiting room. She worries how Joey will take it if Maddie shows discomfort at the idea, or worse... indifference. She doesn't exactly have a perfect track record. Ellie hasn't forgotten the "freak" comment.

But her son seems so sure... so hopeful.

"Okay. Go ahead and ask her. And then ask her parents."

Joey jumps out of bed with a speed that startles a laugh out of his mother as he flies by.

In the family room, Joey skids to a stop and then dives onto the couch next to Maddie, bouncing her on her cushion. He lays on his stomach facing her and props his chin in his hands, flashing her his cheesiest grin. "Hi."

She turns her head slowly and shakes it at him. "You're such a dork."

"I have a question for you."

"What is it?" she says, pushing his shoulder.

He sits up, the gravity of what he's about to say hitting him. He takes a deep breath that holds all his insecurities, trapping them inside until he gets her answer. "We're leaving soon to get my test results."

"Yeah, I know."

He looks down at his hands. "Any chance you would be willing to..."

"Sure, I'll go with you," she says with a smile in her eyes. "If you want."

"Definitely! Let's check with your parents." Joey hops up off the couch, and Maddie follows.

Debbie and David are at the dining table, folding programs for tomorrow's service. After listening to the teens talk over each other, Debbie says, "Yes, you may go with Joey to his appointment."

David is grumbling under his breath as he makes the careful creases in each sheet, but he looks up and nods as well. "You can help your mom pack everything in the car later," he says, and Maddie agrees without argument.

As relieved as Ellie is for the ray of sunshine for Joey, the drive to Jackson is as soul-crushing as always. What was once an anomaly has become routine, and the thought makes her sick to her stomach. Each visit is a reminder. Her baby is dying. Each appointment marks one step closer to his final hour. How many more days until the world turns without him on it?

The trek down the hallway to Dr. Holland's office feels like a funeral march, and she only grows more nauseated, more defeated. She feels herself slump, feels the weight bend her to her breaking point. But she won't break in front of Joey. So, she checks in with the nurse and leads the kids to a row of chairs in the waiting room. She sits across from them, letting them talk in low whispers.

There was a time when this waiting room still held slivers of hope. The hospital meant Joey could get better. The tests were tools to help them understand the cancer and target Joey's treatment. But time after time, any hope she allowed to creep into her chest was abolished the moment the doctor stepped in with that somber look, gripping his charts as if reluctant to let the information inside them leap free to rip her and Joey apart. The sorrow has become so deeply embedded, she doesn't fully notice it until it grows claws and slices her heart. These visits always wake the beast.

She can see Joey's dread not only on his face, but also in the way he leans forward to rest his elbows on his knees and in the way he stops looking directly at Maddie. He expects more bad news, just as she does, and that hurts worst of all. A teenage boy is supposed to feel invincible, naively convinced of his own immortality to such a degree that recklessness becomes mundane fun. Her boy... his mortality looms constantly in the corners of his vision, taunting him.

Each time they visit the oncologists, Ellie's vision of the future gets murkier. Two years ago, she could so clearly see Joey walking across the stage to get his high school diploma. She could see the Jeep packed with all of his clothes and supplies, ready for a move to the college dorms. She imagined herself no different than all of the other freshman parents, crying as she and Kevin put the campus in their rear-view. She imagined a beautiful veiled bride standing beside him, and later, a child in his arms. She could even see the tears of joy rolling down her son's face as he gently bounced that new life, wrapped in a soft hospital blanket.

Now, the future is agony. Now, the future is getting through the evening, making it to the next morning. *One day at a time*, she thinks.

Ellie is pulled from her thoughts by Maddie. She sees the girl reach for Joey, her fingers inches from his shoulder when she pulls back. Joey doesn't see. He has his head bent, his hands interlocked at his nape.

Maddie's sigh is harsh and painful, but when she speaks to Joey, her tone is light and cheery. "It'll be okay."

Ellie strains to listen as Joey looks over at Maddie and smiles. "Thanks. And thanks for coming."

Maddie nods. "Sure."

Joey rubs his face and says, "Every time, it's the same. We wait here and then the nurse calls us into the doctor's office just so he can give us the bad news. Then my mom starts to cry."

Throat tightening, Ellie digs around in her purse to pretend she's not listening. Joey sees her pain, of course he does, he's a smart and compassionate boy, but he shouldn't be concerned for her. This time, she'll fight the tears harder. This time, she won't let him see.

"Maybe it will be different this time," says Maddie, and there is real hope in her voice.

Ellie could kiss Maddie. How is it possible that this is the same girl that called Joey a freak? She has such a kind soul.

Ellie can no longer summon that optimistic tone, no matter how hard she tries. But Maddie still has it, and Joey so badly needs it.

"Yeah, maybe my mom won't cry this time."

Ellie clenches her teeth to keep the tears from springing out early.

"Joey Schumer," calls a nurse from the opened doorway.

Joey gives Maddie an "I told you so" look.

Ellie steadies herself with a long breath before rising to follow the kids into the doctor's office.

The nurse asks them to have a seat. "The doctor will be in shortly." Realizing Ellie is hovering without a chair after gesturing for Maddie to take the spare, she adds, "Let me get another."

Maddie sits straight and sure, smiling Joey's way, but he's stiff and vacant. Maddie looks around the small doctor's office that Ellie already has memorized.

The mahogany desk is the statement piece, and to save room, the cabinets are mounted on the wall. The doctor's family, a wife and two boys, smile from picture frames, all of them healthy and vibrant. One of the boys holds up a rolled diploma in one photo, grinning in a cap and gown and towering over his balding, graying father.

The nurse comes back with a chair and Ellie thanks her as she takes a seat. She is powerless to stop the nervous tapping of her foot.

Dr. Holland at last arrives, even more wrinkled and gray than in the graduation photo. Ellie imagines that constantly being the bearer of devastating news takes a toll on a person.

But the doctor is wearing a new expression today as he takes a seat and drops a manila folder on the desk. Instead of a somber line, his mouth is parted, his eyes wide and blinking too much. He looks... stunned. When he sits, he gives his head a little shake and then beams at Joey.

Ellie sits straighter. The tiniest shred of hope slithers in, as much as she's afraid to greet it. She tells it to go away, but it only digs in.

"Joey, Ellie, good to see you both." He looks over at Maddie. "Who do we have here?"

"Maddie's a friend of the family," says Ellie quickly, silently begging for him to cut the niceties and get to the point.

"Nice to meet you, Maddie. I'm Dr. Holland."

She nods with a tight, awkward smile.

"Where is Kevin?"

"He had to work," says Ellie, not wanting to get into the craziness at home right now. She has no doubt Dr. Holland has seen what's going on in Rindville in the papers and on the news, but in this room, her son is more important than any CDC quarantine or FBI investigation.

"Well, he'll be sorry he missed this one." The doctor opens the folder and folds his hands atop the test results. He looks between Ellie and Joey, and that corny smile overtakes him again, catching Ellie's breath. "The results were truly astonishing. In fact, I had the lab run the tests more than once."

Ellie leans forward, begging the doctor, God, the universe, whoever will listen that the next words are truly good news.

"Joey, the last time you were here, your white blood cell count was over 250,000. It is now..." Dr. Holland can hardly talk around his grin. "9,000. It is actually within the normal range."

Ellie's gasp rips through the room's stuffy air and her hands fly to her mouth to stifle it. Her face is instantly wet, but she does not fight against these tears. Shaking with hope, she whispers, "What about his platelet count?"

"Also, within the normal range: 350,000." The physician lets out a sharp laugh. "To be honest with you... these results don't make a lot of sense."

"That's amazing news." Ellie pulls out a tissue from her purse and wipes away the tears.

Maddie nudges Joey's shoulder, her smile soft and warm. "I told you it would be okay."

Joey takes her hand and says, "You're my good luck charm."

Maddie looks down at their interlocked fingers on her thigh, and her smile grows. Ellie watches the sweet moment, so ordinary and yet so special, so poignant, it pulls a sob from her chest. An exhale of all the pain, banishing it from her body. She nearly throws her arms around both of them. But she stops herself before she embarrasses them.

The doctor clears his throat. "This is great news, but before we can conclude that you are in remission, we need to see the blast count. We should have those results Thursday."

Joey nods, only half looking at the doctor.

Ellie can't restrain the wet, raucous sobs that sound more like wild laughter. She grabs Joey and pulls him into her chest, unable to resist holding him any longer.

He hugs her back, and she kisses the top of his shiny head before letting him go. She stands up to shake the doctor's hand and thank him.

Behind her, she hears Joey whisper, "Mom still cried at the results. Some things never change."

Maddie snorts with laughter, and Ellie puts a hand over her mouth to keep from joining in, letting them have their not-so-secret moment.

The doctor, however, peers around Ellie curiously, and Maddie turns crimson.

The doctor looks back at Ellie and says, "This is great news, Ellie. Clearly the treatments are working. We should get the blast count Thursday. I'll have my nurse schedule an appointment."

Even though he'd been feeling better this past week, once the soreness from hiking the cliff faded. Even though his energy was returning, along with his appetite. Even though he didn't look quite so pale. He'd actually been feeling stronger ever since that day with Maddie. Ever since they found the tower. Ever since he touched it.

"I need to call your father and tell him the good news," Ellie says when they get in the car. "We should celebrate! Ice cream?"

"Sure," Joey says. Is it Ellie's imagination, or does he and Maddie share another secretive look at that suggestion?

Ellie pulls out of the parking lot, already dialing Kevin. When he picks up, voice tense with anticipation, she can't contain her squeal of joy. "You aren't going to believe it!" she shouts. "His numbers are going down! He's getting better!"

Kevin's yelp of excitement is loud enough to hear in the back seat.

Ellie glances at her son in the rear-view mirror. "I don't think I have ever been this happy."

* * *

July 20th, 2016

The church is full. As David lets his eyes scan the pews, he sees people from all walks of life. There are his father's fellow dairy farmers, including Gordon Muller and his son, Ben, in the corner. There are the women his mother taught elementary school with, back in the day. There's the mechanic who fixed all of their farm vehicles for decades and the veterinarian who delivered their new calves. There's his mom's book club, a mix of farmers' wives and professional women. There are the off-duty deputies, paying their respects to the couple who died before their own people lost their lives. There are the church folk, even though his parents were sporadic attendees, at best.

And of course, there are the Schumers, including Jack, sitting in the second row, dressed in their Sunday finest.

"Looks like the whole town came out," Debbie says into his ear.

David nods, feeling choked up in spite of himself.

"Do you still want to speak?" she asks.

"I do."

He hardly slept a wink last night, thinking about this moment. He can barely believe everything that's happened in the past eighteen days. He can barely believe the roller coaster of emotions he's been on. For a man like David, who prefers not to feel too much, it's been exhausting.

But he owes this to his mom.

And, to be honest, to his dad as well.

He gets to his feet and the quiet chatter in the room dies down. He walks up to the podium, where the pastor is waiting for him. He takes his place as the grieving son of the deceased.

"Thank you all for coming," he says. "And for your patience in getting the details ironed out for this memorial service. I know I don't have to tell anyone in this town this, but the last few weeks have been... remarkable."

There's a murmur of agreement from the pews.

"I loved my mom," David begins, glancing at his notes, "and the relationship I had with my dad was... *complicated.* When my sister passed, it definitely changed who I was... and the relationship I had with my dad. But... I loved both my parents and I miss them deeply... every day. I am so thankful that each of you are here today... because my parents... they truly loved this town and each of you." David exhales sharply as he looks at his loving wife and daughters for support. "When we drove into this town eighteen days ago... I was angry. Angry at my father and angry at having to return to this town... the town that I grew up in. But, these last eighteen days have reminded me just how amazing this place is and how much I truly loved my parents. Thank you for being here today and paying your respects to my parents. I can' tell you how much that means to me."

When he is finished, he can't help but notice everyone smiling and nodding at him as if they appreciate his honesty and the outpouring of emotions. He makes his way back down to his family in the front row. When he sits, Debbie pulls him close and squeezes him tight. On his other side, Maddie is wide-eyed and solemn. Past her, Gracie is drawing in a little notebook Debbie got her to keep her busy during the service.

As the pastor takes the podium, David feels a poke in his side.

"Here, Daddy," Grace says, handing him a picture of a rainbow. "I drew this for you."

His eyes well up all over again. "Thank you, sweetheart," he whispers back. "It's beautiful."

The rest of the service follows his parents' written wishes. A eulogy by the pastor, a few hymns, and a slideshow. The only flaw is that the urns on the dais are empty; the government still has possession of his parents' bodies.

Thinking about the government holding onto his parents' bodies makes David think about the feds taking control of the land, too. *Over my dead body,* he thinks, realizing a second too late how inappropriate the sentiment is right now. Still, he has to get a geologist out there, ASAP—

"Are you okay?" Debbie whispers. "You look angry."

"I'm fine," David says, trying to shrug away the tension that just locked up his shoulders and upper back.

They're dismissed shortly afterward, so everyone can head over to the post-service reception at the funeral home. As David stands, he somehow, through the crowd, makes eye contact with Gordon Muller. The old man gives him a gruff nod—which David takes to mean he doesn't know that David was ready to accuse him and his sons of murder two weeks ago.

And in that moment, David gets an idea.

"Excuse me for a second," he says to Debbie.

"Where are you running off to?" Kevin asks, exiting his pew.

"I need to speak with Gordon Muller."

Kevin grabs David's arm. "Oh no, you don't."

"It's not what you think. It's about the IOCG deposit."

"David." Kevin's frown doesn't relax. "Do you really think now is the best time?"

"Fine," David says after a beat. "I'll just ask him if I can drop by his farm tomorrow. Satisfied?"

Kevin nods, exhaling. "Sure. But I'm coming with you."

They make their way through the crowd, both accepting condolences, David for his parents and Kevin on behalf of the lost deputies. But Gordon and Ben are lingering too, talking to a woman David recognizes as the owner of one of the restaurants downtown.

"Hey, Gordon," Kevin says when they're close. "Moment of your time?"

"Sure," the farmer says. He looks at David. "Sorry for your loss."

Ben echoes his father's sentiment, but he stares at David warily, as if waiting for the other shoe to drop.

"I was wondering if I could come by your place tomorrow to speak with you about a matter that concerns both of our properties," David says.

Gordon's eyebrows go up, but he feigns innocence. "What matter might that be?"

"We can discuss it tomorrow," David says. "Is there a time that would be good for you?"

"Mid-morning," Gordon says. "10:30?"

"Great."

"You'll have to use the side access road. Those feds on your dad's land have my main entrance cordoned off now. Something about an expanded perimeter." The old man scowls. "You know anything about that?"

"They don't tell me much," David says, glancing at Kevin.

The chief deputy shrugs. "They don't tell me much either, at this point."

"Well." Gordon harrumphs. "Guess we'll talk tomorrow then."

"Tomorrow," David says, and then returns to his family.

* * *

July 21st, 2016

Joey bounces his leg, willing Dr. Holland's office door to open. At least Maddie is beside him again. He looks to her while he waits for the charts to come back. Catching his glance, she grabs his hand.

"Remember, I'm your good luck charm," she says, and his pounding heart chases away some of his anxieties.

"Yes you are," he says quietly, not caring that both his parents are behind them, watching.

Dr. Holland walks in with chart in hand, his look of surprise milder this time. Joey squeezes Maddie's hand as the doctor sits down and offers a wide smile.

Please be under five. Please be under five, he chants in his head. Only if his blast count dips below five can he be considered in remission. He feels the change. The pain is ebbing. He feels like he could run again. Really run, and leave the cancer in his dust.

"Hello Joey, Ellie, Kevin… and *Maddie,* right?"

She nods.

"Well… I have some great news."

Ellie lets out a little gasp, and Joey turns to see her eyes are already watering, her hand groping for Kevin's.

"Your blast count is twelve percent."

Ellie shrieks, making Maddie jump, but Joey hardly hears it. His ears are filled with a whooshing sound.

"Oh my God, that is amazing news!" his mother cries, sounding to Joey like she's outside the room.

She launches herself into Kevin's arms, grinning so hard it's probably painful, but the corners of her mouth sag when she looks at Joey.

"What's wrong, sweetie? It's great news."

Joey closes his eyes, willing himself not to cry in front of Maddie. "I thought for sure it would be less than five percent. I wanted to be in remission."

Ellie rushes to his side, running a hand over his head with a shushing sound. "Joey, this is great news. This means that the treatments are working. We are headed in the right direction. If we keep up with the chemo, you'll be in remission."

Joey flinches. That's exactly what he was afraid to hear.

"Your mother's right, Joey," says Dr. Holland. "The treatments are clearly working."

"No," he says, trying to sound firm, but it comes out more like anger. "No more chemo."

"What do you mean, no more Chemo?" says Kevin, using his I'm-the-boss voice that Joey hates. "Of course, you have to continue."

Ellie takes his hand in both of hers and draws it toward her face. "Sweetie, it's working."

Joey jumps up and pulls his hand away. "No, it's not the Chemo!"

His parents and the doctor drop their jaws, looking at him like he's gone crazy, but Maddie stares evenly at him, just listening. It's her he looks at while his mother protests.

"Of course it is. What other explanation could there be."

Joey shakes his head, still locked on to Maddie like she's some sort of power source, pumping energy into his veins. "It's something else... it's not the chemo."

He won't do it anymore. Won't lie there helpless while poison is pumped into his veins to kill the monster buried in his blood cells. He won't leave this hospital weak and in agony, stomach roiling.

Kevin folds his arms across his chest. "What is it, then?"

"That object. I know it's the object," says Joey, too loud, his voice bouncing off the walls.

"What are you talking about?" says Kevin.

"When Maddie and I were by the object on her grand-parent's farm, I felt... *different*. I could feel something... I can't explain it. I know it's the reason I'm better."

"Joey's right," says Maddie, her voice a balm for his over-heating brain. "I remember him saying that it made him feel like his whole body was tingling."

"Joey, that's not possible," says Dr. Holland, looking at Joey like he's a preschooler who just proclaimed the sky is green. "It has to be the Chemo."

"You're wrong." He stomps toward the door, brushing past his father. "I'm not going to do chemo anymore."

"Joey?" Ellie grabs for him, but he jerks his arm out of her reach.

He's not a baby. He's not an idiot. Just because they aren't bothering to listen doesn't mean he's wrong. He's sick of being coddled, being told it'll all work out, the adults will fix it.

"No," he bellows, a hand on the knob, "you can't make me!"

"We'll talk about this at home," says Ellie in the aggres-sive whisper she uses when Bethany whines for ice cream at the grocery store. She then turns a taut smile on Dr. Holland. "Thanks, doctor."

Joey barrels out of the office and walks as fast as he can back to the lobby. His parents call after him in hissed whis-pers at first, and then head-turning shouts, but he doesn't slow until he's outside the hospital. Maddie catches up first and stands at his side, turning to face the charging adults whose bewildered faces gawk at Joey from behind the hospital's glass entrance doors.

"They're pissed," Maddie whispers.

He lets out a scoff-like laugh.

"For the record ... I think you're right," she says.

Joey smiles at Maddie as his parents race over the sidewalk toward him.

"What has gotten into you?" says Ellie, matching Joey's quick stride as they all head for the car. "You should be ecstatic. I know I am. This was amazing news... You should be thrilled that the treatments are working."

"Mom, they're not. They have never worked. I know you don't believe me, but it is not the Chemo... it's the object!"

"Joey! Don't yell at your mother," says Kevin.

Joey takes one look at his mother's hurt expression and hangs his head. "Sorry, mom."

* * *

Joey chases Maddie in circles in front of the dock, grabbing at her kicking feet and laughing each time she lets out a surprised squeak.

"You're getting faster," he says, "but I'm still taking it easy on you."

She stops and turns to splash him with a miniature wave created by the heel of her hand. It goes right into his open mouth and makes him sputter. Now it's her turn to laugh.

When both of them catch their breath, Joey says, "Sorry you had to be there today."

Maddie shrugs. "I'm not."

"I know that must have sucked... being there while I argued with my parents."

She makes a "meh" face. "I agree with you. It's the object."

Hearing her say it a second time makes it feel more real, and he smiles knowing someone has his back. It makes him feel a lot less crazy. "I know it is." His voice sounds far more confident in his ears this time. "The Chemo never worked."

"What are you going to do if they try to force you."

"I won't go," Joey says, hands forming fists. He feels strong, and there's no way he's letting the chemo tear him down again. "I need to go back to the tower. My blast count was so close. Maybe if I touch it again, I'll get down below five percent."

"We can't go back. They are too many people guarding it. Like, real soldiers—"

"I'll just go through the cave. No one will see me."

Maddie raises one brow. "You mean, us?"

"No, I don't want you getting in trouble again."

"So, we have to pull a few weeds. I don't care."

"I have to go alone," Joey says stubbornly. "What if it's dangerous to everyone but me?"

"You need me," Maddie says just as stubbornly, head bobbing as she treads water, her ponytail looping around her neck like a snake.

You have no idea why I need you, Joey thinks. But all he says is, "I don't know." Feeling sweaty and uncomfortable despite floating in a cool patch of the lake, he changes the subject. "Do you want to try to dive again? You're close."

"One more time." She gets out quickly and then cautiously approaches the edge.

"Try to really push off the dock as far as you can."

Maddie salutes him with a smirk. She braces herself, knees bent, arms overhead. When she launches herself up, she does a dolphin-like kick and springs into a nearly perfect dive. Her shins smack a little harder than they should, but she comes back up with a triumphant smile on her face.

"I did it!"

Joey smiles along with her, holding the stair railing to conserve energy. "I told you."

With one hard kick, she glides into Joey's arms. He keeps them both afloat by bracing a foot on the bottom step and holds her tight, his hands fanned out over her back. His heart gallops, and he's sick of fighting it, sick of being afraid. He bends his head to bring his mouth to hers, but her eyes widen, and she turns her head aside. He releases her instantly, his ears hot, and she paddles backward so they are no longer touching.

Joey can't look at her face, so he focuses on her shoulder. "Sorry." His throat is tight, and he barely gets the word out.

"Don't be," she says softly. "I'm sorry... I just..."

He holds up a hand, not wanting to hear that she's got some secret boyfriend, probably older. Or worse, that she just doesn't like him like that, that he's like a younger brother to her. "It's fine. It was stupid of me. You don't have to explain." He turns and races up the steps. He hears her get out after him, but he keeps his eyes on the house as they make the horribly silent trek back.

CHAPTER 17

July 21st, 2016

Sarah shoves the mysterious rectangular object from Cheyenne away in frustration, leaving the light device spinning wildly in the center of the table. She's been studying it for days, turning it over, looking for creases, looking for a place where it can be opened. Nothing. It's just a hunk of metal. She's certain it has a purpose, but for the life of her, she can't even wager a guess.

She huffs at it, crossing her arms. At least, with the tower, she's been able to be useful. But nothing about this smaller device makes any sense. How does it work? What is its energy source? It has no transistors, no circuits, no actual wires. It's certainly not solar-powered. There are no anodes or cathodes. Experts before her have already determined that the object has no lithium, cadmium, zinc, graphite... nothing that would indicate a battery. No copper, indium, or amorphous silicon.

Sarah has only one idea left... and it goes against every protocol in the book.

She snatches up the infernal thing and tucks it into her pocket. She hurries out of the tent, scanning the field for Catherine. She can't see the other woman's short brown ponytail anywhere. She must be at the tower. She's hardly left the excavation site in the past two days, as the projected date and time of the next attack draw nearer.

Well, good. Sarah's idea involves the tower, and she suspects it will go over better if the on-scene commander is present. Plus, it's true what they say: sometimes it's easier to ask for forgiveness than permission.

Sarah walks to the makeshift checkpoint at the outskirts of the ominous tower's killing radius. Two soldiers stand in front of the Humvees that act as the gate of the blockade, and one raises a hand as Sarah approaches, halting her.

"I need to talk with Catherine Harris."

The guard isn't one Sarah recognizes. His stance is stiff and impersonal, like maybe he just arrived and is still trying to impress everyone with his vigilance. "Researchers are only allowed near the tower in shifts, ma'am."

"Can you radio her?" asks Sarah. "Tell her Sarah Solheim needs a word."

Just don't ask me what about, she thinks. The Cheyenne device is still classified; most personnel on the site don't know it exists. It's definitely not supposed to be in Sarah's pocket, away from its protective safe under Catherine's desk.

The man hops into one of the vehicles to grab a radio. When he returns, he says, "You've been cleared. She is by the tower. Do you need a ride?"

"No, I'll walk."

"Are you sure? It's almost two clicks away."

"I'm fine, thanks."

He steps aside to let her slip under the blockade's

caution tape. She can't see the tower yet, but it should be a straight shot. The sun is brutal, and the humidity is downright ruthless. She starts to regret her decision to go on foot, but thankfully, when she gets down into the valley, a cool breeze provides much-needed relief.

She rehearses her argument in her mind, running her fingers over the device in her pocket. The FBI Director and others think the tower and the small object are linked somehow. And yet, they've kept the Cheyenne device well clear of the affected zone—what they've started calling the cordoned-off three-thousand-foot radius. It's probably a safety precaution, as well as a matter of security, but what if—

A buzzing vibration runs up her arm. She squeaks in surprise, looking in all directions before pulling the device out to stare at it.

Did the thing just... power on?!

Sarah brings the device closer to her face. A faint blue luminescence has emerged around the device's borders. She turns it over to find symbols made up of dots and rectangles with rounded-off edges glowing at its center. Her mouth goes dry. Is it a language? Some sort of logo? Either way, she walks with new vigor, jogging every few feet. The vibration increases and becomes a steady hum rather than sporadic pulses. By the time the tower comes into full view, she can feel it in her teeth.

The black device is now coated in bright blue symbols.

She sees Catherine standing with hands on her lower back, leaning backward to take in the full view of the tower. Two soldiers sit idle in a Jeep about fifty yards from the tower's base, watching Sarah approach without much interest or urgency. The Jeep's wheels are feet away from the edge of the excavation site. Piles of dirt have been hauled to the base of the nearby cliff.

Catherine spies Sarah and waves her over. Sarah puts the buzzing device back in her pocket and carefully walks across the bridge of planks that spans the excavation area. Up close, the tower's enormous, thirty-yard-wide, spiraling base makes it look like a giant drill with an odd, fat antenna on top that bears a blue gemstone.

The blue of the stone is the same color as the glowing device from Cheyenne.

"What can I do for you?" Catherine asks, shading her face with her hand.

"Don't court-martial me, but..." Sarah holds up the device.

Catherine's eyes bug out of her head. "You got it working? What did you do?"

"I didn't do anything. I mean, I followed a hunch."

The OSC's eyebrows go way, way up.

"It started vibrating when I crossed into the affected zone," Sarah explains. "The symbols started popping up at the same time. The closer I got, the more there were."

Catherine takes the device and traces a few of the markings with her finger. "Incredible." She hands it back to Sarah and says, "Can you hold it up? We have to take pictures of these markings, in case they disappear again." She pulls out her cell phone.

Sarah obliges, holding the device out so the markings are clearly visible.

Catherine takes several pictures, tapping her screen, and then gestures to have the device back.

Sarah hands it over.

"What do you think these markings mean?" Catherine asks.

"I have no idea."

Catherine holds the device flat on her palm, and Sarah can hear it buzzing against her skin. "Clearly it's designed to detect or sense something in or related to this tower."

Sarah puts her hand out. "Or, maybe it's sensing something else."

"Like what?" Catherine asks as she plops it in Sarah's palm.

Sarah's first forty-eight hours on site had involved running every test she could think of related to signals outside the normal audible range for humans. At first, she'd been disappointed to come up empty—no signals detected. Then, she'd realized she'd been given a chance to solve an even bigger mystery.

She pokes at the glowing device. "I reviewed the autopsy and the necropsy reports. All of the victims, including the entire herd, had the same symptoms. I think this tower is creating some sort of signal that in turn creates oscillation with blood."

"For what purpose?"

"Communication, maybe?"

"So, you don't think the tower is a weapon."

"Well..." Sarah considers her words carefully. "I don't think it was *designed* to kill. Do you remember, when I got here, I mentioned the concept of resonant frequency?"

"Yes."

"I believe this tower's frequency is in harmonic proportion to the frequency of our blood. That results in resonant frequency. It could arise from the pi-coupling of bases in the DNA double helix."

Catherine shrugs.

"The natural frequency of our internal organs is believed to be less than 8hz, which of course is infrasound."

Catherine's lips shift to one side, pondering the explanation. "But the tower isn't producing infrasound."

Sarah holds up the rectangular device, excitement building inside her. "This is proof that the tower is generating a signal or wave. We might not have the technology to detect the sound waves or signals this thing is producing... but this device does."

"So... you're saying that this tower is creating something similar to sound waves, and that those waves resonate in harmony with the blood of living beings." Catherine stares at the object with narrowed eyes. "That would explain the autopsy report."

Sarah reaches for the tower and feels its warmth even before her hand touches the surface. "I believe the frequencies resonate, making maximum energy transfer possible. At certain moments—at 5:12 p.m. every five days—the energy transfer is so great that it literally makes the victims' blood... *boil.*"

"And you think we could use that device to measure or evaluate the signals... sound waves... or electromagnetic waves... whatever this tower is producing."

"It's worth a shot." Sarah wiggles the device, proud that she followed her gut in bringing the two strange objects together.

"We don't have a clue how to use that thing."

Sarah's eloquent shrug says, *We'll figure it out.*

"You said the tower might be communicating. With whom?"

Sarah points to the diamond-shaped crystal at the top. "To whoever's up there."

"Space?" Catherine looks to the tower with newfound trepidation.

"Yes."

"If it is sending messages into space, then why does it also send signals here on Earth, to anything within three thousand feet?"

"Anything electronic that sends signals has a certain amount of leakage."

After a moment of silence, Catherine asks, "How do we test this theory?"

"We need to measure the intensity of the signals. If this tower's purpose is to send messages into space every five days, then the intensity of the signal will be greatest at the end of that diamond-shaped crystal."

"True, but we have no way of measuring the intensity."

Sarah taps the device in her hand. "This will. The closer I got to the tower, the more it vibrated. We need to measure the difference in vibrations between the crystal, or whatever it is, and here on the ground."

"Lucky for us, there are two of those things," says Catherine.

"Two?" Sarah startles. "The Director never mentioned having another one."

"Each of the men that was found unconscious in Cheyenne in 1969 had a device."

Sarah starts to grin. "With two devices, we can measure the variance. We should be able to tell if this tower was designed to send signals into space."

Catherine pulls out her phone. "The other one's in storage in D.C. I'll have it here by the end of the day."

* * *

Joey stares at the TV without really seeing the drama play

out. He's not sure who the bad guy is, or why the teen leads are chasing him through a dark office building. His mind keeps drifting to the empty space on the couch where Maddie usually sits. Since their almost-kiss, looking at her has been like gazing at the sun. He has to look away almost immediately.

He's almost glad she seems to be ignoring him.

Almost.

As he turns to sigh at the empty cushion on his right, his father sits on it. When Joey jerks upright in surprise, Ellie sits on his left side, where he'd been lounging.

Kevin clicks the TV off with the remote.

"What?" says Joey, already bracing himself for an argument.

"Your mom and I talked about your treatments and your request not to move forward with chemo. I happen to believe it's the chemo that is responsible for your remarkable recovery—not that weird tower on the Schwarz farm."

Joey rolls his eyes.

"Although I disagree with you," says Kevin, holding up a finger to hush any protests, "we are willing to forgo your treatments for one month."

Joey unravels his crossed arms. Maybe there is hope that he won't have to fight his parents tooth and nail for this. "One month?"

"Yes. In one month, you agree to another bone marrow aspiration to test your blast count. And if it is under five percent, then no more treatments." Kevin looks over Joey's shoulder at Ellie, and when Joey follows his gaze, he can see this was not his mother's idea at all. She nods her agreement, but her frown is deep and her eyes are worried.

"Okay," says Joey, being very careful not to actually make a real promise. If his blast count goes down by even one more percent, he's not doing chemo, no matter what they say.

Kevin pats Joey's knee. "Great. Okay, I've got to get to work. Love you." He hands Joey the remote. "Ellie?"

She stands, although she obviously doesn't want to, and they leave Joey alone in the family room with his aggravating thoughts.

Joey sighs. If only that tower on the farm was a time machine... that also cured cancer. Then he would make sure he never tried to kiss Maddie. He ruined everything. Why did he have to screw things up?

On the screen, the teens are now the ones being pursued. Joey can't bring himself to care. His mind is churning. With this new deal on the table, it makes even more sense to sneak back to the tower. Touching it another time or two will get his blast count below five percent, for sure.

But this time... he'll have to make the journey alone.

* * *

David knocks on the front door of the Muller farmhouse. It's shabbier than his parents' place, probably because this farm lacked a feminine touch. Gordon's wife died years ago, and Ben and Bradley never married. But the porch is tidy and the wooden siding is sturdy. No signs of water or weather damage.

The door swings open. "Well, come on in," Gordon says, already turning to walk back inside.

The old man leads David to the kitchen table. One placemat has a mug of steaming coffee on it. That's where Gordon sits. He points to the other chair. He doesn't offer David a mug of his own.

"Out with it," he says.

"I know about the IOCG deposit."

The words echo in the drafty kitchen. Several hard-to-decipher emotions flicker across Gordon's lined face. Then, he smirks. "I knew it was you. At the lawyer's place."

"The deposit straddles our properties," David says, neither confirming nor denying the old man's words. "I know that's why you wanted to buy the farm from Dad—to own the whole thing. You were trying to swindle him."

Now it's Gordon Muller's turn to neither confirm nor deny.

"But now I have a problem," David goes on.

"The government's occupying the land," Gordon says. "Do you think they know about it?"

"I'm sure they do, by now. They have a whole host of experts there. Scientists, doctors, military... but we have one advantage."

Gordon's eyes narrow. "What's that?"

"They don't know we know about it."

"How does that help us?"

David lays out all his cards. "I can't get a geologist on site to do an assessment now that the feds are on the land. But you already had a comprehensive geological survey done. We can bring that to the person in charge and demand to retain ownership of the IOCG deposit, or to be compensated rightly if the government seizes the land under eminent domain." He leans forward. "I think we need to do this together, in order for it to work. A unified front."

"A unified front." Muller strokes his pock-marked chin with his index finger and thumb. "You mean, a fifty-fifty split."

"Fifty-fifty?" David barks. "At least three-quarters of the deposit's on my land, and you know it."

Muller grins. "But you need *my* geological survey to get anything at all."

David clenches his teeth. "Seventy-thirty."

"No."

"I'll give you thirty-five percent."

"No," the old man repeats, clearly enjoying himself now.

"Sixty-forty," David finally grits out. "Final offer."

Gordon extends his callused hand. "You got yourself a deal."

* * *

Just as Kevin pulls into the parking lot at work, David calls.

"What is it, man?" Kevin asks. "I'm running late." Ellie was in a tizzy all morning. The chance that Joey could go into remission is within sight, a real possibility at last, and now Joey himself is trying to take it away. It took Kevin twice as long to leave the house, with Ellie trailing after him, wringing her hands.

"I just met with Gordon Muller. He's agreed to work with me. But we're going to need your help talking to the government people." This is what David always does: he *tells* instead of *asks*. "When will you see someone in charge?"

"I have a meeting with the on-scene commander and my dad this morning," Kevin says reluctantly.

"Great. Can you ask about eminent domain?"

"I don't know if this is the time—"

"It has to happen soon. The longer this drags out, the less chance we have of getting paid."

"Jesus," Kevin says, pulling the keys from the ignition. "Your parents' funeral was *yesterday*."

"I wouldn't ask if it wasn't important," David replies stiffly.

The conversation from last week pops into Kevin's mind. Debbie offered to pay off Joey's medical bills with their windfall. If Joey's finally getting better, and the astronomical bills are covered... the Schumer family's long nightmare could soon be over.

"Did Debbie mean what she said?" Kevin asks bluntly. "Would you really help us pay for Joey's treatments?"

"Absolutely," David says without hesitation. "If we get what the deposit is worth, it'll be a drop in the bucket, anyway."

Kevin sighs. David can be a real asshole, but he can also be a good friend... when he wants to be. "I'll bring it up."

"Thank you. I really appreciate all your family has done for mine the past couple weeks," David says, sounding uncharacteristically humble. "I truly can't wait to repay you."

Kevin clears his throat. "Okay, well, I do have to get in there. Talk to you later."

"Bye."

Kevin enters the building and goes straight to his dad's office. Catherine Harris has already begun her debrief. Kevin gives his dad an apologetic look as he sits next to Catherine.

Catherine nods to him, barely breaking her stream of thought. "We still don't know for certain that the tower is responsible for the deaths on the Schwarz farm," she says. "But the theory we're currently working with is that it's producing a signal that has a resonant frequency with blood. This could be the cause of death."

"What the hell is a resonant frequency?" Jack asks.

"You know in cartoons, when the opera singer breaks glass with her voice?" Catherine asks, using the example Sarah Solheim gave her to talk to laymen.

The sheriff and chief deputy nod.

"It's like that, except the tower is the opera singer, and our blood is the glass."

Jack winces, and Kevin makes a face.

"Why would a terrorist build a thing like that in middle-of-nowhere Wisconsin?" the sheriff asks.

Kevin massages the bridge of his nose. "Dad, I doubt it was built by terrorists."

"Then who the hell built it?" Jack demands.

"We don't know," Catherine says.

"Any idea how long that thing has been there?" the sheriff goes on.

"We have no way of determining its age."

"How is it possible that Stan and Margaret didn't know about it?" Jack asks next. "They were good, law-abiding citizens. They would've reported such a thing."

"We're not sure it was there before July 2nd. It may have..." Catherine swallows. "Erupted from the ground around that time."

"Erupted?!" Jack looks like his head is exploding.

"We're currently excavating around it to see how deep it's buried."

Jack leans forward. "And then you'll get it out of our town, right?"

Seeing his opportunity, Kevin cuts in, "David Schwarz, Stan and Margaret's son, was wondering at what point he can take possession of the farm."

"We can't move the tower off the lot until we learn more about it," Catherine says apologetically. "We're in uncharted territory. There's no timeline for this."

"Is the government planning to invoke eminent domain?" asks Kevin.

Catherine nods. "We already have. It's what we refer to

as 'temporary taking.' At this point, we have no plans for 'complete taking.' If we do, the Schwarzes will be compensated."

"Who would they go to about the value of the land?" Kevin asks.

Jack waves his hand. "Never mind that, son. Ms. Harris, do you know when this thing will attack next?"

"The signal blast occurs every five days at precisely 5:12 p.m. So, the next strike should hit tomorrow."

"How far away is safe?" asks Kevin. "We can't lose any more men." The Sheriff's Department is reeling.

"We've established a radius of three thousand feet."

"Everything within that radius at the time of the... attack," Kevin says, trying to be clear, "...dies?"

"As far as we can tell, yes," Catherine says. "But our perimeter is airtight. Nothing will get through."

"Excuse me," he says. "You said the tower is producing a signal... that resonates at the same frequency as blood?"

"That's our theory."

Kevin's mouth opens and closes. He looks at his hands folded in his lap, feeling too silly to look the woman in the eye. He clears his throat. "Assuming your theory is correct... is it possible that someone with leukemia could be impacted by the signal, assuming that person got close enough to the tower?"

Jack makes an astonished noise.

Catherine raises her eyebrows. "I have no idea. Leukemia is a cancer of the blood, and we do believe the frequency is the same as blood, but there is no way to be certain. We certainly can't run an ethical test."

"Right, of course," Kevin says, chastened. "Sorry for the interruption."

His father and the OSC resume their discussion of next

steps, but Kevin's mind is spinning. His son was *there*, at the tower… and now he insists it healed him. The numbers don't lie.

But it's not possible. And anyway, that thing is deadly. Kevin will be attending funerals because of it. Joey is a child, and it's Kevin's job to protect him. Whatever it takes.

CHAPTER 18

July 22nd, 2016

Joey slings his backpack over one shoulder as he carefully shuts his bedroom door, keeping the knob twisted until it's fully closed to avoid a click. At the bottom of the stairs, he can see out the kitchen window. The sun hasn't yet risen, but the sky has turned a light gray in anticipation of its arrival. He snuck a sandwich upstairs before going to bed last night, and it's nestled in his bag for emergencies, but he plans to be back before anyone wakes up. He knows the way now.

He tiptoes toward the back door, but before he can open it, someone hisses, "Seriously?"

His heart jumps into his throat. He whirls to find Maddie standing in the kitchen with her arms crossed.

"You were going to leave without me?" she whispers.

Joey catches his breath and says, "I told you, I don't want you getting in trouble for me."

Maddie narrows her eyes. "I'm not worried about

pulling a few weeds. You need my help. I'm coming with you."

"No."

"You don't have a choice," she says, head cocked in a mock threat. "Either I come with you, or I go into to your parents' bedroom and tell them you're leaving."

Joey smiles. That's exactly what he wanted to hear. "Okay."

She unravels her arms and hurries off to get her backpack, ponytail bouncing with each step.

After leaving the yard to cross the green pasture that will lead them to the cave entrance, Joey chances a look at Maddie.

"I'm glad you're coming with me... but how did you know I was leaving this morning?"

"A hunch." She grins and says, "Actually, I looked in your room yesterday and saw that your backpack was packed."

Joey nods.

"So, what's the plan?"

"What do you mean?"

"I'm assuming you want to be near the tower, but what is your plan when we get there?"

"I feel like touching that thing helped me. It's why my test results are better. I just need to touch it again. Does that make sense?"

"No," says Maddie honestly. "Then again, none of this makes any sense. But I believe in you. If you think it will help, then we have to give it a shot."

"Thanks, Maddie," says Joey, stomach flip-flopping.

"What about chemo?"

With a jolt, Joey remembers that Maddie avoided him all day yesterday. "My parents said that if my next blast count is under five percent, I won't have to do any more chemo."

"Do you think that's possible?" asks Maddie.

Joey shrugs. "Yeah... I guess. It did drop from sixty-five percent to twelve percent after the first time I touched the tower, so I would think it would drop again... but I don't know."

"I'm sure it will," she says, tucking her hands into her pockets with a sheepish smile.

The rest of the journey across the fields pass mostly in silence. Joey tries not to look at Maddie as they walk, not wanting to take note of the shine of her hair or the flush of exercise on her cheeks. Those images will just morph into the memory of her eyes widening and her head snapping to the side to avoid his kiss.

When they reach the cave entrance at the base of the first grassy hill, Joey takes off his backpack and pulls out his flashlight. "Are you ready?"

"After you."

Joey's shirt rides up as his bent back rubs against the ceiling of the cave's small entrance. But it's not long before he can stand. His flashlight catches some of the rarer, greenish stones embedded in the gray cave wall. When Maddie catches up, Joey heads for the first fork in the road. He points the flashlight beam down the left side. "This time, we go the right way."

Maddie smirks. "You mean the correct way. The right way would be the wrong way."

Joey snorts. "Real funny. Let's go left, *the correct way*."

They've barely taken ten steps into the tunnel before Maddie stops. "Wait."

"What?"

"It's that same stuff." She rubs loose a tiny bit of the chalky, charcoal-colored substance, and it falls away from the shiny rocks in a miniature shower.

Joey moves in for a closer look, careful not to brush against Maddie's arm. "Yeah, you're right. It's like soot or ash."

"I wonder why it's stuck on the wall?" Maddie wrinkles her nose at the gray stain left on her fingers.

"I don't know." Joey rubs away a wide swath with a sweep of his palm. He squints in surprise when an orange-brown metal is revealed.

"What is that?" asks Maddie.

"Metal… maybe copper?" Before Maddie can ask any more questions, Joey starts walking again. "Let's keep moving. I want to be home before my parents wake up."

Maddie follows him to the exit, both of them jogging until they have to bend to inch out into the fresh air. Joey pauses to peek around the edge of the cave mouth, already tingling from fingertips to forearm.

"Stop," says Maddie as Joey starts to emerge into the sunrise.

"What?"

"We need to make sure no one's around." The last time they were here, the land was crawling with scientists and deputies in white hazmat suits. Maddie creeps forward, hiding behind a boulder, and looks in all directions. "No scientists yet this morning," she murmurs, "but there are some soldiers over there." She points to the field that spans between the tower and the Schwarz farmhouse. "See those two guys by the Humvee?"

Joey follows her finger and sees two men in fatigues with large guns strapped to their backs. "Yeah, but they're pretty far away." Joey can't make out anything about their faces; the distance has boiled them down to their basic shapes.

"Still, they can't see us. Follow me."

Maddie crouches and inches behind the largest of the

nearby boulders and then waves Joey after her. He follows her example as best he can, but his thighs scream at him as he lowers himself into the unfamiliar position. By the time they sneak around the boulder to hide behind some spiny shrubbery, Joey abandons the squat and just bends low at the waist. The tingles race through his whole body now, filling his head with a low hum. Maddie peeks at the men each time she moves to a new hiding place, moving boulder to boulder, bush to bush until they reach the edge of the large moat-like excavation around the object.

"Wow, look how far down it goes," says Maddie.

"This thing is huge."

Maddie looks left to the makeshift walkway that will bring them within touching distance of the object.

"They'll see us if we cross," she says.

"They're not even looking this way."

Both the soldiers' heads are bent over some sort of device, its screen reflecting the sun.

"True," she admits. "Do you feel the tingling?"

"Yeah, it feels stronger than before."

"What are you going to do?" asks Maddie.

"I just want to touch the tower for a few seconds, that's all."

Maddie nods. "Okay, I'll wait here."

Joey scurries on tiptoe to the walkway, keeping his eye on the soldiers. The plank bridge is wide enough to jog across. He makes it in a flash and hops off onto the platform encircling the skinnier top part of the object, then scoots around so that the tower is between him and the soldiers. He looks back at Maddie, and she gives him the thumbs up.

He faces the tower. He can't hear anything over its buzzing now. His veins are singing, the tingles warm and pleasant. He closes his eyes and places his right hand on the spiral. The sensation is like a single, thrumming pulse through his body, like being struck by a sound wave. The following hum is like a meditative chant, tranquil and comforting. The moment he places his left hand beside his right, he is unable to distinguish where his hands end and the tower begins. It is as if he has melded himself with the metal, becoming part of it.

Maddie watches Joey sway, his hands pressed to the tower. He's taking too long. She's bouncing on the balls of her feet, alternating between biting her lip and hissing under her breath for him to hurry up. Her next glance at the soldiers makes her heart jump to her throat. One of the men is walking toward the tower. But... he's not jogging, not shouting. Can he see Joey? Even if he can't yet, a few steps to the left and he'll see just fine.

"Joey," she whispers, hands cupped around her mouth. He doesn't open his eyes. "Joey! Joey!" Her whisper is more like a hoarse shout before Joey finally snaps out of it.

"What?" he calls back, sounding annoyed.

She points toward the soldiers. The walking man... she can't see him that well from this angle, but he's stopped in the middle of the field. Joey peeks around the tower and puts a hand to his mouth. It's not until Maddie sees his shoulders bouncing that she realizes he's holding in a laugh.

Maddie scoots around to the other side of the boulder for a better look. The man is... *oh.* She scrunches her eyes, cheeks heating. She has never seen a man pee before, and she hopes to never see it again.

Joey is shaking with suppressed laughter as he races across the walkway and dives behind the boulder with her.

"The look on your face... too funny."

"For you, maybe. Not for me. I was freaking out!"

"I know. Thanks for getting my attention." Joey glances

back in the direction of the cave. It's getting lighter out, so the route is easier to see. "Let's get back home before our parents wake up."

"So, do you think it worked?" Maddie asks as they retrace their stealthy path.

"I hope so."

They make it back inside the dank cave without a hitch. But then, at the fork, everything goes wrong.

Joey points his light down the right-side tunnel—their way out—and freezes. "What the hell?"

The beam bounces back, glowing from the depths of two large, yellow eyes.

The cave echoes with a low, feline growl that crescendos in a high, yowling roar.

"Mountain lion!" Maddie screams. "Run!"

* * *

Kevin yawns as he dumps the coffee grounds into the filter. One of his eyes is still bleary from sleep, and his back is aching from their lumpy old mattress. Cursing his aging body, he dumps the water and starts the machine.

David walks in wearing basketball shorts and a holey old T-shirt, toting his beloved punching pads.

"Training with Maddie?" asks Kevin.

"Yeah, we fell off our routine, but it's time to get back to it. I'll give her another thirty minutes, then wake her up."

Debbie shuffles in, looking like she needs a caffeine fix as badly as Kevin. She sits at the kitchen table and props her cheek in her palm. She turns groggily toward David, spies the pads, and rolls her eyes. "Why don't you let the poor girl sleep in?"

"9:00 a.m. *is* sleeping in."

"To you, not to her," says Debbie.

Ellie walks in, already showered and dressed. "Is everyone hungry? I'll make us some French toast."

Kevin smiles at his wife but studies her carefully, trying to see if this is just a happy front for their guests or if she's actually feeling less anxious today.

"None for Maddie and me," says David. "We've got training."

Debbie shakes her head. "You can eat afterward. You'll be ravenous."

"All right. I'll save two plates," says Ellie. "Are the younger girls up?"

"Not yet," Debbie says. "But they will be as soon as they smell breakfast."

Ellie laughs. "Isn't that the truth."

Instead of looking at Ellie's smiling face, Kevin studies the way she moves. Her shoulders are back, her steps light. Kevin's smile grows. Perhaps she's starting to get comfortable with the idea of the deal he made with Joey. After all, Joey's count hasn't been this low in over a year; he's already in better shape. It's not likely to bounce back to sixty percent in a month… right?

"How'd it go with Catherine Harris yesterday?" David asks Kevin. He's been itching for details on the meeting, but Kevin had a long shift and didn't get home until almost midnight. And it wasn't like David lacked for things to do yesterday. He'd actually gone to the local public library to look up eminent domain laws. Then, he and Debbie had met with his parents' lawyer to discuss the reading of the will next week. "Did she have anything to say about me getting the farm back?"

"Who's Catherine Harris?" asks Ellie.

"The Federal OSC," Kevin says.

Ellie starts taking ingredients out of the fridge. "And what's an OSC?"

David answers for Kevin. "It's an on-scene commander."

"Thanks, David," says Ellie.

Kevin moves to rub Ellie's lower back as she readies her pans on the stove. "Catherine said that they think the tower is responsible for the deaths on your parents' farm, David. They think it's sending out some sort of signal that has the same frequency as blood."

"Then why didn't we all die when we were on the farm?" asks Debbie.

"The signal only blasts every five days. In fact, the next blast is today at 5:12 p.m."

"How do they know it's today, and the exact time?" asks Ellie.

"They conducted some experiments, after looking at the times of death of the various folks on the property." Kevin winces, thinking of his lost deputies. "There's a specific danger zone, too."

"How big is the danger zone?" asks Ellie, dropping a square of butter in the pan.

"Apparently, three thousand feet from the tower," says Kevin.

"This thing… vibrates at the same frequency as blood?" David is frowning as he speaks. He spent so long pursuing his poison theory, far-fetched as it was, that it's hard to wrap his brain around this new explanation for his parents' deaths. "How does that kill someone?"

Kevin shrugs. "They don't know for sure. It's just a theory."

Ellie turns to him with an egg in her hand, brow scrunched. "Joey swears that tower is why his blast count was so low."

Kevin nods. "I asked Catherine if it was possible that the vibration could affect someone with leukemia."

"What did she say?" asks Ellie, and he hears her breath catch.

"She didn't know." Kevin sighs, watching his wife's gaze drift out the window to the spot where Joey always sits on the dock. "This whole situation is pretty wild."

Ellie nods.

"Did you ask her about me taking possession?" David presses.

"I did, and she couldn't give me a time frame. Sorry."

David huffs, not happy with that answer. "I'm going to wake Maddie."

Kevin grabs the coffee pot the second the machine beeps. He leans against the counter as he pours, watching the java rise in his cup—an addict waiting for his fix.

He's just taken his first piping hot sip when David flies back into the kitchen.

"Maddie's not in her room."

Kevin slams his cup on the counter, the coffee sloshing out, and takes off toward the stairs, but David catches his arm as he tries to pass. "I already checked; he's gone too."

Ellie meets Kevin's eyes, her face white with panic. "The tower," she gasps. "Joey thinks it's the reason for his recovery..."

"He said he wanted to go back," Kevin agrees, already grabbing his keys. "You two, search our property, just in case," he says to the wives. "David, you're with me."

* * *

Joey keeps his beam pointed at the cave floor as he sprints

full speed away from the mountain lion, Maddie breathing hard behind him.

"It's close!" she shrieks, urging him on with her hands on his back.

Unable to stop himself, Joey looks over his shoulder. All he can see at the edges of his light's glow is a dark shape with glowing eyes at its center. The cat's footfalls are silent, but he can hear it panting. He looks ahead as panic swells in his chest. In moments, his beam finds the small crawl space they squeezed inside on their first visit. He stops beside it and waves Maddie in with his flashlight. She dives inside, army-crawling to the other side, while Joey points his light down the tunnel, his muscles tight and breathing shallow.

The cat leaps into the beam, a powerhouse of lean muscle and flashing yellow fangs. Joey dives into the hole with a scream just as the mountain lion lets out another hellish growl and springs. The cat's tail tickles his calf, overshooting its pounce with nothing but air to claw. Still screaming, Joey crawls as fast as he can toward Maddie's outstretched arms on the other side. Her eyes are already wide, but something behind him makes them bulge to the size of plums. She grabs his wrists and yanks, hauling his knees over hard rock. He winces, but when he hears the cat's groping paw scratching the sides of the tunnel, he's grateful busted-up knees are his biggest worry. Joey pops free on the other side and whirls around to see the big cat hesitate on the other side of the tunnel. It paces in front of the hole, debating whether this prey is worth putting itself in such a vulnerable position.

Joey doesn't intend to let the cougar make up its mind. "Help me with this," he tells Maddie as he presses his shoulder into a hefty boulder.

She flies to his side, both of them grunting and huffing

with the effort of getting the boulder rolling. A low growl chills Joey's blood. The mountain lion is in the small tunnel. It must be hungry.

Joey backs up and then rams his shoulder into the rock with all his might, and it starts to roll, leaving an indent in the dirt. Maddie directs it toward the hole, but when the entrance is still only half covered, the cat's fat paw swipes around it, grabbing for Maddie's legs. Maddie falls back onto her butt with a high scream, and Joey takes over, shoving the boulder the rest of the way and forcing the cat to retract its leg with a hiss.

Joey collapses to the dirt floor, sucking in gulps of air. "Damn, that was close."

The cat yowls, lamenting its failure. Its low growl persists, and Joey uses the sound to follow the cougar's frustrated pacing on the other side of the wall. It's still not giving up.

"I'm glad you remembered this place," says Maddie, scooting to come sit beside him. She sighs, and her breath quivers. "But... now we're stuck here."

"Maybe the cat will get bored and go look for other food," Joey says weakly, his chest still tight from panic and exertion.

"Yeah, maybe," Maddie says, not sounding much more confident.

Joey nods, too tired to say anything further. Instead, he thinks to himself, *At least I'm stuck with you.*

* * *

Kevin's sigh is more like a growl when he pulls up to the checkpoint on the outskirts of the Schwarz farm. "Damn red tape." He bounces his thumb on the wheel while he waits for the soldier to lumber over to his window.

"I can't allow you to pass," the soldier says.

"Our kids are missing, and we think they're on this property. We need to look for them."

The man shakes his head. "Sorry."

"Can you radio Catherine Harris and tell her it's Kevin Schumer, the chief deputy? It's urgent."

The soldier retreats while he talks into his radio. Then he strides back over. "She's in the main tent. She said to come on over."

"Thanks." Kevin follows the soldier's pointing finger to the largest white tent. He drives as fast as he dares and has his seatbelt unbuckled before the Jeep is even parked. He and David hurry inside the tent, eyes frantically scanning the various personnel.

Now that everyone's dressed in either lab coats or uniforms, instead of hazmat suits, it's quick work to find Catherine talking with the red-headed scientist the FBI brought in. Kevin hasn't met her yet, but he's seen her photo in the abridged files the FBI passed on to the sheriff's office.

"Kevin," Catherine says, spotting them. "What's going on? Your kids are missing?"

"Yes, my son, Joey, and David's daughter Maddie left the house early this morning. I have reason to believe they went to see the tower."

"We have two men posted at the site. Let me see if they've seen anyone." Catherine pulls out her radio and steps to one side to check in with the soldiers.

Kevin shifts from foot to foot, accidentally making eye contact with the other woman. She gives him a tentative smile. "I don't think we've met. I'm Sarah Solheim."

"Kevin Schumer," Kevin says, extending his hand. He nods at David. "This is David Schwarz."

Sarah gives David a curious look. "Are you the son of Stan and Margaret?"

"Yes."

"I'm sorry for your loss."

"Thanks," David says, but it's more like a grunt.

"Bad news," Catherine says, walking back over. "They haven't seen anyone by the tower." She pauses. "Actually, that's good news."

Kevin and David exchange a look. "That doesn't make any sense. It's the only place Joey would want to go, without telling me or his mom. He thinks..." Kevin fades off. Suddenly, it doesn't seem like the best idea to tell a couple of government scientists that his son thinks the mysterious object they're studying is the cure for his cancer. The last thing he wants is for Joey to become a lab rat. "There was a dare," he says quickly, nudging David. "Right?"

"Uh, yeah. Some kid in town dared our kids to sneak past the perimeter."

"Teenagers," Sarah says, shaking her head. "My two best friends growing up would totally have done that."

"Well, there is no way they could have reached the tower without passing one of our checkpoints," says Catherine. "Unless there's another way onto the property?" She glances at David, raising her eyebrows.

"Where are your checkpoints?" David asks, glancing at a map of the area that's posted on a nearby bulletin board.

Catherine walks them over. "We've got personnel stationed here, here, here, and here." She jabs at the map with her index finger. "And of course, at the main driveway, where you came in."

"Hm." David ponders the terrain in the in-between areas. "The kids would be on foot, so I'm not sure..."

Kevin chews at the inside of his cheek, anxious to get moving. "Even if your men haven't seen Joey and Maddie yet, they could still be heading for the tower. Do you mind if we look around?"

"Not at all, as long as you don't mind an escort." Catherine motions for two of the guards to join them. "Protocol, I'm afraid."

"Of course," Kevin says with a tight nod. "Thanks."

Catherine radios the soldiers by the tower to let them know company is coming, and then they head out. Kevin guns the Jeep, and soon the spiraling metal structure is in view, the military Humvee acting as a sentry nearby. The military presence and the knowledge that the tower is going to send out another deadly signal later today is eating away at Kevin's nerves. Joey and Maddie couldn't have picked a worse day to run off. He tells himself they have plenty of time before disaster strikes... but he doesn't feel reassured. No one really understands how that tower works. It could go off at any second, really.

As they pass the Humvee, the two soldiers wave to their comrades in Kevin's back seat.

Kevin parks. He, David, and their escorts jump out of the car and approach the tower. They circle the odd structure, calling the kids' names, eyes peeled for any movement behind the shrubs or any figures approaching on foot in the distance.

Nothing.

"This makes no sense," says Kevin, unable to bottle up the frustration anymore. "I know Joey was headed here."

"Maybe they went to that cliff." David nods up at the sheer rock face. "We know they've been there before."

"Maybe," Kevin says, but his eyes are still glued to the tower. He turns to the two men assigned to shadow them. "Do you mind if we go up the cliff?"

"Suit yourselves," one of the soldiers says, leaning against a boulder.

"You're not going to follow us?" David snarks. "What happened to 'protocol'?"

The man stares at him, unruffled. "Are you going to do anything stupid up there?"

"No," Kevin says, glaring at David.

"Then we'll wait for you at the base and catch your kids if we spot them."

"Thanks. Come on, David."

Kevin and David drive across the property line to the Mullers' lot, where the hike up to the clifftop begins. "I don't know what's worse—if they're up there, or if they aren't," David says, shading his eyes with his hand as he looks up.

"Let's just get going."

The sweaty trek up the hill, across the terrifying rock bridge, and up the rest of the mountain is enough to morph Kevin's worry into dread. At the summit, Kevin turns in a circle. From this height, he can see for miles and miles. If Joey and Maddie are on their way here, or if they've already come and gone, he should be able to spot them. It's a clear day.

But the teens are nowhere in sight.

Kevin throws up his hands. "Where the hell are they?"

CHAPTER 19

"Does Joey have any friends that he might have gone to see?" asks David.

"No, he really doesn't have any friends... except Maddie." Kevin wracks his brain for another face, another name. "He used to hang out with a boy named Tom Phillips. I guess it wouldn't hurt to ask him if he knows where they might be."

"Do you have his phone number?"

"No. We'll have to go to his house."

"Back down we go," says David with a groan.

They race back to Kevin's Jeep, and then drive back to where the two Guardsmen are waiting for them. "We're going to talk to a friend of my son's," Kevin says. He pulls his card out of his pocket and thrusts it toward one of the soldiers. "That's my cell. Call me if you see anything."

"Will do. Good luck."

Kevin drives across town as fast as he can without going more than five miles per hour above the speed limit. Luckily, Rindville is small enough that it's a quick trip.

The Phillips house is a little piece of small-town heaven, with white painted brick and a baby-blue door. Chickens cluck from a pen in the back, and the lawn is covered in bikes, balls, and gadgets. Kevin steps in front of David and all his imposing muscles before knocking on the door.

"Quit frowning like that," Kevin mutters to David as footsteps approach from inside.

"Like what?"

"Forget it. Just be nice."

The door swings open on a blond man in Wranglers and a faded T-shirt. "Hi, Steve," says Kevin.

Steve nods. "Deputy."

"You remember David?"

Steve takes in David's full breadth. "Yes... from high school. Sorry about your parents."

"Thanks," says David, jaw tight.

"What can I do for you?" Steve asks.

"My son, Joey, and David's daughter Maddie are missing. We think they are in some trouble," Kevin says. "I was hoping to talk with Tom."

Steve narrows his eyes. "I didn't know your boy and mine were still hanging out."

Kevin stiffens but keeps his smile on. "I don't know that they are, but I was still wondering if he knows where he might be... maybe a place they used to go."

"Sure, I'll get him." Steve leans back into the house and bellows for his son.

The skinny teenager flies into the entryway and blanches at the sight of Kevin. He looks to the floor as he comes to stand behind his dad, his bangs obscuring his eyes.

"Tom, Deputy Schumer wants to ask you a few questions about Joey."

The boy flips his bangs clear and at last meets Kevin's eye.

"Hi, Tom. I was wondering if there was a hangout spot

you and Joey used to go to, somewhere you boys didn't tell us about." Kevin stops himself before he can add, *You know, back when you didn't treat him like he was radioactive.*

The boy shrugs, eyes falling again.

"It's really important, Tom," Kevin says, trying to sound urgent without getting testy. Snapping at Tom won't make the teen or his dad more likely to cooperate. "I think Joey might be in some trouble. I know you guys used to go to the cliff..." Tom's head snaps up in surprise, and Kevin presses. "Is there somewhere else?"

"We... we sometimes went to the caves."

"Caves?" says David, trying to scoot Kevin out of the way.

Kevin holds his ground and shoots David a look that makes him step back. "Where are these caves?"

"In the hill by the cliff," Tom says.

David scoffs. "We were just there, and we didn't see any caves."

"They're near the edge of the Muller lot, at the base of the hill. There's a bunch of rocks near the entrance."

"How big is the entrance?" asks Kevin.

"Not very big. We had to duck." Tom's eyes flick to David. "You might have to crawl."

Kevin lets out a slightly hysterical snort of laughter. "Thanks, Tom. I really appreciate your help."

Kevin and David turn to leave. That's when Tom says, "Mr. Schumer... I really hope you find Joey."

"Thanks. We will," says Kevin with a smile.

When they're rolling again, David grumbles, "I lived on that farm until I was eighteen, and I never knew about any caves."

"Crazy." Kevin looks at the car clock. "We don't have a lot of time."

"I know, we need to hurry."

Kevin kicks up dust at the end of the Phillips' driveway.

David's phone buzzes. "It's Debbie. She's asking for an update."

"What are you going to tell her?"

"We think we know where they are." He pauses his typing to add, "I hope."

"Me too," says Kevin.

At the entrance to the Muller farm, they're put through the same rigmarole as this morning. The soldier standing guard at the checkpoint calls Catherine, she gives the okay. The only difference is that everyone seems a bit more on edge, the closer they get to the expected strike time.

"We have to close the affected zone before 5:00 p.m.," Catherine tells Kevin. "I'd really like to pull all of my people out by 4:30."

"Understood." Kevin glances at the clock in his dash display. It's almost 2:00 p.m. now.

Finding this cave should be easy, he thinks... until they get there and he realizes that the hill is a beast, its base stretching for a mile or more.

"You take that way, I take this way?" David says, reading his mind.

Kevin makes a sound like an angry horse but nods anyway. No other choice.

He tries to search at a jog first, only occasionally stopping to peek between boulders that are pressed particularly close together. When he and David finally meet in the middle between the hill and the cliff, Kevin instantly knows David didn't find anything either.

Kevin tips back his head with a groan, staring at the precarious stone walkway high above. "Again."

David nods, grim-faced.

Kevin takes his time now, hugging the rock base whenever possible, poking his head behind every shrub, climbing every set of boulders to look at what might be concealed behind. He's nearly back to the Jeep when another pile catches his eye. The boulders are smaller, but clustered behind a dense thicket of shrubs that had blocked his view when coming from the other direction. He hurries over, squeezes between two of the largest rocks, and lets out a whoop when he sees the small mouth of the cave.

He runs back to the Jeep and calls for David, but he's not back yet. Tapping his foot, Kevin waits ten minutes. Nothing. Growling with frustration, he goes around the opposite side of the hill, yelling at David's distant form. He looks like he's digging into a bush. Kevin shouts and jumps and waves his arms. At last, David comes jogging back.

"I found it! Hurry up!" Kevin races back to the pile of boulders. "This must be it, right?" he says when David arrives.

David scoots in for a look. "Has to be."

Kevin lowers himself to hands and knees, figuring that might be easier on his back than bending himself in half.

"Kevin, wait," says David, a hand on Kevin's shoulder. He looks at his watch. It reads 4:15.

"What?"

"We only have an hour before that thing blasts its signal."

Kevin checks his watch, thinking there's no way. The numbers say David is right, and Kevin's mouth goes dry. An hour to find Joey and Maddie, or they're all dead. "We better hurry," he says, pulling his flashlight off his uniform's utility belt. He doesn't spare a breath to brace himself, just clicks on the beam and starts crawling.

* * *

Joey can hear Maddie's breathing quicken as he scoots the rock over an inch. He maneuvers his flashlight to peek through the crack and down the tunnel. A beige, furry back is pressed against the other end of the exit.

"I can't believe it's still there," he says after he rolls the rock back into place. What he doesn't say is that the cat is either taking a leisurely nap and waiting for the moon to rise to hunt again, or it's starving and desperate to make them a meal. Either way, it's probably not moving any time soon.

Maddie groans around her mouthful of sandwich. They've been rationing out bites since lunchtime, trying to stave off their hunger and boredom. "We're never going to get out of here."

"We will someday," Joey says through a sigh, "but I think it's safe to say our parents are going to be super pissed."

Maddie scoffs. "I wonder what the punishment will be this time."

"I'm sure it will involve weeding."

"At least a week's worth."

Joey sits back down, mimicking Maddie's position with his back against the musty cave wall and legs stretched out.

Joey's exhale is heavy, laden with unanswered questions that won't leave him alone. He wants to ask Maddie about the kiss. Maybe he's missing something. But… what if he isn't? What if she just doesn't like him like that, period? Does he really want to hear her say it out loud?

She looks over at him and notices he's staring. "What?"

He makes a sound as though she gut-punched him, and then it comes pouring out. "I'm sorry," he says, practically shouting in his haste. He grimaces at his own awkwardness and stares at his feet as he explains. "Sorry I tried to kiss you."

"I'm not."

Joey nearly breaks his neck looking back to her. He tries to say, "What?" but it comes out as a puff of air.

"I feel the same way about you," she says, picking at her fatigues and casting him a sidelong glance. "It's just that... I've never kissed anyone before, and I kind of freaked out a little. And then, after... I didn't know what to say to make it right."

Joey's heart works a mile a minute, but his mouth moves in slow motion. "Really?" he finally manages to choke out.

Maddie turns her head, and even in the odd orange glow cast over the bottom half of her face by the flashlight, her eyes transfix him. "Really."

"I thought..." he begins, but now she is moving toward him, those deep, sparking eyes obscured by lowered lashes. His heart lodges near his Adam's apple, choking off his air, and then her lips are on his. He remembers to close his eyes a second too late. His body feels like butter running down hot pancakes. Instead of tingling, he feels a bolt of some strange electricity blast from his core to his extremities. Letting his hand drift to her face, he moves his mouth against hers in a delicious experiment that sends shivers of ecstasy down his spine.

"Joey! Maddie!" a man's voice calls, echoing far away.

Maddie breaks the kiss with a gasp. Joey jumps up when she does, though he's not even sure what's happening. His brain is sluggish. Another call within the cave system snaps him out of it.

"Maddie! Joey! Are you there?"

"Dad!" yells Joey.

Maddie joins in, both of them yelling at the top of their lungs and pounding their hands against the rock.

On the other side of Maddie and Joey's hidden chamber, Kevin and David stop at a fork in the path.

Kevin shines his light down both options, looking for footprints. A muffled call tickles at his eardrum, and he holds his breath, listening. It comes again. Though it is faint, he would know that sound anywhere: it's Joey calling for him.

"Did you hear that?" he says, grinning. "I think it came from over there." He points down the right fork.

David listens. "That was Maddie!"

They jog toward the voices, keeping quiet so they can follow the distant cries of their children.

Kevin waves his light back and forth, checking the walls of the cave for any more holes. Though the voices are growing closer, they don't appear to be coming from directly ahead. Something other than distance is muffling them. As his flashlight bounces from the right wall to the left, he freezes.

David bumps into his back. "Why did you stop?!"

Kevin redirects his light toward the yellow flashes he saw in his sweeping beam and illuminates a beige feline the size of a Saint Bernard. The cat's growl rumbles deep in its chest as it shimmies its shoulders to dip into a crouch.

"Holy shit!" says David.

Kevin whips his gun from its holster and takes aim, propping it atop his flashlight in a practiced grip. "Why would it be in this cave?" he whispers to David, starting to take a slow step back.

"It must have followed the kids," says David, his whisper comingling with the cat's hiss.

Kevin wonders if the mountain lion has been shot at before. It eyes the weapon, hissing and flashing its fangs, but not pouncing. It looks hungry, its ribs visible beneath its pelt.

"Dad, there is a mountain lion in the tunnel!" yells Joey's voice somewhere on Kevin's left.

"We see it, Joey!" he calls, and the cat growls in protest. "Sit tight. We'll get you out of there."

David takes a step toward the cat, and Kevin grabs his shirt. "What the hell are you doing?"

"I'm going to scare it away." He puffs his chest and waves his arms, roaring and bellowing like a maniac. Dirt drops from the ceiling of the tunnel, but the cat doesn't budge.

David wipes the dirt from his hair and looks up. "Oh, shit!"

The mountain lion shimmies again, agitated by all the noise. Kevin cocks the pistol, but David pushes his arm down.

"If you fire your gun, the sound vibrations could collapse the ceiling."

Kevin looks at his watch and says, "We only have twenty minutes until the blast. We have to do something now, or we'll all die."

The cat lets out a yowling roar and springs. With a sharp yell, Kevin fires twice, and the cat smacks into the dirt floor, bleeding from the chest, its paws twitching.

When the light shower of dirt from the ceiling clears, Kevin looks back to find David scrunched against the cave wall with his eyes shut tight. Kevin starts to laugh, but the cat's hiss cuts him off. The creature is wriggling, trying to get its legs beneath it. Kevin walks three paces and fires a third round into its skull.

The sound echoes down the tunnel and then becomes something else entirely.

"Do you hear that?" asks David.

The rumbling is hard to miss, even without the steady powder of dirt crumbling onto their heads.

"Joey… Maddie, we need to leave now!" David yells.

There is a faint scraping sound, and Joey's next call of "We're coming!" is much clearer. Kevin follows it to a hole in the wall and crouches down. Maddie's face appears inside the little tunnel, pale and frightened. Kevin helps her out and passes her off into David's waiting hug. Joey is already halfway through, and Kevin takes his hand to pull him clear.

He doesn't let go once Joey stands upright. "We have to get out of here!" he says, tugging his son forward. Joey falls into his arms and then lets out a cry of pain. Kevin looks him over for an injury. "Joey? Joey, what is it?"

Joey clutches his head, pressing the heels of his palms into his eyebrows.

"What's wrong?" Maddie asks, her voice higher than Kevin's ever heard it.

"Don't you guys feel that?" says Joey through his teeth as he doubles over in pain.

"The tingling?" asks Maddie.

"Yeah, but it's so much stronger now." He gasps in agony, eyes wide and bloodshot.

"Ten minutes!" says David.

"Ten minutes to what?!" Maddie whimpers.

The rumbling in the cave around them is growing louder, like a washing machine with too hefty a load. "I've got you," Kevin says, half-carrying Joey as they all race for the fork.

They make a left, but after five paces, they're forced to pull up short. The tunnel is clogged with a floor-to-ceiling pile of dirt and stone. David attacks the pile, pulling away rocks and scooping out loose dirt. Kevin hands his light to Maddie and starts digging beside David, but no matter how many rocks they yank out, the debris just rolls over itself and creates another obstruction.

"Stop..." David pants. "It's too late. There's nothing we can do." He looks at his watch. "There's only seven minutes left. We don't have enough time."

Kevin grinds his teeth to hold back the tears that try to spring forward at the thought of Ellie sitting at the kitchen table, eyes glued to the clock while she wrings her hands in worry and fear. "No," he says, tugging with all his might on the enormous chunk of rock at the center of the pile. "We can't give up."

The rock is bigger than him by about three feet and probably weighs as much as an elephant, and all Kevin succeeds in doing is cutting up his hands.

"It hurts," Joey whimpers, crouched and rocking in the dark. "It didn't feel like this before."

Maddie looks around the cave, and Kevin can see the cogs in her brain turning. She runs a finger over an odd gray moss-like residue on the wall of the tunnel, studies it a moment, and then says, "Dad, we need to go back to that room."

"What?"

"Trust me." Maddie takes off with Kevin's flashlight, dragging Joey by the wrist.

Turning right out of the fork, Maddie leaps over the dead mountain lion and then urges Joey into the tight crawl space.

Kevin prays Maddie knows what she's talking about as he squeezes himself into the little tunnel after her. He wriggles like a worm, careful to keep his arms out in front of him so they don't hitch up underneath his chest and pin him in place.

He makes it out the other end and turns back to see

David grunting and digging his fingers into the sides of the tunnel, trying to pull his bulk through. His shoulder hitches on protruding bits of rock, sticking him in place with his legs still dangling out the other side.

"Dad!" yells Maddie.

"Help me pull your dad through," says Kevin, waving her beside him.

On his knees, Kevin sticks his arms into the tunnel to grab David's hands. As he heaves backward, Maddie grabs Kevin around the elbows and tugs harder than he would have thought possible.

David angles himself, rocking onto his right shoulder to free his left. With a final yank, Kevin and Maddie help his midsection slide all the way through. As soon as he pulls his legs free, Joey and Maddie scoot the boulder across the entrance.

"Do you still feel it?" asks Maddie, a hand on Joey's shoulder.

Joey looks at her, clear-eyed with wonder. "No."

David sits up and stretches out his arms, beckoning Maddie to him. He pulls her to his side in a one-armed squeeze. "I love you, Maddie."

She leans against him, looking exhausted. "Love you too, Dad."

Kevin throws an arm over his boy's shoulders, hoping his face looks reassuring and unafraid, though his guts are somersaulting. He sneaks a glance at his watch. "We have less than ten seconds until the blast."

Joey looks at him with perfect trust and hugs him around the middle.

Kevin stands tall, his voice firm as he counts down, "Five, four, three, two, one."

CHAPTER 20

July 26th, 2016

Sarah shifts her red braid to her right shoulder to take advantage of the cool breeze blowing in on her left. The walkway over the excavation site is still slick with morning dew, and she treads carefully behind Catherine as they make their way to the spiraling tower. The black, rectangular device from Cheyenne is buzzing like crazy in the pocket of her shorts, and she pulls it out to ponder the blue markings. She, Catherine, and a leading historian the FBI called in still haven't been able to make heads or tails of them.

Catherine looks toward the cave entrance at the base of the mountain, now cordoned off with caution tape. "I still can't believe the four of them survived the blast," she says.

"Apparently, the girl figured out that the room was protecting them from the signal. The boy was fine when they were in the room. When they left, that's when he started to feel pain."

"Not too many teenagers are that observant," says Catherine.

"I know I wasn't," Sarah laughs. Then she sobers, tapping her chin. "That room was covered with the gray substance. It clearly insulated them from the blast. Do we know what it is yet?"

"My DOE team finished their analysis last night." Catherine's face says the answer isn't going to be overly helpful. "What do you know about graphite?"

"I recently did some research for a colleague. Graphite is one of three naturally occurring allotropes of carbon. It occurs naturally in metamorphic rock, mostly in Asia, South America, and parts of North America. My understanding is that it's formed as a result of the reduction of sedimentary carbon compounds during metamorphism."

Catherine chuckles. "Spoken like a true professor."

Sarah acknowledges the comment with a shrug. "So, the walls were covered with graphite?"

"No, not graphite. We believe it is graphene."

"That's impossible," says Sarah, knitting her brow. "Graphene doesn't occur naturally. You need to apply certain techniques like... mechanical exfoliation or chemical vapor deposition to create graphene from graphite."

"Well... I don't know what to tell you, except that that stuff on the cave walls has the same molecular structure as graphene."

Sarah huffs. Another puzzle, just when they had found some answers. "But my understanding of graphene is that it's only one atom thick, so it is almost completely transparent. In fact, graphene transmits about ninety-eight percent of light, and its flat hexagonal lattice structure doesn't offer much resistance to electrons. It's, like, a... superconductor. So, how did it protect them from the blast?"

"Like you said, the signal isn't creating infrasound or electromagnetic radiation. It's something else. Something we can't identify or measure."

Sarah nods, thinking. "You said the walls were covered with graphene?"

"Yes."

"Graphene is only one atom thick," Sarah repeats. "Do you know how many layers of graphene you would need in order to cover the walls?"

"No, but I have a feeling you're about to tell me."

Sarah smiles at the gentle dig. She quite likes working with Catherine. "I don't actually know, but it would have to be in the billions. You could cover a football field with a sheet of graphene and it would only weigh a gram."

"I get that this defies logic, but so does this thing." Catherine jabs a thumb at the tower. "As for how it protected our four survivors, isn't graphene the strongest substance on Earth?"

"Yeah, it's forty times stronger than diamonds and two hundred times stronger than steel."

Catherine's grin grows. "How do you know this stuff off the top of your head?"

Sarah shrugs. "Like I said, I recently did some research for a colleague." She tilts her head to study the tower. "It's just so strange, isn't it? The signal acts no differently than sound waves. Its frequency resonates with blood, but we can't detect any sound waves or electromagnetic waves. So, what is it?"

"Well, we may not know what type of signal this thing is transmitting, but at least we know that it is transmitting a signal... thanks to that device in your hand."

Sarah holds up the device, still just as mystified by it as she was the day the FBI Director put it on her desk, a little over a week ago. "Yes. The signal strength above the tower was much stronger than it is down here."

"Were you able to quantify the difference between the vibrations directly above the tower and those at the base?" Catherine asks.

"Not exactly, but we do know that the signal's strength above it is well over a million times stronger."

Catherine points up at the blue crystal. "So, there's very little question that this thing was designed to send a signal into space, and what we are feeling here on Earth is leakage —a side-effect."

"Yes."

Catherine closes her eyes as she lets out a long breath. "But where is the signal going? Who is receiving it? And why does this thing only send a message every five days?"

Sarah shakes her head. "Who knows?"

Catherine stares at the tower for a moment, and when she turns to Sarah, she looks fearful. "You know..." She sucks on her bottom lip, as if to hold in a secret. Sarah waits patiently, and at last Catherine says, "The two men that were found unconscious in that alley in Cheyenne... *were human*."

Sarah's eyes widen as she gawks at the device in her hand. "Humans created this thing? In 1969?"

"Yes, but these humans were not from Earth. Their blood type and DNA were unlike anyone on Earth."

Sarah blinks rapidly, sure she misheard. "How do you know this?"

"The ER nurse in Cheyenne took blood samples before they regained consciousness."

"What happened to them?" Sarah isn't sure why she's whispering, but she leans in toward Catherine all the same. "Were they captured?"

"No. They simply disappeared."

"Amazing," says Sarah, an awestruck smile creeping onto her face. Not only is she holding proof that there is life beyond Earth, this device is also proof that humans can exist elsewhere in the universe. "I wonder if they built this tower."

"Why would they build a tower to communicate, when their people are already here on Earth?"

Sarah stares up at the tower as thoughts flicker across her mind. "Who knows."

Catherine crosses her arms with a frown. "Why now? Why start to communicate on July 2nd, 2016?"

Sarah hugs herself, suddenly feeling cowed by the enormous object rather than awed. "I have no idea... but whomever is receiving the signal, let's hope they're peaceful."

* * *

August 22nd, 2016

Dr. Holland's waiting room smells like disinfectant, old people, and the doctor's spicy cologne. Joey's stomach is already roiling with nerves, and the mixture isn't helping. Maddie's hand in his, however, is doing a world of good. He's infinitely grateful her family postponed their return to Detroit a few weeks longer, so that she could be here for this moment.

"It's going to be all right," she says, leaning to whisper at his ear. Her fruity shampoo takes away the smell of sickness in the air.

The room is cramped, with the Schumers and the Schwarzes all piled into the few chairs. Grace sits on David's knee, while Bethany leans back against Ellie's chest. Joey catches his father's eye across the space, and with a jolt of giddy surprise, he realizes his dad doesn't have those worry wrinkles around his eyes today. His hands aren't clamped together between his knees. Kevin looks... at peace.

Huh. If his dad isn't worried, maybe Joey shouldn't be either.

The door swings open and a young nurse clutching a clipboard says, "Joey Schumer."

Joey's stomach does a backflip as he stands up, but today it's as much from excitement as it is the usual trepidation. He feels better, he looks better, he has to be better.

Everyone else starts to stand, ready to follow Joey. The nurse's eyes widen and she holds out her clipboard like a stop sign. "Hold on. You're not all coming back here to the see the doctor?"

"Yes, all of us are coming," says Ellie, one thin brow raised as she stares down the younger woman.

The nurse sighs and waves them onward. She leads them past the doctor's checkup rooms to his office in the very back. The eight of them squish in, bumping and apologizing until at last they have shunted Joey and Ellie to the front to take the two available seats. Everybody else squeezes together at the back. David holds Grace on his back to keep Maddie from disappearing into a ficus. Kevin holds Bethany's hand to keep her from touching the short bookshelf in the corner. Doctor Holland isn't at his desk. When he opens the door behind them all, he has to peek in through a crack to keep from jabbing Kevin in the side with the doorknob.

"Well, this is a surprise," he says with a smile. "I wasn't expecting a party."

Kevin picks up Bethany so he can step aside for the doctor, who maneuvers his way to his desk with cheery apologies.

After a few introductions, Dr. Holland says, "This is appropriate."

"What do you mean?" asks Kevin.

"This is a great time for family and friends to be together to celebrate some *extraordinary news*!" Dr. Holland throws up his arms, and his reedy laugh fills the room.

Ellie lets out a cry of delight and bursts into tears. Blushing, she hides her face with her hands. Kevin kisses the top of Joey's head and then pulls Ellie to him, pressing his cheek into her hair to catch his own tears.

"Is it less than five percent?" asks Joey quietly. His blood is singing, telling him it's true, but he's afraid to believe it.

Dr. Holland leans over his desk, looking younger than Joey's ever seen him. "Joey… your count is only three percent. You are officially in remission. Congratulations!"

Joey's whoop of joy comes out a strangled gasp. He feels like he just stumbled off a death-defying rollercoaster, a mixture of queasiness and elation. He jumps to his feet almost without realizing he's doing so. Then arms start wrapping around him, hands start patting his shoulder, and joyful voices fill him up until a smile breaks his stunned face.

Maddie plants a warm kiss on his cheek, hugging him around the middle. "I told you I was your good-luck charm."

Joey tips her chin up to find her eyes and says, "You're more than that."

"You're such a dork," she says through a grin.

Joey turns to his parents and thrusts up his fists as he shouts, "No more chemo!"

"No more chemo!" Kevin shouts through a laugh.

Ellie's tear-soaked face is radiant as she claps her hands once and announces, "We have to celebrate! Dinner's on us. We'll go to Pig in a Fur Coat!"

"Am I invited?" asks Dr. Holland with a chuckle.

Kevin leans around his wife to take the doctor's hand and shakes his whole arm. "Damn right you are!"

Around Joey, the tear-soaked faces blur and the joyful exclamations fade to a murmur. He stands tall in a body that hasn't felt this healthy, this strong in years. He thinks about the tower—the cause of so much pain, and yet, the source of his healing.

Whoever built it, whatever it's really for… he's grateful.

EPILOGUE

Four years later

Joey's breath is like ocean waves as he redirects his focus, peeling his eyes from Maddie's toned body to give all his attention to the red punching pad on her hand. His next punch makes her stagger backward two steps, and her eyebrows jump toward her hairline.

"Okay, that's enough for today," she says through a smile.

In the last year, she's replaced her high ponytail with a long French braid. She tightens the purple hair tie at the end as she says, "I still remember the first time you hit this bag four years ago. You made me laugh."

Joey chuckles around his water bottle. "Well, I was a lot smaller back then."

She drinks him in with lashes lowered, making his stomach flutter. Her eyes scan up from his large calves, linger on his abs, and then make their way over his trapezius muscles to find his face. "That's true."

At 6'2" and weighing in at two-ten, he's certainly not a string bean anymore, though he still gets taller every year. Plus, training together these last four years has morphed

Joey into a force to be reckoned with—though he isn't quite at Maddie's level.

Maddie saunters toward him, that look still in her eye, and Joey drops the water bottle to catch her in a kiss. When he pulls back, Maddie holds his face in her hands and stands on tiptoe to steal a second one.

"Love you," she says with a wink.

"Love you too."

Her nails trace patterns on his scalp, buried in his thick brown hair, as she laughs and says, "I bet four years ago, you didn't think you would be nominated to homecoming court."

"I didn't think I would be alive."

She wraps her arms around his neck, and his brain goes fuzzy. "Well... you are, and no one is happier about that than me."

"I was only nominated because you're my girlfriend."

"Probably true," she says through a chuckle.

Joey tickles her side. "You're so modest."

"Well, you know..." she says, swatting away his hand. "Remember when I had to defend you from bullies?"

"You mean Jeb and Wilbur?"

She chuckles. "What idiots. I wonder where they ended up going?"

"Juvenile Hall, probably." He snorts and retrieves his water bottle. "You don't have to defend me anymore," he says, patting the bench beside him. "I can take care of myself."

She sits and loops her arm through his, one hand cupping his bicep. "That's true." She leans in for another kiss, a sweet peck that makes him smile.

"Thank God you guys moved here," Joey says. "High school would have sucked without you."

Maddie's family had only been back in Detroit for a few months before David discovered that battling the government for his property rights was a job better done in Rindville. Right before Christmas of 2016, he and Debbie had given notice at work, and they'd packed up and relocated.

Maddie and Grace hadn't argued. Not even a little.

"I'm sure you would have met someone else," Maddie teases Joey. "Maybe another sheriff's daughter."

Joey gives her a crooked grin. She likes to complain about being the sheriff's daughter who can't get away with anything, but no one cheered louder than her when David was pronounced the winner last year. After he resolved the land rights issue, he'd been itching to get back to law enforcement work. Where else to start, but with the county's top job?

"You could have found another chief deputy's son," Joey teases back. His dad is perfectly happy not being the man in charge... yet. He reminds David constantly that the sheriff is an elected official, and he could choose to run against his old friend at any time.

"I could never find anyone else like you... you dork," Maddie says. She wipes Joey's brow with a gym towel and then digs in her beat-up bag for her phone. Despite the hefty trust fund sitting in the bank, thanks to the millions in gold, copper, and graphene under her grandparents' fields, Maddie has no real taste for luxury. Her sports bra is off-brand, she barely wears jewelry, and besides a few pink streaks sophomore year, she doesn't dye her hair.

Her biggest splurges are for Joey's birthdays. Thanks to Maddie, he's got an electric skateboard and the latest VR console.

"Did you send in your application to UW?" he asks.

"Yes, I did."

"God, I hope we both get in."

"Me too."

"I wonder if our parents will let us share a dorm room?"

"Seriously?" she says with a snort. "The University won't let us."

"Then we should get an apartment."

"Our parents would never let that happen."

"True." He wraps an arm around her shoulders. "I never thought I would get the chance to graduate high school and go to college." Thoughts of his battle with cancer still strike him during poignant moments in his life, milestones he never thought he'd reach, and he welcomes the sense of awe and disbelief. It makes the world around him brighter, more beautiful.

Maddie nuzzles her face into his chest. "Well, you are. And I can't wait to go with you."

"I hope it never comes back."

"It won't, but if it does, we'll just go to that crazy tower."

"You really think we'd be able to sneak past the perimeter a third time?" Joey asks, shaking his head.

Four years later, the farm is still occupied by a small contingent of scientists and military personnel. The tower is still transmitting its deadly signal every five days at 5:12 p.m.

The town mostly tries to pretend the Schwarz farm never existed. It's like a dark spot on the map. People drive the long way around to avoid it. Kids dare each other to approach the fence by the road, to set foot on the grass. They run away goosebumped and squealing. They have no idea that the tower's signal caused all those deaths years ago. They think it was due to some unknown contagion. Maddie and Joey know the truth. For them it was a life saver. *A miracle.*

* * *

The 7th book in the Frozen Pandemic Series, Tethered, is a three part manuscript that ties together the previous six books in the series. Characters from each of the six books will appear in Tethered.

The book will not be published on Amazon until June or July of 2021. However, if you would like an advanced copy at no charge, please request a copy along with a brief review of the series. You can email me at ccb@frozen-pandemic.com

Made in the USA
Las Vegas, NV
06 January 2021